LEGACIES OF SPRING

MATT BANNISTER WESTERN 11

KEN PRATT

Paperback Edition

Published in the United States by Wolfpack Publishing, Las Vegas

CKN Christian Publishing
An Imprint of Wolfpack Publishing
6032 Wheat Penny Avenue
Las Vegas, NV 89122

christiankindlenews.com

Paperback ISBN: 978-1-64734-632-4
eBook ISBN: 978-1-64734-631-7
Library of Congress Control Number: 2021940809

LEGACIES OF SPRING

Dedication

This book is dedicated to my friends, Pastor Dan and Nancy Wentworth.

"The greatest legacy one can pass on to one's children and grandchildren is not money...but rather a legacy of character and faith." – Billy Graham.

I, too, am part of the legacy of your character, faith and ministry. I love you both.

Author's note

The Matt Bannister Series is a sequence of people and events that arise in the life of U. S. Marshal, Matt Bannister. Through this series of books, Matt has faced multiple enemies and situations that have left some open-ended storylines. Many of those are designed to be that way for future events. Every book takes place in a short time period, a week at most usually and they are spaced out a month apart, generally speaking. I have every intention of bringing past characters back here and there to close those open-ended storylines. Dragon's Fire ended as a cliffhanger leaving the reader wondering what would happen to Wu-Pen Tseng. Legacies of Spring is a story of urgency becoming the priority. This story does not address Wu-Pen Tseng, but what I have planned for Wu-Pen could not happen without this story. Legacies of Spring brings some past characters back and puts an end to one or two of those open-ended storylines. Believe it or not, timing is a big factor in this series and there are some big and exciting things ahead. This story is an abrupt change of direction but a lawman never knows what tomorrow will bring or where it will take him. And that is what makes it exciting.

1

It was Friday morning and Pamela Collins did not have much choice rather than knocking on the door of the Monarch Hotel's security guard William Fasana's room. She knew he wasn't an early riser and had just gone to bed a few hours before. The hotel manager, Roger King, was late for work and the fighting in the luxury room upstairs on the third floor was troubling to the other guests and could be heard by Pamela at the front courtesy desk of the hotel. Her anxiety was growing stronger the longer she had to listen to the distant enraged man's voice and the cries of his wife. When William didn't answer quickly enough, she got the key to his room and entered. He was sleeping soundly in his bed.

"William, you need to wake up. I need you upstairs. There's a fight happening and it's a bad one."

He took a long deep breath as he lifted his head tiredly. "What?" he asked, struggling to keep his eyes open.

Pam tried to sound calm but her voice revealed the urgency, "A man is screaming at his wife upstairs. Please, can you calm him down? We're getting many complaints and nobody wants to confront him."

William nodded as he sat up in his drawers and reached for his pants. "Yeah. Who is it?"

"Hiram Stewart and his wife. They're in room Sixteen."

"I'll be right there. What are they fighting about?" he asked with a yawn. He rubbed his eyes and stood up to put his pants on.

Pam turned her face from him uncomfortably. "It sounds like where she was last night."

William chuckled. "Where was she?"

Pam shrugged. "I don't know."

William finished dressing and walked upstairs with a cup of coffee. He could hear the upset man throwing something made of glass shattering against the wall. It was not the first time he had walked up those stairs to interrupt an argument and check on the safety of any guests taking the brunt of a fight. William never had a guest be too disrespectful to him nor ever needed his weapons to ask a guest to quiet down. He carried a derringer in his pocket if it was needed but it was far too early to put on his gun belt for a moment's job before he went back to bed. William had met the Stewart couple multiple times over the past week that they had been in town. Hiram Stewart worked for the Union Pacific Railroad but was in town to survey the best route for the Oregon Short Line rails to cross town to reach the silver mine, sawmill and granaries. Hiram and his wife were a nice couple, albeit the age difference was most noticeable. Hiram Stewart was in his late fifties and his wife, Sherry, was in her early twenties. William had thought Sherry was Hiram's daughter at first and didn't hide his surprise to learn they were married. Hiram was a crusty old toad with just enough energy to sit on a log talking about business and numbers with the businessmen in town. On the other hand, Sherry was a lovely blonde ball of fire roaring to have a good time when Hiram wasn't around. It was William's opinion that Sherry was just as beautiful as a copperhead snake and about as trustworthy as well.

"Who is it!" Hiram yelled through the door when William knocked.

"Mister Stewart, good morning." He yawned. "It's William from the hotel. Can I talk to you for a minute?" He sipped his coffee tiredly.

"William!" Hiram shouted with surprise. "Hold on."

William narrowed his brow curiously when he heard Sherry's whimpering voice say, "Hiram, don't..."

"Shut up!" he yelled and the door unlocked. "Come in, William."

William opened the door and stepped inside, closing the door behind him. He saw Sherry kneeling protectively in the corner of the luxury living room with a bleeding lip and swollen eye. She was crying. The room was in shambles and it took a moment for William to glance around and realize Hiram was nowhere to be seen. A flowing sense of alarm drained down his spine like a glass of cold water when he noticed Sherry staring behind him by the door. William turned while reaching for the derringer but all William saw was the stock of a shotgun swinging towards his head and the solid blunt force of the wood slamming against his head. He fell to the floor stunned and saw a drop of blood drip onto the carpet before he heard Sherry scream and felt the rifle stock hit the back of his head.

William woke up slowly with a splitting headache. Water was splashed on his face and all he could see was a pink liquid dripping over his brow and onto his white shirt and the carpet that was already soaking up his blood. William was lying on the floor with his hands tied tightly behind his back. He sat up and leaned against the wall, trying to understand what was happening to him. Sherry was sitting on the floor next to him; her hands were also tied behind her back. Hiram sat in a dining chair he had pulled close to them and held a shotgun across his lap. Sherry was weeping quietly with a sock shoved in her mouth.

"Why did you hit me?" William asked, realizing he had been knocked out and tied up. "What are you doing?"

Hiram had seemed like a determined business-oriented fellow but a nice man in the past week. Now, sitting with an angry scowl and madness in his eyes, he didn't appear so docile anymore. "I'm glad you joined us, William. I'm a fine man and

I believe in commitment. I believe in being faithful to my job, my employers, my employees and my wife. Unfortunately, Sherry doesn't believe in that. I brought her to spark up some fun and have a nice little vacation with my wife. I didn't think she'd be sparking up the night in your room!"

William grimaced and shook his aching head. "What?"

Hiram shouted. "I saw how you stared at Sherry when we got here! Don't act like you're surprised. She came walking in at seven this morning and her shoes were still here, so where else is she going to be, William? And then you have the gall to come here with a gun in your hand!" He held up the derringer William had been reaching for when he was hit. "I'm glad you came, though. Trust me; you're not going to be walking out of here the same. You don't mess with another man's wife and you're going to learn that today! Were you two planning on running away together?"

William glanced from Sherry and back to Hiram. "I have no idea what you're talking about. Take the gag out of her mouth and ask her."

"I did. She said you were playing cards with her all night! Imagine that."

"What?" William gasped irritably and glared at Sherry. If he could, he'd reach over and yank the sock out of her mouth and demand an answer for himself. He had not seen Sherry since she was with Hiram the night before in the restaurant. "No," William laughed nervously. "I was in the lounge until five o'clock this morning and women are not allowed in there. I haven't seen your wife since dinner. And I have never been alone with her."

Hiram stood up and kicked William's crotch. He watched William fall to his side and curl into a fetal position in agony. Hiram leaned over him and shouted, "I don't believe you! You are a womanizing liar with a long history of gambling and drunkenness, from what I heard. Well, let me tell you something, William, I'll never touch my wife again because I don't want your syphilis, gonorrhea or whatever else you might spread across the whorehouses in town. You can have her! You can take her right into eternity with you."

Many times, William had been sarcastic and belittling while in questionable circumstances to escalate the hostility but now wasn't the right time. He bit his bottom lip and tried to breathe through the internal agony of the blow. He took a few breaths and glared at Hiram with fierce blue eyes that indicated that he would beat Hiram to death if he could get his hands free. He shouted, "Hiram, I didn't touch your wife! I have never spoken to her without someone being there. I may be a lot of things but I'm not stupid. I'd lose my job if I womanized with a guest's wife, daughter or sister. And I have an easy job," he laughed bitterly. "I came up here as a friendly fella just to say quiet down."

"Of course! And that's why you were reaching for your little gun, right? Did you think you could kill me and keep her for yourself, William? Were you going to claim self-defense while trying to save the damsel in distress? Good plan but it isn't working. I caught you and your whore both in the act. Didn't I?"

It was no laughing matter, but it was a nervous reaction; William chuckled. "She might be someone else's whore, but not mine. Pull the sock out of her mouth and ask her again now that I'm here."

There was a knock on the door.

Hiram turned agitatedly towards the door. "What?" he yelled.

"Mister Stewart, I am the United States Marshal, Matt Bannister. May I come in?"

"No! I'm busy."

William shouted, "Matt, he has a shotgun pointed at me and my hands are tied."

Matt's voice came through the door, "Mister Stewart, William is my cousin and I suggest you release him."

William could see the concern enter Hiram's expression. He was rightfully so, an angered man, but he wasn't a killer and had a sense of reasoning. Matt's name often brought a bit of realism of life and death to a man acting foolishly. William spoke softly, "I didn't do anything with your wife, Hiram. You have the wrong man if there is a man. I promise you that much. I don't know where your wife was but she was not with me."

"Then who was she with?" he yelled.

William shrugged. "Ask her, not me."

Matt knocked on the door again. "Hiram Stewart, open the door so that we can talk. Tell me why you have William tied up and under your gun? Don't force me to come in shooting, please, because I'd rather not."

William lied, "It wouldn't be the first time Matt has kicked a door in here. You would not get that longarm halfway around towards the door before you're dead. Trust me, I've seen it before. Honestly, unlock that door and tell Matt what's happening here. I promise you we will find out where Sherry was last night and then you can apologize to me because I have nothing to do with it."

Hiram stared at William for a moment while he thought it over. It might be dismissible if he had overreacted but to accuse the wrong man was wrong, plain and simple. Hiram was taking an adulteress woman's word for it, and if she's going to spend the night with another man, she'll probably lie too. Hiram began to question if he may have made a big mistake.

William continued, "You have a great career and a lot of work to do here still. Don't lose your life over this. Open the door while you can."

"You didn't tell me Matt Bannister was your cousin." Hiram didn't verbalize it but the thought of the famous marshal bursting through his door scared the fire out of him.

William shrugged, feeling easier now that he could see worry replacing the rage in Hiram's composure. "I get tired of bragging, I guess. Open the door before he comes in here and kills you for holding a gun," he chuckled. He looked at Sherry with disdain. "And you, you're going to explain why you said you were with me. I want to know where you were now, too."

Hiram laid the shotgun on the bed and opened the door to see a tall man with broad shoulders and appeared to be quite muscular. He had his long dark hair in a ponytail and had a neatly trimmed dark beard and mustache covering the lower features of his square-shaped handsome face. Hiram was shocked to see Matt's hardened brown eyes behind the Colt .45 revolver that was pointed at him. "I'm unarmed!" Hiram exclaimed and held up his hands.

Matt stepped inside the room with his Colt pressed against Hiram's chest and looked at William and Sherry sitting against the living room wall. The sight of William's blood-covered face and hair angered him. Matt backhanded Hiram with the barrel of the gun, knocking him to the floor. The strike wasn't hard enough to leave him unconscious or break the skin but a knot was forming. Nate Robertson helped Hiram back to his feet. Matt put his attention on his cousin. "Are you okay, William?"

William grinned, happy to see Matt knock Hiram down. "My head hurts. Other than that, I'm just humiliated to have you see me like this."

Nate Robertson spun Hiram around and shackled his wrists while Hiram yelled, "You hit me! You had no right to hit me like that!"

Matt picked up the shotgun and checked the chamber. "It's not loaded."

"Of course, it's not loaded!" Hiram spoke irately. "I wasn't going to kill him. I just wanted to find out where my wife was last night and scare William enough to leave the married women alone! My wife said she was with him all night!"

"I wasn't with her," William asserted before Matt could ask. "Pull that dang thing out of her mouth so she can tell us where she was!"

Matt pulled the sock out of Sherry's mouth and asked, "Ma'am, were you with William last night?"

She shook her head and wept. "No. I am so sorry, William. I didn't mean for you to get hurt."

Hiram shouted, "Where were you? Did I break his head open for nothing? The least you could do is tell the truth!"

Matt cut the binds on William's wrists. "You need to get those cuts on your head sutured."

"I will when I find out where she was," William answered. He stood and pointed a finger warningly at Hiram. "Where's my derringer? You better hope I don't shoot you for the hell of it!"

"You're not shooting anyone," Matt answered as he cut the binds on Sherry's wrists.

"That's my blood on the floor. I think I owe him that much at least." He kicked her foot lightly to get her attention. "Where were you?" William asked Sherry bitterly.

Sherry's face deformed into a grievous scowl while she covered her face with her hands and wept shamefully.

"Where were you?" William demanded loudly, standing over her. Matt watched him closely to make sure he didn't try to grab her.

"She's my wife. I'm the one that should be screaming at her!" Hiram snapped.

"You had your chance. Now it's my turn," William answered Hiram sharply. He leaned over

Sherry and yelled, "My head is busted open because you lied! Now, where were you?"

"I was upstairs."

"With who?" Hiram demanded. Nate continued to hold him.

Sherry whimpered, "Roger."

"Who?" Hiram demanded.

"Roger."

"Roger King?" William asked, stunned. She nodded affirmingly. "Why would you tell Hiram you were with me?"

"The manager?" Hiram asked loudly.

She nodded.

Now that the truth was told, the answer was shocking. Roger was the last person in Branson that William would expect to spend the night with the promiscuous young lady. William sighed heavily and sat on the davenport. "Someone needs to get Lee. This turn of events is far above me," he said with a shrug.

Matt spoke, "Nate, run to my brother's office and bring Lee here. If he's not there, run to his home. Tell him he's needed."

William stared at Sherry, perplexed. "Roger? Really? He's married."

Hiram glared at William. "So is she!"

William grinned awkwardly and chuckled. He felt no pity for the man who beat him over the head. "Well..."

"Save yourself some trouble and keep quiet, William," Matt suggested quickly. He knew William was going to say something to enrage Hiram further.

William laughed. “Yeah, maybe I better keep quiet.” He turned back to Sherry. “Roger, huh?” He grinned. “Not many young or older women who come here find him so attractive.”

“William,” Matt warned. “Go get a towel for your head or something.”

2

Matt stood from kneeling in front of Sherry Stewart; he had brought her a cool rag with ice for her swollen eye. William sat in a chair holding ice on a large bump and cut on the back of his head. Hiram Stewart sat on a smaller davenport glaring while Matt tenderly cared for Sherry. Lee fixed himself a drink and stood in the doorway to the bedroom impatiently. He had already gotten an earful of hostile language about his hotel manager from Hiram. Sherry admitted to spending the night with Roger in a room upstairs. There was minimal discussion left to say while waiting for Pamela and Deputy Nate Robertson to locate Roger King and bring him to the room.

Hiram addressed Lee, "When this is over, I want my now ex-wife thrown out of this hotel. I don't want to see her here again. My company's paying my bill and I won't pay a dime for her. Understood?"

Lee was in his early forties and already a very

successful businessman. He wore a gray pinstriped suit and a derby if he wore a hat at all. He shared many of Matt's physical features of being tall and broad shouldered, except Lee kept his dark hair cut short and combed respectfully to the side. He was clean shaven except for a mustache that he kept well-groomed. Lee nodded agreeably. "There are other hotels you can put her up in," he said to Hiram.

He scoffed. "You don't understand. I don't ever want to see Sherry again. I'm not wasting another dime on her!"

Sherry pleaded with her husband in a high-pitched voice, "Hiram, I made a mistake. You can't throw me out of here without any money. Where will I stay?"

The expression on Hiram's face told her all she needed to know. "I don't care. We are through and you're not leaving here with me. You can find your own way back to Ohio."

"What am I supposed to do?" she raised her voice.

Hiram shrugged his shoulders carelessly. "They have a whorehouse; go there. You'll feel right at home."

"That's enough!" Matt spoke firmly with a severe glance at Hiram. "No one wants to hear you two fighting."

Hiram was too upset to be quiet. He shouted at Sherry, "Take what's yours and go! I never want to see you again, Sherry. Don't come whimpering back to me with the poor me crap either. When I get home, I'll load your things in a wagon and take them to your mother's house along with a certificate of divorce."

A tear rolled down her cheek. "And how am I supposed to get home?"

"You spent the night with your first customer; that should be at least two bits. Right? Well, here's Roger, ask him for it." His expression turned to stone as he glared at Roger King. "Congratulations, Roger! Take her home with you and introduce her to your wife, why don't you? She needs a place to stay. I'm sure your wife won't mind."

Roger King was in his mid-fifties and dressed in the same suit he had worn the day before. His round clean-shaven face was flushed and his breathing was noticeably rapid. He knew he had made a big mistake and had been hiding in a room upstairs, afraid to come down after hearing Hiram yelling at his wife.

"Roger," Lee Bannister said to end any arguing between the two men. "I want to hear it from you. Did you take Missus Stewart upstairs into a room and spend the night with her?"

His head lowered. He spoke softly, "Lee, can we talk in private?"

Lee's brow narrowed angrily. "No, we cannot. Look at William, Missus Stewart and Mister Stewart. The only one not affected so far is you. Tell me, is it true?"

Hiram spoke with disgust, "Do not call her Missus Stewart. Call her by her name, not mine."

"Hiram..." she whimpered and began to weep.

Roger wiped his sweaty palms on his suit jacket. His voice trembled, "I'm sorry. I wasn't thinking and it…it…just kind of happened."

Lee's shoulders slumped slightly as the scales of disappointment gave way to a wave of rising anger. "Your wife might buy that but I don't," Lee stated coldly. "Taking an empty room key and walking up four flights of stairs with a guest doesn't just happen. It's a decision. I won't have that happening in my hotel. The Monarch Hotel guests are to be treated like royalty, not like this!" He took a breath and added, "I'm sending Nate and William down with you to pack up your personal belongings out of the manager's office and I want you out of here."

"Lee, please," Roger gasped. His eyes filled with terrified tears and his voice trembled, "I made a mistake. I swear, I won't do it again. This place is all I have. Please…"

Lee shook his head slowly. "You should have thought about that before. You know the rules. You're fired, Roger. My mind is made up."

A surge of fury filled Roger. "Are you sure you want to do that? This place will fail without me."

Lee addressed William, "Take Nate and escort Roger downstairs, pack up his stuff, get his keys and throw him out. And I don't care if you or Nate do it forcefully."

Roger stared slack-jawed at Lee. "I made this place what it is! Without me, this would have just been another hotel. I built its reputation and now you think you're going to fire me?"

Lee spoke in his usual tone, "Well, that part is true, Roger. But we'll make do without you. Don't forget to tell Martha why you're home early."

Roger gasped with emotion. William gently grabbed his arm. "Let's go, Roger." He led him out of the room.

Lee paused for a moment to set his heavy disappointment off to the side. Roger had been a loyal and dedicated administrator that was also a good friend. Lee was heartbroken to have to fire his friend. He turned to Hiram. "I apologize with all my heart. I cannot imagine the pain you're experiencing. If there is anything, we can do aside from making the rest of your stay pleasurable, please let me know. Pamela will be the one you can talk to or William. They'll both be taking over as co-managers for now."

Hiram scoffed with disgust. "The first thing you can do is throw Sherry out. I can't stand to even look at her."

Sherry removed the cool rag from her eye and scowled at her husband. "I can't stand you either! You're so boring and pathetic. I swear..."

"That's enough," Matt said, raising his voice. If there was one thing that bothered him more than anything else, it was a couple in a heated argument. He didn't want to hear it.

Lee addressed Sherry, "Miss, I'm afraid I'm going to have to ask you to pack your things and exit the hotel. I'm sure Matt will be willing to escort you to another hotel down the street."

Sherry answered anxiously, "Seriously? You're going to throw me out?" She turned to Hiram with a desperate expression. "You're going to throw me out? Are you going to give me anything to survive on, Hiram? I'm your wife! You can't just throw me out. Where am I going to go without the money to stay somewhere? You owe me a ticket home if nothing else." She asked Matt, "Marshal, doesn't he owe me a ticket home?"

Hiram answered before Matt could, "Give me, give me, give me! It's all I ever hear from you. I'm sitting here just hoping you didn't give me a harlot's disease. I already paid for a year of your life. Now, you're on your own. I told you from the beginning if you committed adultery, I won't waste another day on you. You can knock on Roger's door for the pennies he owes you from last night. As I said, I don't want to see you again. Get your case packed and go! Don't come back."

Matt carried her heavy trunk of clothing along the boardwalk while Sherry wept lightly. She didn't have a dollar to her name nor access to one now that Hiram had cut her off financially. She was abandoned in a strange town without knowing anyone or having any place to go. Not too unexpectedly, Matt took the responsibility upon himself to make sure she was safe. There was only one place that Matt could think of that might take her in and help her. Helen Monroe had married Sam Troyer and moved out of Bella's Dance Hall to start her new life as his wife. To Matt's knowledge, Bella had not yet replaced Helen and had a spare bedroom upstairs. Matt hoped Bella and Dave would allow Sherry to stay there until she was wired enough money to get back home.

"Where are you taking me?" Sherry asked with a sniffle. "I don't have any money."

Matt had spoken very little to her. It was the most uncomfortable of circumstances and he didn't know what to say to her. He knew she was humiliated and afraid, if not heartbroken. Sometimes saying nothing during awkward silences was the best thing to do. He answered her question, "A place called Bella's Dance Hall. I'm hoping Bella will let you stay there for the time being."

"I'm not a whore," she said defiantly.

"No, Ma'am, I never said you were. And the dancers are not either. It's a dance hall and the ladies dance, that is all."

"Do you go there?" she asked with interest.

Matt nodded once. "My fiancé is a dancer there."

"What's her name?" There was a sudden cold tone to her voice.

"Christine. If Bella allows you to stay there, you'll meet her."

She began to weep. "Matt, what am I going to do?" She slowed to a stop and turned to him and put her arms around him to be held. He uncomfortably set the chest down and put his arms around her to let her cry.

"Um...just take it one day at a time," he answered awkwardly.

"I'm so scared," she squeaked into his shoulder.

"It might be scary for now but it will get better. I just hope Bella has a room available," Matt said, moving his hands to guide her away from holding onto him.

Matt introduced Sherry to Bella and explained quickly what had happened at the Monarch Hotel. He left the details of what happened the night before out so Sherry could explain that herself if she wanted to.

"Sherry…I like the sound of your name," Bella said while reaching up to touch the swollen black eye to see how swollen it was. "Dave, get us some ice, would you?" she asked her husband. She continued, "How long have you been married?"

"Just over a year. It hasn't been a very good year," Sherry answered.

"Luckily for you, I can put you in a room. Come into my office and let's talk some more," Bella invited.

Christine came downstairs and hugged Matt. "Did you come to see me?" She was in a robe with her long dark hair hanging freely past her mid-back. One of the other ladies had let her know Matt was downstairs.

"Of course. How are you feeling this morning, Beautiful?" Matt kissed her.

"I'm feeling good." She had started dancing again after being shot and was back to her usual self. Her brown eyes shined as they gazed up at Matt. Her long dark hair hung freely down the back of the white robe that she had on. The morning sunlight beamed through the glass of the window and reflected upon her giving an angelic glow.

Sherry watched Christine in Matt's arms. "My, you are beautiful. I'm Sherry Stewart. I might be staying here for a little while."

Christine frowned when she saw the black eye and cut lip. "I'm Christine." She shook Sherry's hand.

Bella spoke, "She's going to be staying here for a few days or maybe a while. But we need to talk. Come along, Sherry."

Christine grinned and lifted her brow with excitement. "I know you're not excited but I want to remind you of the Spring Fling Dance at the Branson Community Hall tomorrow night."

He groaned. He wasn't as excited about the community dance as Christine was. "Don't you have to work or something?"

She laughed. "No, I don't. I am looking so forward to going to the dance with you and your family. Annie wrote to me and stated she'd be here for it and we ladies are all getting dressed at Lee and Regina's house. It's going to be so much fun! It's a big deal, so, dress nice."

Her excitement caused him to grin. "I'll dress nice."

"You're going to dance. It's been a long and terrible winter for us and now spring is finally here. And we're going to celebrate it! I'm expecting to have a whole lot of fun."

"Of course. I'm glad Annie will be there for you because you know I don't like big social events."

"Matt, we'll have fun, I promise. It's not like we dance here, it's just like a barn dance I hear. You ought to feel right at home being born in a barn," she joked.

"Funny. I was thinking, on Sunday, we could

skip church and take a buggy and give Annie a ride back home to Willow Falls. We could stop by Reverend Ash's place and ask if he would be willing to come here and officiate our wedding. I could introduce you to him and his wife. And maybe even Gabriel's mother, Elizabeth and Tom. You've never been to Willow Falls and you'd get to see the Big Z Ranch where I grew up and meet Darius and Rory too. You could spend the night at Annie's and we'll come back on Monday. What are your thoughts on that idea?"

"Yeah. I love to. Do you think I would get the opportunity to put a matchstick between your uncle Charlie's toes? I still can't believe he did that to me at Christmas. I plan to get even with him."

Matt chuckled. "It's hard to find him without his stockings on. But you could do something else though."

"I have an idea. Do you think he'd be mad if I brought Aunt Mary a nice gift and I brought him a gift too, but instead of chocolates or new stockings, it was a box of horse manure?"

Matt grinned. "No, I don't think he'd be mad at all. But be careful with him because, once you start the jokes with him, it escalates fast. And he doesn't like to lose. I once thought it would be funny to put a chicken egg under his bed to rot. So, I put three under there. When it began to stink, yeah, I got in trouble but I thought it was funny. Four or five days later, he asked me to grab a shovel from the shed and, when I opened the door and stepped inside, a bucket of spoiled milk fell on me. The milk was curdled and stank. He let it set out in the sun for three or four days planning that. He thought that was funny. Aunt Mary didn't though. All I'm saying is if you start it, expect a worse payback."

She laughed. "I'm doing it. Wouldn't it be funny if I coated them with frosting?"

"Ah. I'm guessing you wouldn't like the pay back."

"I'll ask Annie. But when we go, I'm going to get him back," Christine said confidently.

"You do that. I'll just watch," Matt replied with a smile.

3

Roger King looked at himself in the mirror. He had gained a lot of weight over the years and now at fifty-five and portly, his puffy cheeks rounded out his head like a chalk circle on a schoolhouse's blackboard. Roger's thinning brown hair was cut short and neatly combed to one side. However, he could never grow a well-shaped beard or a mustache thick enough to look professional, so he shaved every morning before work. Roger never claimed to be the most handsome man in the city but he wasn't looking at himself in the mirror to appreciate his beauty. He pulled the collar of his shirt and bowtie down from his neck once again and sighed at the dark purple patch Sherry Stewart had left on his skin from a long passionate kiss. He covered it up quickly as his wife walked past him.

His heart quickened. He had met people from all over who came into his luxury hotel. He always greeted them with a friendly smile and made it known he and the other employees were there to serve the guest's every need. He had often met attractive women and none had ever gazed at him quite as seductively as Sherry had. No other young lady had ever stirred his desire as she had. There was no explanation for it other than lust. She was such a pretty young lady with long blonde hair, an oblong face and the most expressive, sultry blue eyes he had ever seen. Her attention never left him and, for four days, he had welcomed her into his office to talk and made himself available to her, including taking a buggy ride around the city to show her around. Sherry was fun, exciting and started a fire inside him that could not be extinguished. Roger knew she was a miserably married, lonely young lady and had, to his shame, exploited that to his advantage.

The passion burning inside him had led to planning a night at the hotel with a bottle of fine wine. His foresight saw no further than the moment of pleasure. Roger lied about his marital happiness to align with hers and said whatever he needed to say to build that bond with Sherry. Her name, beauty, and body were like gallons of camphene burning oil tossed on a flame. He had become obsessed with fulfilling his passion. He didn't plan on her staying the night but they fell asleep in each other's arms and she awoke in alarm. Sherry had left her husband's bed while he slept and hoped to sneak back into bed beside her husband before he awoke. The sound of Hiram's furious voice coming from the third floor and her cries let Roger know she had failed. He knew right then that he had made a terrible mistake.

Roger knew better. He was a Christian man who loved his wife. He and Martha had been married for thirty-four years and raised a good family. They had a happy life together and Martha was a wonderful wife to him. Now, standing in front of the mirror, he could not stand the idea of telling Martha what he had done. He didn't want to tell her that he had lost his job and the income they enjoyed. The plans of taking a month off this coming summer to travel were going to be an impossibility. Roger didn't know how to tell her he lost their income because he lusted for one night with a twenty-two-year-old girl he would probably never see again. He had done the worst thing he could do to his beloved wife.

He had been humiliated in front of Lee, his employees and guests of the hotel. The rumors were going to spread throughout the town and it would not take long for the talk to reach Martha. He would become the subject of scorn and gossip rather than a pillar of respect in the community. No matter how long he stared in the mirror, just like the mark on his neck, there was no way of hiding what he had done. Everyone would know he had committed the most heinous crime within a marriage. Roger knew he had to find some courage and admit his guilt before Martha heard the rumors from someone else. She was active in many community areas, such as being the community Spring Fling Dance's main organizer this weekend. There was no way under heaven that Martha was not going to find out. After all, she was friends with Regina Bannister and others who would know what happened before the workday was over.

How does one explain to his wife that he was attracted to a younger woman who had made him feel young and alive again? How could he admit to lying to his wife about having to stay last night at the hotel for security reasons while William left town? To his shame, all he planned was now proving harder to confess than to do.

He entered the family room where Martha was separating clothes that were brought back by their laundress. He stood by the fireplace anxiously.

She took notice of his uncommon anxiousness. "You look worried, Roger. What's on your mind?" She was a plump heavy-set woman with her gray curly hair in a bun and silver framed spectacles setting on her nose. She was a pleasurable woman with a kind heart and loving spirit, friendly with everyone she came across. She was a sincere Christian woman that deserved far more than he had to offer her.

His pulse pounded through his veins so hard that he swore she could see his heartbeat through his clothes if she watched for any length of time. He fought to control his breathing and tried to remain calm. He could not tell her what he had done. He wanted to tell her the truth and come clean but he didn't have the heart to hurt her or see her cry. Roger had always hated to see his wife crying. He could not break her heart by his actions and then double her agony with financial worries. He could not afford to keep paying for their home if he couldn't get his job back. The house was Martha's pride and joy with a yard and a large rose garden that took years to cultivate. Maybe she would forgive him for the adultery if he could save his job and keep providing for his bride. He cleared his throat. "I need to go back to work for a bit."

"Okay," she responded softly.

"I love you, Martha." He had never meant those words more in his lifetime.

She smiled at him. "I know. I love you too." Her brow raised inquisitively. "Are you okay, Roger?"

He nodded. "Yeah. I'll be back."

Roger had already been on his knees pleading with the Lord for forgiveness. Still, the shame of his actions haunted him and there was no sensation of being spiritually cleansed. He felt as dirty and lecherous as he had that morning.

Roger was desperate as he opened the door to the Branson Home & Land Brokers Office. "Good Morning, Lois. Is Lee in?"

The middle-aged Lois Reynolds glanced at Roger and then looked away with a clear expression of disappointment. Lois went to church with Martha and him. "He is. I'll ask if he wants to see you."

Sweat beaded on Roger's nose and under his arms as she walked back to Lee's office.

"Roger, he will see you." There was none of her usual cheerfulness when he came to the office. It verified that the rumors were already starting.

Lee Bannister stepped out of his office. "Did you

want to see me, Roger?"

"If I could, yes."

Lee waved him into his office. Roger closed the door behind him and took a seat in front of the large desk. He took a deep breath to calm his anxiety and get control of his shaking hands. "Lee, I messed up and I know it."

Lee rubbed his face with both hands before looking at him with a disappointed scowl. "Roger, I'm sorry. It's done."

"Can I just talk, please?" he asked quickly. "Look, I know I messed up. I've been your manager since the hotel opened and I've never wronged you or any employee. We've made the finest hotel, restaurant and lounge in the county, if not the state altogether. I'm good at what I do and I love the Monarch Hotel. I love the people and the guests..."

Lee sighed. "Yeah, and loving the guests became the problem."

"Oh, you know what I mean! You've never had a problem with me until now. I know it's my fault, but..."

"But what?" Lee asked harshly.

"Lee, she initiated it."

Lee grew irate. "I don't care if she tried to corner you. My biggest rule is to leave the guests alone. The Monarch Hotel's reputation is tarnished now and I don't like that. Who's to say the next time a pretty lady comes on to you, you won't grab a set of keys again and this time get William or Pamela killed. No, if you're here to get your job back, the answer is no."

His voice trembled, "Lee, I need my job back. Please. There's nowhere else where I can work. Give me another chance. I'm begging you." Desperation showed in his eyes.

"The answer's no," Lee said plainly.

Roger slammed his fist down the desk irately. "You have prostitutes hidden away in the lounge; how respectable do you think that's going to be when everyone finds out? Huh? Don't sit here and pretend like I'm the bad guy when three-quarters of your high-class friends cheat on their wives every day and you're supplying the means to do so! Hell, you're getting rich off them women. You're just a pimp, Lee!" he shouted.

Lee took a deep, controlled breath. "Then you should've taken advantage of one of them and called it a job perk, not a guest's wife. What happens in the Monarch Lounge stays there, you know that. I'll have your last check for you tomorrow. Goodbye, Roger."

Roger took a deep breath to calm down. "I apologize. Lee, will you please give me another chance to prove myself?"

"No, I won't."

"My reputation is going to be ruined. I could see it in Lois's face; you already told her. I'm begging you; please give me one more chance. I did something I can't forgive myself for and I'm desperate," he pleaded. Roger was leaning forward in his chair taking heavy breaths. His face was reddening while his eyes longed for mercy.

"Roger, you may think this is easy for me but it's

not. I know you're a good man and made a mistake but I can't afford to keep you there. It's business and I know you understand that. I'm sorry. Now, if you'll excuse me, I have work to do."

"What am I supposed to do, Lee?" he asked with outstretched arms. "How am I going to provide for my family?"

Lee folded his fingers together on his desktop. "I'm sorry, Roger. I really am. We built a good thing but it's over. I wish you luck but there's nothing I can do."

Roger began to weep as he stepped out of Lee's office. Defeated and broken, Roger walked hopelessly back towards home.

4

The excitement was growing for the Spring Fling Dance that was happening on Saturday night at the Branson Community Hall. Although Matt Bannister was dreading it, his young deputy, Phillip Forrester, was excited to have an evening dancing with his fiancé but no one was more excited than Nate Robertson. He had plans of asking a young lady's father for permission to court his daughter. He planned to make it official at the dance if the young lady agreed to court him. Other young men wanted to court her but he hoped to be the first to win her heart and commitment.

Matt couldn't help but grin while he listened to Nate. He recognized the vast expanse of anxiousness caused by the heart yearning to love a lady and not knowing if the desire would be reciprocated. He remembered how intimidating it was to put his heart on the table and a knife in Christine's hand. It wasn't easy for a man to open himself up, lower his guard and expose his heart to a lady holding a knife. A lady, even with the kindest soul, could drive that knife so deep into a man's heart that it felt like the end of the world. But if she laid that knife down and shared that yearning to love, the risk of being hurt could become the most beautiful blessing a man would ever know. It was a scary place to be in and Nate's nervous excitement showed on his face. Matt put a hand on Nate's shoulder as he walked towards the woodstove. "She'd be a fool to say no. And if she does, let her go because she isn't bright enough for you, anyway."

"Were you nervous when you asked Christine?"

"I was. I felt just like you do, probably. I thought if Christine said no, my life would be torn apart. Christine had a lot of men wanting to court her. Do you know what I found out? She was falling in love with me too. All those other men bringing her flowers and presents were getting nowhere because she already belonged to me. I just didn't know it. A lady already falling in love with you is what you want. How long have you known her?"

"Years. She's my cousin's best friend."

"She's not your cousin, though, right?" Matt asked with a teasing grin.

Nate chuckled. "No, she's not my cousin."

Matt poured himself a cup of coffee and sat down at the table where Nate was sitting with Phillip. "I wish you luck but I don't think you'll need it. Introduce her to Christine and me if she agrees to be courted. We don't want to meet her if she declines, though." His attention went to the office door opening and the cowbell being rung. He stood up to greet the man who stepped inside.

It was an old cowboy who allowed the door to close behind him while he gazed from man to man with a lopsided grin. He was dressed in blue jeans, worn boots with spurs that jingled when he walked. His gray flannel shirt was covered with a brown jacket that was cut above his gun belt. His tan hat was dirty and misshaped. He was a rough-looking old man with a few days of whiskers on his weathered, triangular face. A wide scar deformed the left side of his upper lip and pulled it upwards, leaving him unable to close the left side of his lips. Deep wrinkles surrounded his expressive hazel eyes that revealed a friendliness and humor that didn't quite fit his rough exterior.

"Well, I'll be!" Matt exclaimed with a broad grin.

The old cowboy's disfigured grin grew. "Hey, golden boy! How are you, kid?"

"I'm good, Marvin. How are you?" Matt asked, opening the partition gate and shaking the man's hand vigorously.

"I'm here." Marvin's grin held while his eyes glimmered. "I got your letter and wintered in Cheyenne. Thought I'd be here for spring roundup. I wanted to stop in and get pointed towards your sister's ranch and try to get there before dark to make introductions."

"Your timing is perfect. My sister, her name is Annie, is coming to town today for tomorrow's Spring Fling Dance. You can ride back to the ranch with us on Sunday."

His grin slowly faded. "Well, I would but I've been sleeping on the ground and, to be honest, I was looking forward to sleeping in a bed tonight. I'm not as young as you folks," he said to the youthful deputies with a wink. He continued, "I don't mind sitting in the saddle but the ground gets a little harder and colder the older you grow."

Matt waved a hand. "Don't worry about that. I'll get you set up in the Monarch Hotel for a night or two. They have food, a lounge, baths, just about everything you can think of."

Marvin was hesitant. "I spent about all I had getting through the winter. I told the boss man I was leaving him in the spring and he let me go and tossed me out of the bunkhouse. I had to rent myself a little cabin like you had in Cheyenne and spent my earnings surviving. I don't have the money for a hotel but I can set up camp out of town somewhere. Another day or two won't matter."

Matt wrinkled his nose. "Don't worry about it. You won't be charged for a thing. I just want you to enjoy your stay."

Marvin put up a hand. "No, I don't want no charity. If I can't pay, then I can't stay. I'll camp out and I'll be fine."

"Marvin, I'll give you a choice, you can go stay in my jail all night or stay in a hotel with good food, a lounge, a laundress, baths and mirrors where you can shave and look your best when you meet Annie tomorrow. Because I doubt, she'll let you miss the dance tomorrow night."

Marvin's head rolled towards the deputies at

the table as he laughed. "Did you hear him? I need a bath and a shave." He turned back to Matt. "All right, but I'm going to owe you. I don't want anything for free, Matt. I should tell you, I picked up a couple of stragglers around Boise City looking for work and they came with me. I don't know them well, but they came along anyway."

Matt glanced out the window and saw Marvin's horse at the hitching rail and his packhorse tethered to it. "Where?"

"They went to the saloon as soon as we entered town. I told them I was not waiting for them and was heading towards the ranch within the hour. I'm supposed to stop by the saloon and tell them where to find it before I leave. They plan on showing up on Sunday sometime."

Matt shook his head disagreeably. "You can let them know you're taken care of for the next two nights but they are on their own. What kind of men are they? Annie's my little sister and I don't want unscrupulous men around her."

Marvin nodded in agreement. "They seem decent enough. I just met them on the way through, so I can't vouch for their character. All I know, so far, is they've got cowboying experience and they're friendly enough. Like most young cowboys, they enjoy raising a little hell when they're free to do so but I was known for that too." He chuckled. "I figure when you or your sister meet them, you can make that judgment call. I'm not attached to them."

Nate Robertson, who had spent a week or so in Felisha Conway's boarding house in Sweethome,

Idaho, stepped near with his cup of coffee. "I spent some time around Sweethome and met a handful of the Thacker cowboys. It's not too far from the Boise City area. What are their names by chance?"

Matt explained while motioning with his hand, "This is my deputy, Nate Robertson. We had some trouble over in the Sweethome area and Nate helped me out. My top deputy is named Truet Davis and he's courting Annie. He's presently bringing her here to Branson. You'll see a lot of him occasionally on the ranch."

Marvin put his rough hand out to shake. "Marvin Aggler. Nice to meet you, Nate."

"Likewise," Nate answered.

Matt explained, "I invited Marvin to come here to help Annie at the ranch. Marvin has a reputation for being able to ride anything that bucks. They haven't caught the mustang yet that can throw him."

Marvin laughed through his twisted lips. "That's a crock. How do you think I got this?" He pointed at the scar on his lip. "Down Arizona way, I hopped on a mustang and got thrown like a child right onto a rock. I didn't lose any teeth but I lost a chunk of my lip and haven't been overly handsome since."

"You can ride better than most, then," Matt offered with a grin.

"I don't even know about that but I know enough to get by." He let his eyes roam around the Marshal's Office. "Hey, it looks like you got yourself a nice set up here. I heard you came west and was made into a federal marshal. Well done, young man. Are you still out there chasing the worst of them or are you sitting in here and letting the younger bucks do the dirty work for you?"

"I do a little of both."

"I figured."

Nate repeated, "What are the names of the men that came with you? None of them go by the name Thacker, do they?"

"No, no Thackers. Elias Renner and Jude Maddox are who I picked up. Do you know them?"

"I don't think so." He explained to Matt, "I didn't want Bob Thacker or his son Brit coming here to bother Abby. You know his ex-wife?"

"Bob and Brit are both in prison," Matt answered simply.

Matt introduced Marvin to his other deputy, Phillip, and then said, "Well, let's get you registered at the hotel and let you rest up. Tomorrow, I'll introduce you to my fiancé, unless you want to meet her tonight? I'll take you to the dance hall and let you dance with her once."

Marvin questioned the two deputies through a laugh, "Do you hear this? No wonder he wants me to bathe and shave. Looking like I'm just coming off the trail embarrasses him but what he doesn't know is once I clean up, this old mug can steal his fiancé away." He laughed. "I'd love to meet her, Matt, but if you don't mind, I think I'll stay in and rest tonight."

5

The Spring Fling Dance was second only to Branson's Independence Day Celebration. People from the local area came to celebrate the end of winter and have some fun before another season of hard work consumed their days. The community hall's ground floor would be filled with tables and chairs, with a food line in a potluck-style dinner. The folks came to celebrate the arrival of spring and have a rare night out of socializing, eating, dancing and have a good time. It took a lot of work to prepare and organize such a big event but it was made easier with the help of volunteers. It was Friday night and a small number of people showed up to decorate the community hall.

Martha King was the President of the Branson Oregon Woman's Club and the Branson Quilting and Needlework Club. The woman's club organized the festivities and it was a responsibility that Martha enjoyed. She took a great deal of pride in her work to give back to the community that had blessed Roger and her. Martha put on her coat and set a floral hat on her gray curly hair. She glanced at Roger, who sat in his chair, lost in his thoughts. She knew he was troubled by something but had yet to share with her what it was. For the first time in the five years that she had organized the event, Roger was not interested in decorating the community hall. She knew her husband well and figured he'd show up to help even though he declined to leave with her now. He always showed up when she needed help.

"Roger, are you sure you don't want to help decorate?" she asked, standing near him.

"Sweetheart, I'm...I'm not feeling like it tonight," Roger replied with a nervous stutter.

"Very well. I'll be home in a few hours." She leaned down to kiss him. "You should change out of your suit and get comfortable. Are you sure you're feeling okay?"

He nodded. "I'm fine." It was his last opportunity to tell her the truth before she heard the rumors from one of the ladies at the community hall. His stomach felt like it was going to turn inside out and choke him to death at the same time. He knew what he had to do but the words were stuck in his throat. He gulped down the last of the bourbon. "Martha," he stated anxiously.

"Yes, dear," she turned to face him.

He couldn't do it. He could not break her heart. "I love you."

Martha smiled warmly. "I love you too. Go

change your clothes and take a nap. Maybe you'll feel better."

Martha walked into the community hall and greeted the ladies decorating the tabletops and walls with paper-made flowers and hand-painted pictures made by the local school children. Every year, she asked the school to have the children paint pictures of what reminded them of springtime. Sunshine, flowers and green leaf trees were the three most common themes. She was quite happy with the decorations downstairs and climbed the stairs to the dance floor. She could hear the city band getting ready to practice together as the guitars, bass and fiddle sounded intermittent. Several ladies were decorating the walls with colored drawings of daisies, strawberries, wheat, and yellow smiling sunshine. Albert Bannister was on a ladder running a string across the chandeliers with paper tulips of various colors across the large room. The upstairs had tables on either side of the room for seating but the floor was cleared to leave plenty of room to dance.

"Albert, that looks fantastic. I sure thank you for helping us tonight," Martha was pleased to see him helping.

"You're welcome, Martha."

She walked over to where Regina and Mellissa Bannister worked with Georgina Dalton to hang a banner that read, Spring Fling 1884.

"I love it, ladies. I think this might be the best dance we have thrown together yet," she said with a satisfied grin. "Every year, the prize drawings get better and this year should be the best yet. I suspect there will be some delighted people tomorrow night."

All three of the ladies appeared uncomfortable. Regina took a deep breath and exhaled. She spoke softly so as not to be overheard by others across the open room, "I'm sorry to hear what happened. I hope it doesn't impact our friendship, Martha. Because I think the world of you."

Martha's brow furrowed curiously. "I think a lot of you too. But I don't know what you're talking about. Did something happen at the hotel? Roger seems uncharacteristically melancholy today."

Regina sighed inwardly. The last thing she wanted to do was be put in a position to tell her friend that Roger had committed adultery. It was the worst feeling in the world to know a secret that would break a friend's heart and having an obligation, by the very definition of the word friend, to tell Martha even though it broke Regina's heart to do so.

"Regina?" Martha asked with concern. She could see the hesitation in Regina's large brown eyes. Regina was truly a stunning young lady with her curly long black hair, but despite her beauty, Regina couldn't hide troubling secrets or lie worth beans.

Regina's eyes began to tear. "Lee had to let Roger go this morning."

"What?" Her shock was evident. She glanced over and saw Mellissa and Georgina standing behind Regina with compassionate expressions on their faces. "Why?" she asked with a touch of emotion in her voice.

Regina hated to say the words. "Martha," she grabbed Martha's hand gently. "I hate to tell you this. I wish Roger had told you, so you don't have to hear it from me."

Martha sighed heavily as her heart dropped. "Did Roger steal money?" she asked with shock and disappointment.

Regina shook her head slowly. "Worse. He spent the night with one of the guests and the lady's husband caught them."

She pulled her hand out of Regina's grasp. "That can't be. He worked for William last night."

Regina placed her hand on Martha's shoulder empathetically. "William got his head broke open by the young lady's husband this morning because he thought she was with William. The truth came out when Matt got there and Roger is the one who spent the night with the young lady. He admitted it to Lee."

Martha stared at Regina, dumbfounded. "Roger wouldn't do that. I know him," she argued lightly. "You must be mistaken."

"I'm not," she replied softly. "Roger admitted it, Martha. It broke Lee's heart to do so, but Lee had to let him go. I'm so sorry."

Martha's mouth opened but no sound was uttered. Her eyes grew moist as the words she heard took root. She felt faint and, for a second, felt like she was going to collapse while pressure built in her chest. "Roger wouldn't do that," she heard herself say.

Regina's sorrowful face nodded emphatically. "It was shocking to Lee as well. I didn't believe it myself, but it happened. Did you know he was staying the night at the hotel last night?"

"Yes. Roger said he had to work for William. William was leaving town."

"William was there all night."

Martha's lip began to tremble. "I'm…not feeling so well."

Regina hugged her and whispered, "Go home, Martha. We'll take care of this. If you need anything at all, just come over. You don't even need to ask."

Roger King drank another shot of bourbon. Tears rolled down his cheek and he wiped them away. The lantern put out enough light to see the twenty-gallon wooden keg that stood upright. Roger sat in a wobbly wooden dining chair and poured another drink into his glass. Numb. All he wanted to feel was numb. He didn't want to feel the guilt or the shame that weighed more than he could bear. Thirty-four years of marriage to the love of his life and one moment of lust ruined it. His reputation at the hotel, his friends at church and his own family would be tarnished for good.

The relationship with his wife was broken, she would be broken, and he was responsible for hurting her. He did not want to see Martha cry and he couldn't stand to disappoint her. However, his infidelity was going to cut her deep enough to end their marriage. Even if he could ask Martha to forgive him, the gossip among their peers would drive them apart and bring shame to her as well as him. Adultery is a nasty word that never really goes away in a small town once tagged to a person. Roger couldn't do it. He couldn't live with the stain of what he had done. He knew there was nothing in his future except heartache and pain. It would be better if he were gone by the time Martha returned home. Then she would understand that he could not live with what he had done. He had written a note and placed it on the table beside his bottle of bourbon.

He took his last drink and stepped up on the wooden keg, reached for the rope he had tied to the crossbeam in the basement. He wiped the tears away and slipped the rope over his head and placed it around his neck. One step forward and his life would end. The shame would end. The guilt would end. Just one step and it all would end. He could not do it. That step into eternity was just too far to step.

He began to sob. "Jesus, forgive me. Forgive me, Lord." He turned his feet on the barrel to remove the rope from the crossbeam with the slip knot noose around his neck. He leaned to one side too far and the barrel kicked out from beneath him and rolled away leaving him hanging with the rope tightened around his throat, cutting off his air supply. Desperately, he kicked and flailed hopelessly and then reached up towards the crossbeam and was able to slip his fingers into the tight space between the floor and the beam. He pulled his weight upwards just enough to use one hand to loosen the slip knot barely enough to get a gulp of air before needing to hold on with both hands to support his weight.

"Help!" he tried to yell. "Help!" His bodyweight pulled on his fingers, dragging them across the beam. He readjusted his other hand and held on as tight as he could. If he lost his grip, he would undoubtedly hang. He did not have the strength to hold himself up with one hand for more than a few seconds. The slip knot was still against his throat and threatening to tighten the more his fingers ached from holding his weight. Terror gripped him in death's eternal embrace and he knew what a fool he was to put himself in such danger. He didn't want to die, he wanted to live, but to do so, he would have to fight hard to survive. "Help!" he yelled. His hope was someone outside might hear him and come to his rescue. "Jesus, help me!" he cried as he shoved his right hand deeper into the crevice to hold on. His left hand had been dragged across the rough wood by the two hundred and some pounds he was trying to hold up. His right hand was sliding across the wood as gravity pulled on him continuously. He shoved his left hand deeper into the narrow space as his right hand slipped off the beam. "Help!" he screamed. His fingers were already aching and his arms were growing weak.

The basement door opened, casting light down the stairs.

"Help!" he cried out desperately.

Martha came down the stairs as quickly as her

aging knees could take her. She gasped in horror to see Roger desperately trying to hang on for his life. "Oh, my Lord!" she exclaimed. She looked desperately for anything that would help and grabbed the dining chair and pulled it over for him to stand on but his feet weren't low enough to reach it.

"Help me!" he cried desperately. He once again shoved his fingers deeper into the crevice to hold on.

"I'm trying," Martha frantically murmured. She stepped up on the wobbly chair and reached for the knot trying earnestly to loosen it with her shaking hands. When she got the knot to loosen, she pulled the homemade noose off Roger's neck. Roger could no longer hold himself up and dropped down to the floor. His knees collapsed and he fell into a pile on the floor, slamming into the side of the unsteady wooden chair Martha stood on. The force of his body hitting the side of the chair legs knocked Martha off the chair and she fell towards the floor face first. She put out her arm to protect herself and landed on her extended arm and then hit her head as her body slammed against the concrete floor.

"Are you okay?" Roger asked frantically while crawling towards her.

"Get away from me!" she hollered painfully. She slowly sat up, holding her arm and sobbing immediately. A cut on her forehead bled, trickling blood down her face.

"I'm sorry, Martha! I'm so sorry. Are you okay? Let me see."

She slapped his hands away from her and glared at him angrily. "What are you doing? You were going to hang yourself?" she was stunned. He didn't answer. "Roger, why in the world would you try to hang yourself? Answer me, damn it!" she shouted.

"I'm sorry."

"Answer me, Roger. Tell me why you tried to hang yourself!" Tears slipped down her cheeks beside a line of blood that streamed lightly down the middle of her face.

He maneuvered across the floor, reached up on the table, and handed her the letter he had written. "I can't face you, Martha. I'm ruined and I can't do it."

She read the note with a sour expression. "So, you're taking the easy way out, so you don't have to face the consequences of your actions? Do you think killing yourself is going to make things better for you? For me? For our children? Do you know how selfish that is? Do you realize how much pain you would cause all of us?" she shouted in a high-pitched voice. "Roger, I love you. Do you even know what that means? How could you try to hang yourself? Don't you realize how loved you are by your family and friends? Thank God I came home when I did or I wouldn't have you anymore. Don't ever do that again! It's not worth it."

He sat with his legs crossed and his head buried in the palm of his hands, sobbing. "I'm so sorry... God forgive me, I'm so sorry."

"Do you love me, Roger?" she asked angrily.

He removed his hands, revealing a face covered by tears and red eyes draining his body of water. "Martha, I messed up. I did something I should never have done and I am so sorry. I didn't mean to hurt you."

"And you think killing yourself is going to make me feel better?" she asked with disgust. "Roger, we'll talk about what you did later. I cannot believe you would do this to me! Don't ever try killing yourself again. You scared me, Roger. You scared me so much!" She began to weep.

He slid across the floor to hold her. "I'm so..."

"Don't touch my arm!" she screamed. "I think it's broken."

He wiped the blood off her face with his handkerchief. "Let me take care of you."

A sincere tear rolled down from her sorrow-filled face. "You have for thirty-four years. Don't stop now. Don't you understand that what you do impacts me? Even by trying to hang yourself, you broke my arm and made me bleed. Just imagine what you would have done to me if you had succeeded in killing yourself. You can't take that kind of pain back. And it always hurts others more than you know."

6

Elias Renner and Jude Maddox had gone to the first saloon they came to and had a few drinks while waiting for their dinner. After speaking with Marvin Aggler and learning Marshal Matt Bannister was putting Marvin up in a hotel for a couple of days, the two men were happy to hear it. They wanted to stay in Branson and spend their money on the excitement of Rose Street. They were quite pleased to find a bunk bed at the Lucky Man's Bunkhouse available and have the freedom of the weekend to have some fun before leaving town to find work. After riding for five long days with little to eat, they ate heartedly and went back to the bunkhouse to take a nap before they ventured into the night on Rose Street.

Elias Renner was a tall and thin-shouldered man in his late thirties. He had short dark hair and a graying dark beard about four inches long that extended his oblong face. His most prominent features were his high cheekbones and brown eyes. It was late and the busyness of Ugly John's Saloon had slowly died down. He turned his body around to peer at the empty tables with a scowl. "Where is everyone? It can't be that late. The dance hall is closed but I know they don't stay open all night. Does this town have a curfew or something? What time is it? We just got into town from riding for five days from Boise City and everyone's gone to bed, just when we'd like to liven up a good time!" He grinned at Big John Pederson, who was working behind the bar.

Big John checked his pocket watch. "It's three-thirty in the morning. Most folks work on Fridays and have been up since the sun rises. Most of them go home by this time. They'll be back tomorrow night, though, refreshed and fired up to stay later. It happens every weekend. It's about closing time for me too."

"Oh, come on, is there anywhere else open? We're just a couple of cowboys passing through town with a hearty appetite for fun."

Big John asked, "Where are you fellow's passing through to? If you don't mind me asking."

Elias was quick to answer, "We met up with an old cowboy heading to the..." He looked at his friend. "What is it? The...?"

"Big Z Ranch," Jude Maddox replied. He quietly sat at the bar holding his drink halfway to his mouth. It was almost empty.

"That's right, the Big Z Ranch. We're heading there to inquire about hiring on. We hear they're looking for horsemen. Have you heard of the spread?"

Big John nodded. "I've heard of it. I knew the owner, Kyle Lenning. He used to come in here and gamble sometimes. He drowned in the river this past summer. His wife's the actual owner and runs it. I've never met her but I hear she's young, pretty and tougher than most men around here."

Elias chuckled. "That's what I like to hear. She sounds like a better business opportunity than the job. Huh, Jude?" he nudged his friend with his elbow and a grin.

Jude Maddox was in his mid to late thirties. He was a bit shorter but broader in the shoulders than Elias. Jude had straight sandy blonde hair that was over his mid-ear. He had a week's worth of whiskers on his usually clean-shaven, square-shaped face with light blue eyes and a somber expression that stayed on his face. He smirked slightly. "Yep. I'll have to clean up before we go, so I make a good impression."

Big John scoffed at the two men lightly. "She's Matt Bannister's sister, so any funny stuff might get you killed instead of fired. I hear she's tough."

Elias laughed. "Well, I knew Matt was around. The old cowpuncher we met up with is Matt's pal and was asked to help with the ranch. Old Marvin didn't say anything about her being Matt's sister, though. We just figured we'd see some new country and get paid for it. I guess it pays to have Matt as a friend, though, because Matt's paying for that old coot to stay uptown in that nice hotel. Matt's paying for his meals and all, but we get to sleep in that bunkhouse clear down on Second Street."

"The Lucky Man's Bunkhouse," Jude added, taking a drink of his whiskey. "It's better than the ground."

"The Lucky Man's namesake doesn't fit it, though, at least not for us tonight. I was really hoping for a hoot and hollering good time. The night started all right but it fizzled out before we did. Hard to say when we'll have another opportunity, so this night has been a bit disappointing. I thought this would be a wild cattle town, not a mining community."

Big John quickly smashed a spider that ran across the top of the bar with his hand. He wiped it off onto the floor. "The silver mine's our biggest employer but we're a pretty diverse city. We have all kinds here. The true cattle towns are north of here."

"Well, there's a couple of new cowboys on the block now. Once we start working and get some time off, we'll be back and raising some hell. Big John, I gotta tell you we started up the right side of the street and are working our way back down the left side and so far, I like the feel of your place best."

"Thank you."

Elias set his empty glass down on the counter. "John, we've boughten three shots a piece and a beer from you, so far, and now we're out of money. What are the chances you spot us another drink before we head out?"

John answered sternly, "Not good. I get nothing for free, so I give nothing for free. I'll see you men when you get paid."

Jude stood and put his hat on. "Let's go."

Elias stared at John with a questionable grin. "It's going to be hard for us to be friends with that attitude, John."

John shrugged uncaringly. "I'm not your friend. I sell drinks."

Elias laughed. "Well, that settles that. It's late and we probably have an early morning. I hear the new lady boss is coming to town tomorrow for a dance of some sort. I imagine I'll be whooping it up with her on the dance floor. I imagine her life's going to change for the better tomorrow night. Love grows where Elias goes." He laughed. Elias tapped Jude on the arm, "If she's pretty, I might end up marrying her and becoming your boss!" he chuckled.

John smirked doubtfully. "I wish you luck. It's my understanding that she's courting Truet Davis. Matt's deputy."

Jude glared at Big John with a sudden hostile expression. "Truet Davis? The same Truet Davis from Sweethome, Idaho?"

"I believe so. Heck, of a nice guy. Do you know him?"

Jude's cold blue eyes glanced at John with a bitter scowl on his lips. "No." He turned to his friend. "Let's go."

They walked up Rose Street back to a smaller saloon named Ebenezer's. Earlier, a young gambler named Dean McDowell had been winning steadily against some other men at the poker table. They hoped Dean might advance them a few dollars to join back into the game and buy them another drink. Dean had been a liberal drink buyer with those who played against him while he hardly drank at all.

Dean had not moved from the poker table and glanced over at them with a smile when they entered. "You boys back for more?" Dean had taken a fair share of their money earlier in the evening.

Elias approached the table where two other men sat with Dean. Neither of them seemed as excited as they were when they sat down earlier. "You already took all our money. We're here to beg for a chance to win some of it back. But you'd have to advance us a few dollars. If you're up to the challenge?"

Dean snickered. He was a young man in his twenties, clean-cut and well dressed. He was a friendly man with a warmness in his eyes. "These men are about to leave me anyway. Heck, why not? Sit down, let's play. The worst that can happen is win my money back. Do you want a drink?"

Elias grinned. "We'd love one."

An hour later, Dean, Elias and Jude left Ebenezer's together when it closed for the night and walked down an empty Rose Street towards Dean's hotel. Elias laughed as Dean told them a story.

"You're a funny man, Dean. You might've taken all our money but you're one humorous follow," Elias said.

Dean chuckled. "You have to have fun, you know? You have to be able to enjoy life and laugh the sorrows away. Do you know how many people walk around here with sour stomachs on their faces and meanness like you wouldn't believe? Far too many. Like your friend, Jude. I haven't seen him smile until now. You need to lighten up, Jude. You act like you have all the world's problems on your shoulders and you don't."

Jude glanced at him. "You don't know me well enough to say one way or another."

"True. But I have to read people because gambling is a tricky trade when you take someone's money. All I've been saying becomes important when you meet up with a man angry at the world. You just never know when they're going to overact and turn violent, so you have to be ready for that too."

"What do you do when that happens? Run?" Elias asked with a chuckle. He couldn't imagine Dean was a threatening fellow. Dean didn't carry a gun and the knife on his waistband appeared to be more of a child's toy with its thick fancy brass-colored decorative handle that stood out like a red flag in a snow-covered field.

Dean laughed good-naturedly to Elias' question. "I run as fast as I can if need be. But mostly, I'll read the person and call their bluff. And if anyone tries to attack me, I have a surprise waiting for them. I have this." He pulled the fixed blade knife out of a sheath on his belt. The knife handle was about seven inches long and thicker than most knife handles. It appeared to be brass plated with intricate designs on the handle that greatly appealed to the eye. The blade was thinner than most knives and about eight inches long that came to a sharp point.

Elias snickered. "That's a nice little dagger but most men carry a broader knife that will fillet you right open. You want to leave a bigger hole than that if you're going to poke someone. Needle pricks heal too fast," he teased.

Dean grinned. He was glad to hear Elias make fun of it because he looked forward to showing them what his knife could do. "Watch." He moved his fingers on the handle and, suddenly, there was a flash of metal and the blade flipped outward from the handle, expanding the blade from eight inches to fifteen inches long.

"What the..." Elias started to ask as he stared at the long blade. "No way!" he shouted out, impressed. "How did you do that?"

Dean chuckled. "It's a knife my grandfather gave me. I don't know if it is Italian or British, or exactly what you call it even. But it is the neatest knife you have ever seen, right? I've never seen another like it."

"Yeah, no doubt. How's it work?"

"Well, there's a small little lever down here that unlocks the blade and then you have to push this lever to release the blade and it just opens up real quick. It doubles the blade length right before your eyes."

"How do you put it back?"

"Press this lever here and you fold it back into the handle, like this. And now it is a fixed blade just like any other. No one would know it was different until I release the extra seven inches of blade. So, when I get into a knife fight, I just do this." Dean released the expanding blade and it quickly flipped the blade out to fifteen inches long. "And the other person usually walks away because it becomes a small sword." Dean laughed.

Jude Maddox asked, "How many knife fights have you been in?"

Dean laughed. "None! I don't like to fight. Making friends is much easier," he explained.

"Can I try your knife out?" Elias asked.

"Sure, but you can't have it."

"No, of course not. That's incredible, though. I've never seen anything like it. Are these new?"

Dean shrugged. "As I said, my Grandfather gave it to me years ago. He was from England, so it could be from there or be Italian. That's what a fella once told me anyway but I don't know. Grandad just called it an expanding blade knife. And that's all I know about it."

Elias held the knife blade in his hand and stared at it with a growing smile. "That is amazing. How do you close it again?" He closed the blade and opened it up again. "How much do you want for it?" he asked.

Dean laughed. "Oh, no. I won't sell it for any price. I got it from my grandfather. It's a family heirloom." He held his hand out for his knife.

"All right, let me close it for you," Elias said, glancing around on the empty street carefully. He folded the blade back into the handle. "That's an amazing knife. It's too bad you won't sell it, though. It might've saved your life."

"Huh?" Dean asked and then laughed at the humorous statement.

Elias pushed the lever expanding the blade and then turned his body quickly towards Dean and drove the long dagger in a sharp, upwards arch into Dean's abdomen, forcing the blade up behind Dean's sternum. Dean bent over slightly with a gasp, slack-jawed and in shock. Elias pulled the blade halfway out and then drove it upwards again at a different angle, puncturing a lung and then the heart. Dean dropped to his knees. Elias twisted the knife around so the cutting edge was upwards and then pulled it out of Dean's abdomen at an upwards angle slicing through his flesh up to the bottom of the sternum bone. Dean fell into an expanding pool of blood in the middle of Rose Street.

Elias wiped the long blade off on Dean's back. "I think I'll get our money back," he said and bent down to take Dean's leather billfold out of his coat's inner pocket.

Jude searched the street to make sure there were no witnesses. His attention went to a faint light in an upstairs window in the dance hall. A young blonde-haired woman stood in the window holding the curtains open, staring at them, mesmerized by what she was seeing. Jude cursed and his hand went to his revolver, automatically removing the hammer thong, pulled his gun, and fired towards the window. The bullet penetrated the glass and the woman disappeared behind the curtains. The shot was amplified by the silence of the early morning. "Come on," Jude ordered and ran down the alley behind the dance hall disappearing into the darkness between the buildings.

They ran into Chinatown and hid behind a corner of a building that was unlit. "What were you shooting at?" Elias asked bitterly. He was irritated about the shot drawing attention to them.

"A woman in the dance hall watched you kill him. I tried to kill her, but I missed."

Elias cursed. "I should've led him into the alley. How far away was she?"

"Half block, maybe."

"If she was in the dance hall, she's never seen us before, so we should be okay as long as she doesn't see us again."

Jude was frustrated. "What were you thinking, Elias? You didn't have to kill him! You could've stolen the knife before we left town tomorrow night. Now, we have to kill barkeep before he leaves because he knows we left with Dean! We're going to get caught if we let him live."

Elias cursed. "I didn't think about that. Let's go." They ran up Flower Lane behind Rose Street to stay out of sight. They made sure the street near Ebenezer's was clear of people before Elias peeked into the window and saw the barkeeper sweeping the floor before he went home. Elias knocked on the door. Four blocks down Rose Street, a couple of men circled the dead body of Dean. Elias tried to remain hidden in the doorway of Ebenezer's.

The barkeeper hollered to be heard, "We're closed."

Elias faked a sense of urgency. "I dropped my room key. I need to look for my room key. Please."

"It's not here."

"My drunk friend tossed it into one of the spittoons. I'll look really quick if it's okay with you." He placed his hands together prayerfully. "Come on, buddy, I have to get some sleep."

The barkeeper sighed and came to the door. "That's some friend. You have one minute." He opened the door.

Elias stepped inside and walked back by the bar and began looking into a spittoon. "I know. My luck's never been good when it comes to finding friends. I can't see," He used his boot to tip the spittoon over, spilling the liquid contents out onto the floor.

"I just swept the floor!" the bartender griped as he stepped angrily away from the door towards Elias.

"I know," Elias said and pushed the pin and lever on his new knife and rammed the expanded blade upwards into the abdomen of the barkeeper just as he did with Dean. He pulled the knife halfway out and rammed it back up inside of the man at another angle to pierce the lungs and heart. Elias turned the handle upwards and sliced the man open as he dropped and then Elias pulled the long blade out. He cleaned the blade off on the man's back, then put the knife away before locking the front door. He pulled the man's body behind the bar and went to the back door. "Jude, let's get a drink on the house."

Jude chuckled. "Sounds good. Did you use your new knife?"

"You bet. I love this thing already," Elias said with enthusiasm. He opened the unlocked cash drawer and collected the money. "Look at this, Jude, we're already making money." He laughed.

"How are we going to explain our late night? We're bound to wake someone up when we go into the bunkhouse," Jude said, taking a drink of a bottle he pulled from behind the bar.

Elias sat down behind the bar to count the money and opened a bottle of his own. "No one's going to be watching the time if they wake up at all. We gambled here for a while, went to Ugly John's and went to bed around three-thirty. We just can't be seen walking back there."

"You might want to clean the blood off your hands and face before we go too far. Your duster too."

Elias chuckled. "With the money we earned tonight, I can buy a new duster in the morning. The river is not far, I can put some rocks in the pockets, tie this duster in a bundle and throw it in. I'll wash up here where there is a mirror though."

Jude looked sternly at his friend. "Maybe you ought to get moving on that. I'd like to get some sleep before anyone wakes up in the bunkhouse."

7

Sherry Stewart couldn't sleep. She was in an awful void, not knowing if she would get back to Ohio or be left stranded penniless in a town two thousand miles from the only home she knew. Bella offered her a job dancing once her face healed but Sherry was hesitant to commit to it. She had not considered the repercussions of her actions and now it was laying heavy on her mind. Hiram had given her a lovely home. Although he could be as dull as a dead turtle, she was warm, well-fed and secure. He said he loved her and she said the same in return but, in truth, she believed Hiram asked her to marry him in a fog of infatuation and the love that he had professed was wearing off. She met Hiram at Elvira's Red Room Parlier, a high-end brothel in Cleveland. Sherry was the prettiest and most expensive lady of the evening with a very select group of customers. Mostly all older men with money. After Hiram's wife passed away, he became an infatuated customer. Hiram wasn't the most handsome of men but he was a professional and responsible man who promised to take care of her for the rest of his life if she would marry him. He was in his late fifties and the investment of a will and life insurance sounded good to a young lady with an entire life ahead of her. She knew he was lonely but the proposition left her with a choice to continue selling her body or eventually becoming a semi-wealthy young widow. She accepted his marriage proposal and they were married just over a year ago. They didn't live in a mansion by any means. Still, they did have a respectable home with a view of Lake Erie and the finances to live a comfortable lifestyle. It was a much nicer way to live than entertaining men. Now, that she'd been caught in another man's bed, she was afraid of losing what she had and being forced back to Elvira's Red Room Parlier.

Being twenty-two years old and a bit restless and adventurous in spirit, she didn't want to live like an old maid sitting at home day after day knitting afghans and dusting the same coffee table. She wanted a social life and to adventure outside and see new things. She wanted to travel the country and see what could be seen, not stay in a hotel and wait for a tired old man to come home from work and not have the energy to do anything. Young, bored and restless was a recipe for disaster and it had come together in a big way with Roger King. Strange, Roger King wasn't handsome either, but like a cuddly bunny, he was cute, gentle and lovable. Loneliness, like harshness, can tempt someone into another's arms to fill the emptiness that isn't being met at home. It wasn't Roger who seduced her; she had seduced Roger to break up the monotony of her life. The bottle of wine was to blame for her falling asleep in his arms instead of going back to her room. She did regret the wine now that Hiram had thrown her out of the hotel. Had Hiram never known she had left their room, it would have been best. Breaking the monotony of her life's routine had broken her marriage vows and Hiram caught her. Only one question remained: Now what?

In the quiet of the small room she was given, she realized the consequences of her actions. If Hiram refused to pay for her trip back home, her stepfather might but his expectations in return were not worth the cost. Her stepfather was a horrible man. If Hiram insisted on a divorce, she would have lost a comfortable life that every woman in her former business would consider her a fool to lose. Now that her moment of fun was over, she feared being left behind in a strange town two thousand miles from the only city she had ever known. She couldn't care less if she ever saw her mother or stepfather again. Her mother turned her head and intentionally looked the other way every time her stepfather abused her. They were the reason she ended up in Elvira's Red Room Parlier.

Sherry sat close to the window at a small desk, writing under the light of a kerosene lamp. The dance hall music, dancing and the men talking and whooping it up were considerable for most of the night. But the random noise and yelling on Rose

Street was more annoying when she tried to sleep earlier. It was no wonder the lady who stayed in the room moved into Helen's room on the other side of the building when Helen moved out. Now that it was quiet outside, Sherry was unable to sleep. She used a quill and ink to write a letter just shy of pleading for her husband's forgiveness. In truth, she didn't miss him at all but, if he'd forgive her, she'd have her comfort and security back.

The sound of laughter on Rose Street at that late hour brought some curiosity to see who was out at four-thirty in the morning. She peeked out of her thick curtain and saw three men walking in the faintly lit street. Her curiosity turned to horror when she watched one of the men stabbing another with a long knife. She was horrified and couldn't look away until the third man noticed her, drew his gun, and fired, shattering the window and leaving a hole in the wall behind her. Terrified, Sherry found herself on the floor with her nose buried in the rug, too afraid to scream, whisper or even move. Through the broken window, she heard one of the men say they needed to go but she was frozen to the floor with a thousand-pound block of fear on her back. Breathing short, shallow breaths and frozen like a dead dog in ice, she remained motionless, expecting to hear the sound of the door being kicked in downstairs. It was no more than a minute or two when she heard the other ladies talking in the hallway as the gunshot had woken them up.

Sherry leaped onto her feet and swung the door open and ran into the hallway sobbing.

Christine Knapp was enveloped in a hug raising her concern. "Are you okay? You look as white as a ghost."

Sherry sobbed. "They shot at me! They stabbed a man and shot at me," she whimpered through her sobbing as the terror of the moment overwhelmed her. She clung to Christine tightly.

"Who?" one of the ladies asked.

"Who shot at you?"

"I don't know. Out there!" Sherry pointed towards the street.

Christine broke loose of her and entered Sherry's room and could see the broken glass and hole in the wall. Cautiously, she pulled the curtain back and peeked out the window. A lone body laid motionless face down in the middle of the street. "Oh, my goodness!" she exclaimed and left the room quickly to run downstairs to pound on Bella and Dave's door anxiously.

Dave opened the door with a concerned expression, "What's the matter?" The other girls had followed her downstairs and stood around her chaotically speaking all at once. Sherry was being held by a dancer named Susan.

Bella was quickly beside Dave. "Girls, quiet down! Now, what is it?" she asked with great concern.

Christine answered anxiously, "Someone stabbed a man outside and he's lying there. They shot at Sherry!"

"Who did?"

"I don't know! Sherry saw them, not me," Christine answered.

"Where?" Dave asked, not entirely coherent with a few hours of sleep.

"Outside…He's lying on the street. Sherry watched him being stabbed."

Sherry tried to compose herself and spoke between heavy breaths and shaking voice, "They saw me and I'm afraid they're coming after me next."

Dave answered quickly, "No one's coming for you. Susan, go wake up Gaylon and tell him to bring his shotgun." He left the ladies to go put on some warmer clothes and grab his revolver.

"Tell me what happened," Bella said, bringing Sherry into her apartment and sitting her down on the davenport. She asked the group of ladies. "Will one of you make us some tea?"

"Of course," Angela replied softly and went to the dance hall kitchen to get it started.

Sherry was scared. "All they have to do is break the window and unlock the door and come in here! What if they come back?"

Bella answered reassuringly, "They're not coming here, Sweetheart. Dave and Gaylon are both here and so am I. We won't let anyone harm any of you, ladies. I promise. Do you know who the men were? It wasn't your husband shooting at you, was it?" Bella asked with a heartbroken frown on her lips.

Sherry shook her head quickly.

"Did you recognize them at all?"

"No."

"What did they look like? You need to tell me everything you remember so you don't forget anything when Matt gets here."

"Matt will be here?" Sherry asked, looking at Bella quickly. There was an underlying tone of interest in her voice.

Bella motioned towards Christine, who stood nearby listening. "When he hears someone shot at one of our ladies, there isn't an army of men that could keep him away from checking on Christine."

Gaylon Dirks carried his shotgun out front and found Dave kneeling over a body of a young man. Dave had turned him over to look at his face. "Oh, my goodness," Gaylon gasped. He had been slit open.

"Do you know him?" Dave asked somberly.

"No."

"The killers are gone. Gaylon, I'm going to stay here and protect the ladies if they do come back. I need you to run to the sheriff's office and get the sheriff."

"Not Matt?"

"I wish. This is the sheriff's jurisdiction."

Before too long, a small crowd of curious men gathered around the body and one of them knew the deceased young man and said his name was Dean McDowell. Dean was new in town and spent most of his time in Ebenezer's gambling at the poker table. Dean had come to Branson in late November and was planning to make his way to Portland in the spring. He was easy to get along with, according to the man who knew him. It took an hour but, finally, the sheriff, Tim Wright, showed up with his deputies, Bob Ewing and Alan Garrison.

Tim sent Alan to fetch the undertaker, Solomon

Fasana, to collect the body off the street. Solomon's mortuary had burned down a few weeks prior, so he was now renting a small house as a temporarily funeral parlor.

Tim Wright stepped into the dance hall and sat down at a table near the bar with Bob Ewing and Dave to wait for Sherry to come out of Bella's apartment. The sheriff wasn't too comfortable talking business to the very people he had once tried to blackmail. Tim could convince most people that he upheld the law with integrity but Dave and Bella knew better. They knew he was a crooked man that went where the winds of opportunity took him. It made for an uncomfortable atmosphere. Tim waited at the table and sighed with his palms getting sweaty.

Tim asked Dave, "It's early for a drink but after seeing a sight like that, I have no appetite for breakfast. Dave, can I get a shot of your strongest whiskey? Maybe a few shots? It's kind of hard to see a body like that, you know?"

Dave was hesitant but reluctantly had Susan grab a bottle and two shot glasses for Tim and Bob. She set the bottle on the table.

"Thank you," Tim said. He poured himself a drink.

Bella opened the door of her apartment and was followed out by an attractive blonde-haired lady. She spoke gruffly, "This is Sherry. She's the one that witnessed the murder." Bella had no use for the sheriff and did not pretend to like him. Christine had stayed in Bella's apartment.

Tim put his attention on Sherry. "I'm the Branson sheriff, Tim Wright. If you wouldn't mind, can you tell me what happened?"

Sherry shook his hand while taking a seat across from him. Bella sat beside her protectively. "I was in my room…" she paused as an unexpected knock on the front door drew all of their attention. Gaylon Dirks quickly answered the door and, a moment later, let a middle-aged lady step into the dance hall.

Gaylon interrupted, "Sheriff, this lady is Felix Young's wife. She says he hasn't come home, and Ebenezer's is closed and locked."

Tim frowned irritably. "Ma'am, I'm in the middle of something. If he's not home yet, maybe he stopped off at the bordello or somewhere."

The lady grimaced angrily. "How dare you! My husband would never do that! He's always home by five-thirty at the latest and it's almost six. Something is wrong! I know my husband."

"Ma'am, if the place is locked up, I don't know what to tell you," Tim said with a shrug.

Dave spoke, "Actually, you better go check it out, Tim. That is where Dean liked to play poker, according to... I forget the man's name already."

Tim directed his deputy, Bob Ewing, "You and Alan go check it out with her." Tim turned his attention back to Sherry but was interrupted by Dave asking Gaylon to walk Missus Young to Ebenezer's saloon with them and then home if need be.

Before long, Alan Garrison burst through the door, out of breath from running. "Sheriff, you need to get to Ebenezer's. Felix Young is dead! There's blood everywhere!"

8

Matt had plans of buying a pair of black boots to match the black suit Christine had picked out for him to wear to the dance but those plans had changed. The murders on Rose Street had taken an urgent priority, and the Branson Sheriff, Tim Wright, had no leads on the two suspects. The only witness who had come forward so far that had gotten a good look at the two suspects was Ed Taylor. Ed was in Ebenezer's the night before and witnessed two strangers playing poker with Dean McDowell. However, a stranger to one man did not make the two men strangers from out of town. According to Sheriff Wright's information, the two murderers both wore Stetson hats, spurs, and a duster over their gun belts. Matt had a reasonable suspicion that it might be the two cowboys that came into town with Marvin Aggler. Every profession had a specific dress code. Miners didn't wear spurs or gun belts but were the only ones to use the six-inch iron candle holders with a sharp point that they'd hammer into the rock walls for lighting called candle picks, for self-defense occasionally. Lumberjacks did not wear spurs or a gun belt either but cork boots or a fifteen-inch hatchet on a belt sheath wasn't all too uncommon. Both miners and lumbermen were hard-drinking men and tough as nails with the endurance to fight long and hard but they were armed with tools they used in the rough nature of their profession. Cowboys were unique with their clothing and the tools of their trade. There were plenty of ranchers in Jessup County and it was not that rare for a group of cowboys to come into town and cause a bit of trouble with the lumbermen and miners.

The Big Z Ranch was just north of Willow Falls and there were other small ranches spread out along the base of the Blue Mountains. However, the big ranches and cattle towns were north of Branson in Cold Water, Cato Springs, Elmore, Trinity Lake, and the ranching community hub, Hollister. Most cowboys went to Hollister to let loose and cause trouble on the weekends but Branson was much larger and had more to offer. Sherry had mentioned the three men were walking northward towards the dance hall so, by that bit of information, it put the men on the south end of Rose Street, narrowing down where the men had visited. Ed Taylor had gotten the best look at them and described two men as being in their thirties. One was tall and thin with short dark hair and a graying beard. Ed couldn't remember the man's name, but the tall one did most of the talking and laughed easily. The second man was shorter but broad-shouldered and muscular. He hadn't shaved in a week or so and had exceptionally light blue eyes and sandy blonde hair. Ed couldn't remember his name either but said the shorter man was not friendly. Ed Taylor stated the two men had left Ebenezer's for an hour and then came back complaining that Ugly John's Saloon had closed.

Matt confided in Tim that he might know who the killers were and asked Tim to cease any investigation until Matt could verify it was the two men he suspected. In the meantime, to minimalize the risk of the murderers fleeing, Matt had Tim start a rumor that he had arrested the two men accused of the killings.

Matt and Truet walked to Big John Pederson's house and knocked on the door. It was common knowledge that John worked late at night and let his bar manager and employees open the saloon during the day. Matt was not surprised when John opened the door, a bit cranky about being woken up.

"What?" Big John shouted. His expression changed when he recognized Matt and Truet at his door. "Matt? What are you two doing here?"

Matt apologized for waking him up. "You may not have heard but Felix Young was murdered last night as was a young gambler named Dean McDowell."

John's brow furrowed at the news. "Felix is dead? Who would want to hurt him? He's the nicest man on Rose Street."

"That's what I'm trying to find out. Any strangers come into your place last night? In particular, a pair of cowboys?" Matt asked.

Big John nodded. "Yeah. I know who you might be talking about. They came in late and stayed about an hour. You ought to know them. They said they were here to work for your sister. I wouldn't let her hire them if I was you. Is that who killed Felix?"

Matt answered casually, "No, they didn't, but they might've played poker with the man who did. Out of curiosity, why do you suggest I tell my sister not to hire them?" Matt asked with interest.

Big John peered at Matt skeptically. "Those two men are troublemakers and that's why I don't believe you. You should arrest them before they even get a look at your sister or her property. The shorter one took an interest in you, Truet. When I told them, you were courting Matt's sister, he got some fire in his eyes. Said he didn't know you, though."

"What did he say? Anything?" Truet asked. His short brown hair fluttered lightly in a westwardly breeze. His brown eyes remained steadfast on John with interest.

"He just asked if you were the same Truet from Sweethome."

A cold chill ran down Truet's spine. "Did he say his name?"

"Not that I remember."

Matt answered, "Marvin told me their names. The one John's talking about must be Jude Maddox. He must be related to Farrian. The other one's named Elias Renner."

Truet had killed a local gunfighter named Farrian Maddox in Gold Hill, in the Idaho Territory. If there was one thing Truet knew about, personally, it was revenge for a loved one. Whether Jude Maddox was Farrian's brother or other relation, Truet knew he had to put his guard up and become more aware of his surroundings immediately. He asked John, "Did he say anything else?"

"I don't remember, Truet. I don't think he liked you, though. He didn't say much at all. It was just the look on his face."

"Did they say anything else that might help us?" Matt asked.

John yawned. "Just that they came here to work for your sister. That's about it." John set his hand on the door jamb and leaned against it comfortably. "I don't own a saloon to make friends, I own it to make money. I'm not known for being sociable and I don't care to hear the customer's problems or life stories. I don't particularly like to talk to anyone at all. But doing what I do for as long as I have, you get to recognize bad characters. Don't let them get near your sister."

"Thank you, John."

"Oh, Matt. Even though I'm not particularly friendly, there are people that I come to like a lot. You know Chusi Yellowbear was a friend of mine, don't you?" John asked with a sourness in his voice.

"I do."

John scoffed with disgust while making a sour expression. "You should have shot that coward Frank Ellison for killing him. I should've pulled the trigger when I had Wes Wasson in my sights that night out back. That would have saved Chusi's life too. I guess we both have our share of regrets."

Matt nodded sadly. "I suppose we do."

"You find those two cowboys and string them up somewhere. The Rose Street head gate worked fine for Ballenger; it will work fine for those two men as well. I'm letting you know now that if they come into my saloon tonight, I'm grabbing my shotgun and filling them full of lead. Felix was my friend. And I'm tired of seeing my friends being killed and the killers walking around free."

Matt and Truet walked to the Monarch Hotel and knocked on the door to Marvin Aggler's room. He welcomed them inside with a friendly smile. He had bathed and shaved, gotten himself a haircut and dressed in his nicest clothes which were still work clothes.

Matt declined to enter his room. "Marvin, I only have a minute. I have a big dance tonight I need to get prepared for. But I wanted to let you know Annie is in town today and thinks it would be a great opportunity for her to get to know you and your companions over lunch. Can you let your two companions know that Annie wants to meet you three gentlemen at two o'clock in the Monarch Restaurant? She'll be buying lunch so let the other two fellas know. Can you do that? She's excited to meet you."

Marvin nodded. "I will. I look forward to meeting her."

"What are your two friends' names again?"

"I don't know about the friends' part but their names are Elias Renner and Jude Maddox."

"Which one is which?" Matt asked.

Marvin laughed. "Elias is taller. Jude is the shorter and quiet one. Once you meet them, you'll be able to tell them apart. Are you coming to lunch with us?"

Matt nodded. "I wouldn't miss it."

Marvin grinned his crooked smile. "Are you going to have your cousin, William, join us? I have to tell you, he's quite a character. We've had some good laughs already."

Matt's lips rose slowly. "He'd be mad if I didn't invite him. I'll see you then."

9

Roger King had slept in the guest room and woke up to the quiet unmistakable sniffling of Martha weeping in their bedroom. He had slept uncomfortably due to the rope burn that removed a layer of skin from his throat and his fingers throbbed from clinging to a support beam while gravity beckoned his two-hundred and forty pounds towards the end of the rope. His aching fingers had trouble buttoning his shirt around his neck and the missing layer of skin stung against the cotton fabric of his shirt. It had never taken so long to tie a bowtie but he refused to let Martha see the purplish mark Sherry had left on his neck.

Roger had asked the neighbor's boy to request Doctor Ambrose to make a house call to tend Martha's broken arm. Doctor Ambrose took her to his office to set the bone in a cast made of plaster of paris and strips of cotton fabric. Martha had enough decency to spare Roger any more humiliation by saying she had fallen down the stairs. When they returned home, Martha told Roger to make his dinner and sleep anywhere but with her. She did not want to talk about what he had done nor offered any indication of what she was thinking. Martha went upstairs to their bedroom and closed the door. Their home had become uncharacteristically silent and cold.

Roger read his Bible and focused on reading Psalm 51. King David wrote it after committing adultery with Bathsheba and having her husband killed to protect his name and reputation. Bathsheba had become pregnant while her husband, Uriah, was at war. Roger was not reading the story and the following Psalm to justify his sin but to reassure himself that he could be forgiven. It was strange how the words written by King David in Psalm 51 over two thousand years ago shared the same brokenness and shame that Roger was experiencing. The honesty in the psalm dug deep and brought out the sorrow of betraying not only Martha but the Lord, too. Sexual sin was an all-encompassing action that only led to his disgrace before God and the terrible guilt and shame he felt while facing his wife. The church and the community would know he was an unfaithful man and his reputation and representation of Jesus as a Christian would be tarnished. Everything he once held sacred had been compromised by his lust for a beautiful young lady with an amorous nature. As King David had centuries ago, Roger found the consequences weren't worth surrendering to the moment of temptation.

He knocked on Martha's bedroom door softly and opened the door slowly. He peeked in and saw her sitting upright in bed with puffy eyes and a handkerchief in her hand. "I brought you a bowl of soup and some crackers."

"I have no appetite," she said with a sniffle.

"You must be hungry. You have to eat something, Martha. The dance is tonight and everyone will expect you to be there."

"I'm not going there with you," she snapped sharply.

"I wouldn't expect you to." He set the tray with a bowl and crackers on the bedside table. He sat on the edge of the bed near her feet. His emotions could find no stable ground to slow the frequency of his tears. "I can't take back what I did. But it is killing me. I wish it never happened."

Her lips were pursed tightly into a small down-turned ball. "Then why did it?" she asked with a nasty tone he had not heard in close to twenty years when they had fought over his whipping their youngest daughter too hard. It wasn't a whipping; it was a beating he had given when he found their fourteen-year-old daughter kissing a boy behind the outhouse. Martha wasn't angry at the idea of whipping her but she was furious at the anger that had taken over him.

Roger shook his head slowly, unable to justify his decision. "Lust."

"Lust?" she questioned. "What's another word for that, Roger?"

"I don't…" he stuttered.

"Horney. Don't make it sound less sleazy than it is. You committed adultery against me, our marriage and against the Lord. Why do you think the Bible condemns adultery over thirty times? Reverend Painter just talked about this a few weeks ago. Don't you remember what he said? In times of sexual temptation, ask yourself, if I do this... then what? You're supposed to think about the consequences before you do them. You never asked yourself those words before you decided to stay the night with some young woman who is younger than our daughters! How do you think our daughters will feel about that, Roger? You have destroyed the trust, the honor and the sanctity of our marriage. I know you have never done this before but it only takes one time to ruin everything you have. You have ruined your job, your reputation, your home and our marriage. And you can count on it ruining your relationship with our children and grandchildren. That's the present tense, now what! Instead of having the wisdom to ask yourself, then what? before you give in to temptation." She paused and added softly, "You hurt me, Roger. You couldn't cut me deeper with a calvary sword."

His bottom lip quivered while the floor grew blurry from the amount of water in his eyes. "I never wanted to hurt you."

Martha chuckled bitterly. "You can't pretend like you didn't know it wouldn't! Don't lie to me, Roger. You didn't care if it hurt me as long as your horniness was gratified. You just didn't want me to know and, now that you're caught, I don't know if you're sorry for what you've done or if it's because you were caught. If you weren't caught, would I ever know? Or would you be, to use your word, lusting after all the pretty young ladies that came into the hotel?"

A tear rolled down his cheek. "It isn't because I was caught. I made a mistake that I don't ever want to do again. I can't do anything about it now but I am sorry. I can only ask you to forgive me and swear to you that I will never do that again. I love you, Martha." He looked on his beloved wife. "Do you think we can put this behind us?"

She hesitated to answer and took a deep breath. "Do you know why the Bible warns against adultery and sexual immorality? Let me remind you; it's because the consequences can be everlasting. What if I forgave you today and we decided never to mention it again and for a moment we were happy like we were a couple of days ago. But in a few weeks, what if you discovered you had syphilis and had given it to me? Could we forget about it? What if you gave me Gonorrhea Can we forget about it? Trust me; if she's going to spend the night with you after knowing you for a few days, she's going to do the same with other men a lot sooner. You aren't the first, I promise. And even if you're lucky enough to be spared those reminders, what if in three months we are happily planning a new move to start your new job somewhere and that young lady knocks on our door to say she's pregnant with your child? Can we just forget about it? I'm too old to raise another child, Roger. Are you going to divorce me and marry her to be that child's father? A child needs its father, Roger. How would you feel knowing you have a new son or daughter out there in the world somewhere without you? Could you forget about it?" She paused. "Sometimes you can't put things behind you because the 'now what' consequences are everlasting. That's why Reverend Painter was emphasizing asking 'then what?' before giving in to temptation. And I wish you had."

"Me too." A wave of anxiety flowed through him. He had not considered any risks of disease or pregnancy at the time. Fear of diseases that couldn't be healed or the chance of becoming a father again brought a sense of panic and urgency to pray. His life had the potential to become a nightmare and he had not even thought about it until now. He used a handkerchief to wipe his face dry. "Are you willing to give me another chance? Or are you thinking about leaving me?"

"Roger, I would like nothing more than to slap the snot out of you and leave you to rot on your own. But I love you. I always have. Don't you understand that if I had delayed any longer last night, I wouldn't have you and that would kill me? The Bible says love endures. And it will. I can't stop loving you but you hurt me deeply. You broke my heart like it's never been broken. I know I'm not young anymore nor attractive like I used to be. But I'm the only woman in the world that loves you just the way you are. I hope you can say the same about me."

"I can. I don't want to lose you. I've spent the last twenty-four hours praying for the Lord to forgive me and I know the Lord has. But I can never forgive myself if you won't forgive me. I am sorry for betraying you. It will never happen again."

She closed her eyes and a single tear slipped out and slowly rolled down her cheek. "I could say the words but I'm not ready to forgive you and I have that right. I can divorce you and no one would say I was in the wrong. To be honest, I don't know what I'm going to do. Do I love you? Yes. Am I willing to raise another child? No. The consequences I mentioned a moment ago are truly relevant and will affect our marriage. I won't be liable for the consequences of your stupidity. No, I can't say I forgive you and act like it didn't happen," she finished with a penetrating glare. She sighed, "I don't feel like it but I have to go to the dance tonight. Are you coming to help?"

"No, I'm not," he said uncomfortably.

"Then we have nothing more to talk about today. If you would please leave my room so I can get dressed, I'd appreciate it. I am very disappointed in you. Please leave."

"Martha..."

Her eyes were sharp enough to slice his skin. "Leave now."

10

Elias Renner and Jude Maddox walked towards the Monarch Hotel for a lunch meeting that only Elias was excited about attending. He had boughten a new black duster, had his hair and beard trimmed and wore a new red shirt to make a grand first impression on his new boss. If Matt's sister Annie was as pretty as he heard she was, then he had every intention of winning her heart. Elias and Jude had awoken to the news of the murders on Rose Street but any details of suspects had been suspiciously quiet. They didn't like knowing there were a few men who had seen them playing poker with Dean. Those men could identify them quickly enough if they were seen again. However, it was the lady in the window who concerned them the most. She had witnessed the actual crime of Elias killing Dean. The two men were packing up to leave town for good when the news reached them that the sheriff had arrested two men and accusing them of both murders. The announcement came with a sigh of relief and Elias and Jude could breathe easily enough to go shopping and prepare to meet Annie. They were told the day before that Annie Lenning would be in town, so they had no reason to be suspicious of the lunch meeting. But a natural part of breaking the law was a sense of paranoia that every step was a trap or a lawman taking notice of you. They were in the clear but wanted to leave Branson and ride out to the ranch to stay out of sight before any of the witnesses could identify them. After meeting Annie, they would ask for permission to do just that. Elias came up with the excuse of being broke and unable to afford to stay another night. The murderers had robbed Ebenezer's Saloon, but if they didn't have any money, then it couldn't have been them. It was a little extra insurance in case the Marshal had any suspicions.

"Relax, Jude. If they already arrested someone, then we are in the clear. Let's go in there and meet the Marshal and his sister and tell them we're looking for honest work. Which we are. Right?" Elias asked with confidence. "Don't worry, you won't have to say much because I'll be working my love grows where Elias goes magic."

Jude answered with a sour tone, "I'm not going to the dance or waiting until tomorrow to leave. We're not children. We don't need to be taken by the hand and guided here or there and I'm going to tell the woman as much. Just tell me where the ranch is and I'll find it."

Elias grinned at his friend's bitterness. Jude

didn't like social dinners with strangers who would be asking him a bunch of questions. Elias didn't mind them, though. "You heard Marvin. The Marshal just wants to meet his future brother-in-law." Elias chuckled. "I hope his sister is pretty like the barkeep said. I'm telling you, Jude, this might be our greatest opportunity yet. It's every cowpoke's dream to marry a beautiful, ranch-owning woman especially if she's a pretty and rich woman."

Jude ran his teeth over his bottom lip. "You forget that the barkeep said she was courting Truet Davis," There was a hint of resentment in his voice.

"Yeah, I know. But they're not married and anything can happen. You know, to break them up." He grinned. "You've seen that Elias magic work before. She'll be puddy in my hands."

Jude wasn't in the mood for Elias's empty talk. Truet Davis was a name that Jude had never expected to meet in person. Now that he was, it changed everything. "I'll be taking care of Truet for you. Good luck with her."

Elias questioned his friend curiously. "How do you know him? I've never heard of him."

Jude peered at Elias dumbfounded. "You know who he is. And if not, you've been kicked in the head too many times."

Elias laughed. "Remind me because I'm drawing a blank." He was unable to recall meeting anyone by that name.

"You don't know who Truet Davis is?" Jude was surprised. Elias had been his best friend since they were young and if Elias thought about it, he'd know who Truet was too. "I'll tell you later."

Elias grabbed the handle to open the door of the Monarch Hotel and paused. He spoke sincerely, "Okay. I know you don't like this kind of thing but don't cause a scene or be rude once we get inside. Let's just eat a good lunch and make a good first impression to charm our new boss lady." He stepped inside of the Monarch Hotel's entry and wiped his boots on a carpet before reaching for the second door leading to the hotel lobby. He tapped Jude's belly good-naturedly. "Smile. We want to make a good impression."

"Kiss my..." he paused as Elias opened the door and stepped into the lobby of the Monarch Hotel.

A rough-looking man with long, blonde, wavy hair stood in front of the hotel clerk's oval counter near the restaurant's door. He was dressed in a black suit with two reverse-handled ivory-handled Colts in his gun belt. His face was weathered and had a well-maintained goatee. He smiled warmly. "Welcome to the Monarch Hotel, gentlemen. My name is William. May I assist you somehow?"

Elias looked around the beautiful hotel, impressed. "This is where Marvin got to stay. Can you believe that?" he asked Jude. "Dang, it pays to have friends in high places."

William chuckled. "Can I help you, gentlemen? If you'd like a room, you can check in with this young lady right here. The restaurant is by reservation only and the lounge is only available to registered guests and members."

Elias spoke, "We were invited to have lunch with

Matt Bannister's sister and him. We're supposed to meet our friend Marvin Aggler here at two."

William turned behind him and grabbed a paper off the receptionist's desk. "Your names?"

"Elias Renner and Jude Maddox."

William nodded. "Very good," he said as he handed the reservation list back to the hotel clerk. "I'll have you seated in a moment. I do need to ask you to leave your weapons behind the courtesy desk here with this beautiful young lady if you would."

Pamela Collins blushed with his reference to her.

Elias began unbuckling his gun belt when he heard Jude say, "What if I don't want to?"

William shrugged uncaringly. "Then, you won't be able to have lunch here. We have a strict policy about weapons in our facility. You can take them to your room if you'd like to rent a room but no weapons are allowed in the restaurant or the lounge. You can understand that, I'm sure."

Jude asked William, "And who's going to enforce it? You? I notice you're wearing quite a setup," Jude challenged.

William's lips turned upwards just a touch. It was easy to recognize the Maddox ice-blue eyes and handsome facial features that Farrian had shared. Undoubtedly, Jude was the elder brother that Farrian had mentioned to William a time or two. William wanted to say more like he knew Farrian personally but he was given strict instructions to be professional and not ruffle any feathers.

William stepped a touch closer to Jude and spoke humbly just above a whisper, "It is my job to look the part, you know? I was hired to look good and give the place a sense of security. I would appreciate it if you would just do as you're asked so that I can keep my job. Listen, I have five kids to feed; I need my job. If you insist on defying our rules, Marshal Matt Bannister will be here any moment and I suppose he could be the one you'll have to challenge about the rules. Not me, okay? I'm just trying to do my job, fellas."

"Jude, let him have your gun belt." Elias chuckled while handing William his gun belt.

"Thank you, Sir. You can pick this up right here when your lunch is over."

Jude reluctantly turned over his gun belt and William handed them to Pamela to put below the counter. William entered the restaurant doorway and waved to get the attention of an attractive young waitress. "Catherine, these fine gentlemen are named Elias Renner and Jude Maddox. Would you escort them to the banquet room and seat them at their plates, please? Get them whatever they would like to drink."

Elias smiled as he scanned Catherine up and down. "Wow, it must be top service here. Like we're rich or something."

"Nothing but the best, sir. Enjoy your meal." William's smiling face turned to stone once they followed Catherine into the restaurant.

Elias and Jude watched the attractive teenager as she led them through the multiple tables of the restaurant towards a private banquet room at the back of the restaurant. The door was centered to the room and was opened outwards. There was only one window that was beside the door. The mahogany wainscot walls with white wallpaper with a light blue flower design gave the room a soft and yet elegant touch. In the center of the room was a long table about ten feet long. It seated twelve people altogether and was rented for any meeting or family get-togethers. Elias and Jude couldn't help noticing the aroma of freshly baked bread mixed with gravy and toast. Elias's stomach growled as he entered the private room separated from the restaurant.

"Gentlemen," Catherine said, "You'll find your name tags beside your plates. Please have a seat. Can I get you any appetizers or drinks while you wait for the others in your party?"

"Who's paying the bill?" Elias asked curiously.

"Dinner parties are always charged to the individual who makes the arrangements. In this case, Annie Lenning is responsible for the bill."

Elias chuckled. "Then yeah, I'll take an appetizer and a drink. Both of us will."

"What would you like?" Catherine asked.

Elias shrugged. "Surprise us. Whatever costs the most but make it good." He sat beside Jude along the left side of a large spacious table. There were six plates set on the table but theirs were the only two on the left side of the table facing everyone else. "Can you believe this place? I bet the food is great!" Elias said. He was excited to meet Annie and to eat a full meal.

Jude was placed at the farthest from the door and window and felt trapped which he did not like. He wanted to be on the other side of the table where he could see out the window and nearest to the door. If there was any one thing he couldn't stand, it was being closed in without an escape route nearby. "Elias, let's rearrange this a bit. I feel trapped over here." He switched all the name cards placing the other four names on the left side of the table and his name on the plate nearest the door and window to see into the restaurant. Elias sat down beside him.

After a few moments of waiting, Jude nodded towards the door. "Here comes Marvin. It must be the Marshal with him."

Marvin Aggler walked into the room with a big, crooked smile. He had been shaved and bathed. "Boys," he greeted them with a chuckle. "This is my pal, Matt Bannister. Matt, this is Elias Renner and Jude Maddox."

"Gentlemen, it's nice to meet you," Matt said, shaking their hands. He was irritated with William for not having the table set up how he specifically had drawn it up. There was a reason Matt wanted the two suspects to be on the blind side of the table and separated from the public. Now he and Truet were at a disadvantage if Jude and Elias saw the Branson sheriff, Tim Wright and his deputies enter the restaurant before Matt did. What was supposed to be an easy snare of two criminals was now potentially a risk to the public, which frustrated Matt. "Thanks for meeting us here for lunch. Annie will be here soon. This is my deputy, Truet Davis." He pulled out a chair across from the men and sat down where his name was set. Truet sat two seats away from Matt at the farthest point away from the door next to a plate with Annie's name. Marvin was supposed to be seated at the far end of the table but was now nearest to the door across from Jude.

Matt knew the two men had left their gun belts with Pamela but he had no idea if either of the men carried a concealed weapon. "Marvin says you want to work at my sister's ranch. I'm kind of protective, so tell me about yourselves. Where did you work before now?" Matt asked to make conversation.

Elias groaned. "Oh, I don't want to repeat myself when your sister gets here but I did a spell at the Specter A Ranch, Split Wing Ranch and a few others. Mostly in the Idaho Territory, Wyoming and Utah. You name the job; I can do it. If you know much about ranching, that's quite a skill set."

Matt answered, "I know quite a bit about it. I grew up on the Big Z Ranch. So, what brought you over here with Marvin? Hold on a minute." He turned to address Marvin. "Since Annie, Truet and I will be talking to these men, how about you and Truet switch places. That way, we don't have to yell back and forth?"

Marvin agreed and Truet moved next to Matt across the table from Jude. "That's better, so what brought you over here?" Matt asked Elias again.

"The job. We were hoping to be hired on and experience new places and people. You graze cattle over there for twenty years and you get pretty bored with the sagebrush, you know?"

"I can believe that." He glanced at Jude and caught him glaring at Truet. "So, Jude, are you both from the Boise City area?"

Jude nodded his head. "Thereabouts."

Matt casually lowered his hands to adjust his chair and removed the thong from the hammer of his Colt. "I was in Sweethome last summer. Did either of you ever work for Bob Thacker?"

Elias answered, "No. I knew some of his cowboys, though. They were a rowdy bunch. We heard what you did to them. I can't say that I blame you." Elias's eyes widened and his grin faded while he suddenly remembered where he knew the name Truet Davis from. Truet had killed AJ Thacker and some of the ranch hands for murdering his wife. More significantly, Truet Davis was the man that murdered Jude's younger brother, Farrian Maddox. It finally clicked and he stared at Truet with his mouth agape. Elias wasn't a praying man but he hoped Jude could keep his mouth shut and control himself long enough to get hired onto the ranch. There would be plenty of time for killing later on.

Matt noticed the change in Elias's expression and smiled slightly. "The Thackers broke the law; Truet and I brought them to justice." He shrugged humbly. "It's about as simple as that."

Truet could feel the hatred burning from across the table where Jude sat but he did not want to say anything and spark a possible fight in a public restaurant. He tried to change the subject before Farrian's name came up. "Annie will be here shortly. There's a community dance tonight she went shopping for."

Jude's tongue rolled across his cheek while his

focus remained on Truet. Sitting across the table from the man that murdered his little brother was more than he could stomach. Jude had no interest in working for Annie since he heard Truet was in town. He put his elbows on the table and placed his thumbs together while tapping his fingers together rhythmically. He spoke in a low and soft tone, "I heard you ran away from Sweethome. Did you really think you were going to get away with shooting my brother in the back?"

Truet rested his chin on his folded hands, mirroring Jude. "You look like Farrian."

Jude raised his eyebrows. "He was my younger brother. And you shot him in the back without giving him a chance." His upper lip twitched with animosity.

Matt did not like the direction of the conversation between Truet and Jude. Matt had asked Tim to wait five minutes before entering the restaurant to let the two men begin to relax and catch them off guard. He already knew his plan would not work as he hoped.

Truet answered Jude, "Shooting a man in the back doesn't put a slug in his chest. You've heard wrong. I didn't go looking for your brother; he came looking for me. He was drunk and missed twice. I didn't. It was self-defense."

Elias chuckled uneasily. "Jude, let's keep our mind on the task at hand. You two can talk about that stuff later. Our new boss is coming in here soon."

Jude slammed his fist into the table. "Screw the job! I'm going back the Idaho way. And I won't sit with the man that killed my brother either. See you later." He slid his chair back and stood to leave. He was stopped by Matt drawing his revolver.

"Sit down!" Matt ordered, pulling the hammer back until it clicked.

Truet pulled his revolver and pointed at Jude as well.

Elias was stunned. "What's this?"

Jude answered with a scowl on his face. "I told you it was a trap!" He sat slowly. He nodded at Truet. "Is that the gun you murdered Farrian with?"

"It's the gun that killed him, yes. Keep your hands on the table or it will be the one that kills you too," Truet answered.

Elias stuttered, "Marshal, what's going on here?"

"You're under arrest. The sheriff will be here momentarily to take over. Sit and be still," Matt said sternly.

"What? No, we came here to meet your sister?" Elias asked, trying to stay in the character of an innocent man.

"She's not coming. As Jude said, it was a trap."

"A trap for what? What are we being arrested for?" Elias raised his voice.

Jude's peripheral vision caught a slight movement in the restaurant of a man carrying a shotgun walking down the center aisle. The restaurant guests spoke in whispers and gasped with concern as three men walked towards the banquet room. Jude's eyes shifted quickly from man to man and then towards the door as his mind moved rapidly to find a way out.

Matt answered Elias just as Tim Wright entered the room holding a shotgun. His two deputies also had shotguns. "Tim, they are your prisoners now."

Tim leveled the barrel of his Parker shotgun at the two men. "Stand up and turn around. Put your hands on the wall. Now!" Tim spoke loudly so everyone in the restaurant could hear him. "Bob, you and Alan search them good and shackle them."

Jude glared at Truet, refusing to stand.

The corners of Truet's lips rose upwards slowly. "You better get up before I slam you against the wall headfirst," he warned.

Jude's eyes narrowed with a cold smirk. Deputy Bob Ewing stepped forward impatiently and grabbed him. When Jude felt Bob's hand touch his shoulder, he quickly swept his right leg over his left leg under the table with a spin of his body, intentionally jamming his spur into Truet's shinbone. Truet jerked in pain and scooted his chair back while reaching for his leg. Jude held the fork in his hand, turned his body to ram his shoulder into Bob's belly, and drove him backward into the wall. He spun around Bob, grabbed his chin with his left hand, and jerked Bob's head back, and pressed the tip of the tines of the fork into Bob's neck over the carotid artery hard enough to penetrate the skin and bleed. "Get back!" Jude screamed. "I'll bleed him out like a stuck pig!" Jude was smart enough to keep his head tucked behind Bob's as he circled towards the door. "Put your gun down, Marshal. I'll kill him!"

Bob grimaced in a combination of fear and

rage. He didn't put up a fight, knowing he was at Jude's mercy. One push of the fork and he could bleed to death.

Matt aimed carefully but hesitated to shoot. He spoke calmly, "Jude, you have nowhere to go. If you stab Bob, you're a dead man. Surrender now and you'll be better off."

Jude ignored him. "Elias, grab the shotgun! No one had better stop him or I'll stick this fat pig!"

Elias, who had stood to be searched, broke free from Alan Garrison's grip and reached for the shotgun on the table.

"Elias, you're one move from being dead! Get back against the wall," Matt demanded dangerously. He spoke to Jude, "No deal, Jude."

Jude backed out of the doorway into the restaurant holding Bob close to him. "No one follow me or he's dead!" Jude planned on demanding his gun belt, Elias' and taking Bob's gun before piercing the artery and making a run for freedom.

William Fasana had no intention of being left out of an arrest and stood back watching from inside the restaurant while Jude stepped back, coming closer. William held his revolver in his hand, waiting. Jude backed up the aisle of the restaurant while keeping his attention on Matt who matched a step forward to every step back Jude took.

Matt spoke to keep Jude's attention on him, "Jude, if you jab that fork into Bob, I'll shoot you. It's just that simple. You should know I'm not afraid to shoot, so tell me what your plan is? I'm a bit confused about what you think you're doing."

"Get away! I'll stab him!"

Matt sighed. "No. You won't. William."

William swung his left-handed revolver with all his might and connected the silver-plated barrel against Jude's ear as hard as he could. Jude fell against a table forcefully, ruining a couple's lunch as their drinks and plates crashed off the table to the floor along with Jude Maddox. Jude's momentum had pulled the fork out of Bob's neck and it dropped to the floor. Jude held his ear while groaning in agony and thrashing his legs in pain.

William knelt and tapped Jude on the leg to get his attention. "Stop bellowing like a branded calf. I wish you cowboys would toughen up a bit, you're making the weakest of the sodbusters look tough," he said and then laughed.

Bob felt his neck and stared at the blood on his fingers. He kicked Jude in the gut and was quickly pulled away by Tim and Truet.

Matt stepped back into the banquet room, where Marvin sat quietly through it all with a perplexed expression. "Thank you for bringing them today, Marvin. They murdered a couple of men last night and robbed a saloon."

Marvin nodded slowly. "I figured it must've been something like that. I'm sorry I hooked up with them. We're still having lunch, aren't we?"

Matt chuckled appreciatively. "Yeah. Give us fifteen minutes or so."

11

The second floor of the Branson Community Hall thundered with the stomping and clapping of couples dancing the Virginia Reel, Oh Susanna, the Heel Toe Polka, the Gallopade, which were various square dances. Almost every dance involved stomping, clapping, twirling your partner around and then changing partners to do-si-do and connect elbows and swing around to a new partner or stepping back and clapping to wait your turn to glide or promenade in a circle. The band played various instruments from a cello and fiddle to a banjo, guitar and piano, while the dance steps were called expertly. It was a great deal of fun and the joy and laughter could be heard in the whooping and hollering as the dancing continued. It was good to see the wide grins of the men who labored from sunup to sundown day after day as they danced with their wives. Moments of romance and fun were two of the last priorities on a family farm struggling to get by or in the miner's everyday life. It was a rare opportunity for a man to bring his beloved lady out for an evening of food, fun and socializing.

Martha King was proud to be involved in the planning of the Spring Fling Community Dance. To see the joy on the many faces and hearing the laughter and stomping of the dancing made every meeting and hour of preparation worth it. Her usefulness for picking up and washing dishes or even carrying trays of drinks upstairs was limited by her broken arm which was in a sling. Every year, her husband helped her but he had refused to come to the dance because Roger feared he would be the topic of conversation to every gossiping man and woman in the building. To Martha's surprise, not one person had questioned her about what he had done but most all inquired where he was and what had happened to her arm. She had answered them by saying Roger was not feeling well and she had fallen down the stairs. She had cast away the heartache and forced a smile while continuing her duties with the grace and joy that everyone would expect.

Martha stood behind the food table with a large spoon serving potato salad to the folks who brought their plate down the row of tables with a hearty appetite. In years past, it was a lesson learned that allowing the people to serve themselves usually led to empty bowls of food and too much extra food thrown away by people with hungrier eyes than room in their belly. "Are you feeling better?" she heard someone ask.

"I am, thank you," Roger King answered.

Martha was surprised to hear his voice. He stepped across the table from her and frowned. "I haven't missed one of these yet and figured you could use the help."

She felt a smile come to her lips. "I can. Are you hungry?"

He nodded pitifully. "Starving."

"Go grab a plate. In about twenty minutes, the band is going on break and we're going upstairs for the drawings. You can help me with that. You bought the new plow so you can announce the winner of that drawing. I was wondering who I could get to holler out the winners because quite frankly, I don't feel like shouting right now," she emphasized with a twinge of forewarning in her voice.

Roger smiled. "Well, I'm here to help you." He paused to gaze upon her affectionately. There was a sadness in his expression but the affection was as sincere as it had ever been. "I can't hide from what I've done. Lord willing, I'll be spared from anything you mentioned but the worst thing that could ever happen to me is losing you."

"Roger, this is not the time to talk," she responded softly, not to be overheard. "Go grab a plate and eat while you can. We're going upstairs shortly."

Upstairs, the fiddle played while the other band members clapped their hands in time to the caller who called out the steps to the Cumberland Square Dance. Matt left his gun belt with his brothers at the table while he and Christine danced. The dance floor was made up of multiple sets of four couples in square formations. Matt had worked up a bit of a sweat with a giant grin on his face as he danced with Christine and the other three couples. He held her hands in an elongated position drawing close and slid together for eight steps and then back to their place to start the dance. Through a series of moving to the center of the square with one other couple or all four, a series of instructions were given by the caller for what to do next, including right stars, skipping circles to the left, to the right. Until finally, they heard the call to take your partner's arm and promenade in a circle to their home position, where at last he bowed to Christine while she curtsied to finish the dance.

Matt couldn't help but share the joy glowing on Christine's face when he put his arm around her shoulders to walk her off the dance floor. "That was fun," Matt said, glancing at her fondly.

She beamed. "You have no idea how long I have wanted to come to dance like this! Nothing fancy, just good fun. Thank you. Do you have any dances left in you or have I worn you out?"

The grin on Matt's face answered her question. He hadn't expected to enjoy the dance as much as he was. "I'm sweating a bit but, if you don't mind that, I can dance all night with you. I'm having a great time."

She giggled with excitement. "I am so glad to hear that. Because I want to dance every dance."

The band leader shouted above the crowd noise, "Ladies and gentlemen, we're going to take a short break to wet our whistles and get some grub. If you're having a great time tonight, please give the lady responsible for all of this a big hand. Please, welcome, Martha King and her lesser half, Roger, onto the stage. Put your hands together in prayer, too, because they're going to draw the winners of those amazing prizes right now."

"Lesser is right!" someone hollered from the back of the room to cause some laughter.

Martha walked onto the stage with a humored grin. She was followed by her husband and three older ladies who carried a wide mouth jar in each of their hands. Each jar was labeled for the drawing.

"Thank you," Martha shouted as the crowd quieted down and told others to hush so they could hear. There were multiple prizes, including cash prizes, bowl sets, knives, and other small household items, where the winners would be posted downstairs. The more valuable drawings were being drawn on the stage. The people crowded together to hear who would win the donated items, such as a white porcelain gold inlaid vase, the Jessup County Quilting Show's winning quilt. There was a beautiful sixteen-piece porcelain china set inlaid with a flowering branch design of three blue flowers in the center with an outside border of blooming white bamboo flowers. The dish set had caught everyone's attention and the jar was filled with names entered to win the donation by Wu-Pen Tseng of the Chinese Benevolence Society. It was a wonderful donation from a man who wasn't allowed to attend the dance because of his nationality.

For the men, there was a drawing for a pair of new custom-made boots of their choice, courtesy of the Lesko Clothing and Shoe Repair Store. A Remington twelve-gauge shotgun was the most sought-after donation for the men. For the farmers, a Moline Flying Dutchman plow was the most expensive donation that had brought high hopes and excitement to many who owned small farms and couldn't afford such modern equipment.

Martha and Roger stood in the middle of the stage. "Thank you," she repeated for the warm greeting. "This dance would not have been possible without the help of several ladies and some gentlemen who worked hard to make it happen. The Branson school children made the art you see hung on the walls everywhere. If you see some made by your children, feel free to take them home with you. We had more donated gifts this year than any other year and I want to thank everyone who donated something. I think we are blessed to live in such an amazing community. Don't you?"

The crowd applauded loudly. Someone yelled, "What happened to your arm? Did your fat ass husband roll over on it?" A round of laughter followed.

Martha smiled but was not amused as she watched Roger's cheeks redden. "No. I've been asked a dozen times and I slipped on the stairs and broke it. Okay, the first drawing is for the beautiful vase donated by Marsha Hatfield." She reached her good hand into a jar and pulled out a piece of square paper. She handed it to Roger.

He spoke loudly, "And the winner is Lynette

Conner."

"Congratulations, Lynette. It is a beautiful vase," Martha said, taking the piece of paper. "Next, we have a drawing for one hundred dollars. The donor wanted to be anonymous." She reached into a separate jar, a much larger pickle jar, pulled out a piece of paper. She handed it to Roger.

"The winner is Mister Joe Thorn."

"Congratulations, Mister Thorn," Martha said.

Joe Thorn stood up with a stunned expression. He yelled, "Really?"

Martha chuckled with some of the crowd. "Yes, really. You can meet me downstairs when we finish here to collect your money."

Joe turned to Billy Jo Fasana and held his arms out to her. "I can buy you a wedding ring! I can buy her a wedding ring! We're getting married! I can get you a ring! Thank you!" He hugged and kissed Billy Jo.

Roger could not help but to grin while he watched Joe's excitement. "Congratulations," he said. It was good to see someone who needed the money win it for such a beautiful purpose.

A voice yelled from the back, "I'll give you my ex-wife's ring for free! I have Roger to thank for that, too. Thank you, Roger!" The voice didn't sound as excited as Joe Thorn's.

Roger's face turned white as the blood drained down his spine. He peered towards the back of the community hall but he couldn't see who he feared it might be.

Martha gasped. She shouted, "Now, if you'll

excuse me." She reached into the jar held by one of the women and pulled out a piece of square paper. She handed it to Roger. "This drawing is for the sixteen-piece beautiful china set donated by Wu-Pen Tseng of the Chinese Benevolence Society."

"It really is China!" someone hollered, causing some laughter.

Roger read the paper. "The lucky winner is Mary McNichols!"

"Congratulations, Mary," Martha said.

The man's voice came over the applause, "Congratulations, Mary! Watch out for the slippery snake on the stage. He might steal it from you!" The hostility in his voice was unmistakable.

Roger watched Hiram Stewart step out of the crowd towards the back into an open area of the dancefloor. He held a glass of what appeared to be whisky. Hiram was noticeably drunk by the way he stepped and the slurring of his words. Roger could feel himself slinking lower and lower in the view of everyone's eyes and the shame he felt turned his spine to mush. He lowered his head in silence, wishing Hiram would go away.

Martha shouted angrily, "I don't know who you are but you are interrupting and I don't appreciate it! If you don't stop, I will ask any of these capable men to remove you so we can continue uninterrupted."

Hiram walked towards the stage. He took a drink from his glass. "Missus King, my name is Hiram Stewart, I work for the Union Pacific Railroad but I'm here in your precious community working for the Oregon Short Line to get you all out of the dark age. I'm doing you all a favor by being here." His head swayed as he gazed towards the stage.

Roger pointed towards the stairs and shouted, "Someone get him out of here!"

Hiram's face twisted into a vicious snarl. "Of course, you want me out of here!" He spoke to Martha, "Your husband spent the night with my wife Thursday night at the hotel. Don't believe me? Ask the Marshal, his deputies, Lee, William or any of the other guests that stayed in the Monarch Hotel. Better yet, just look at his neck. My little serpent of a wife likes to leave her venomous mark and it's on your husband's neck!"

Martha shouted, "I don't care who you are. You are drunk and causing a scene. Someone escort him out of here!"

Hiram chuckled slowly. "I am good and drunk. So, you might as well take advantage of me and share my room tonight. What do you think?" he laughed. "Roger, I must be drunk as a blind skunk to think your wife's pretty enough to grace my bed. It looks like she'd break the bed frame to me. Can I get a key to an empty room?" He laughed.

"You son of a..." Roger yelled. Anger took over and he ran forward and leaped off the stage to the floor. Being an older, heavy man who wasn't so limber, his right foot landed on the floor with a jarring impact that buckled his knee and Roger collapsed to the floor. He cried out in pain and rolled to his back with a terrible grimace while holding his knee with both hands.

Martha gasped with concern and moved quickly towards the stage stairs to be with her husband.

Hiram sneered with curled lips and stomped on Roger's face and tried to shove his boot into Roger's mouth. "Do you like the taste of my boot? Eat it, you pig!" He laughed and began to lose his balance when he stepped back and was caught by Matt's hand bracing his shoulder.

"That's enough, Hiram!" Matt said firmly.

Hiram glanced back at Matt and then swung his right hand with the glass held in his palm towards Matt's head. Matt stepped his left foot forward to enclose the distance and swing his left arm over Hiram's elbow to catch the punch in an over hook. However, Hiram threw the glass before Matt could trap the strike. The thick glass hit Matt above his left eye with such force that the heavy glass shattered against his skull. The sudden blow forced Matt to take a step backward and turn away from Hiram. Dazed by the power and speed of the blow to his head, Matt was suddenly aware of the sensation of a steady flow of blood running down his face. Matt bent over to get his bearings and watched the blood drip onto the floor.

Hiram, seeing Matt's back to him and bent over, stepped forward and brought a rigid right leg up connecting with Matt's groin with his chin bone.

Matt grimaced from the jolt to his groin. He wanted to lay down and curl up in agony. The blow to his groin felt like it could paralyze him if he remained still. Matt turned and drove a right-handed fist deep into the abdomen of the drunk man. Hiram bent over, opened his mouth to catch his breath and ended up vomiting liquid onto the floor. Matt, careless of the vomit, grabbed Hiram by his jacket and swung him around to gain more momentum and threw him into the side of the stage. Hiram flew six feet and hit the stage horizontally with a hard bang.

Matt followed and pushed a man out of his way who tried to interfere. Matt yanked Hiram up to his feet and pulled Hiram's head back to slam it down on the stage when an arm hooked Matt to stop him. Matt released Hiram and turned around to face whoever stopped him.

Joe Thorn backed up when he saw Matt's blood-covered face and wild eyes intent on hurting him. Joe raised his hands with his palms up. "Matt…it's over. He's done. Matt…don't," he said with concern.

Lee Bannister quickly pushed his way between Joe and Matt. He stopped Matt's advancing by putting a hand on his chest. "Knock it off, Matt! Settle down, little brother." His brow lowered slightly when he saw the gash in Matt's forehead.

Matt glanced back at Hiram and Albert Bannister was standing between him and Hiram. "You finished him. It's done," Albert said with finality. "Let's go sit down."

Matt took a deep breath to calm the fury that had taken over him. He could see drops of blood falling over his eyebrow steadily. He glanced at Hiram sitting on the floor against the stage, catching his breath. Matt's wrath was hell bent on making him bleed too and it took a moment for him to calm down. He took a deep breath and put his attention on Doctor Ambrose and a group of men leaning over Roger.

Truet Davis and Sheriff Tim Wright circled Matt. Tim spoke, "Truet and I will take Hiram to your jail. We can't have that happening to the lawmen around here,"

Truet asked with concern, "Are you okay?"

Matt nodded. "I'm fine."

"Go do what you have to do. I'll take care of Hiram," Truet said and walked over to where Hiram was being helped to his feet.

Hiram laughed as his senses came back to him. "Is that all you got, Marshal?" He was swaying on his feet.

"He's drunk. He won't feel anything until tomorrow," Lee said and put his hand on Matt's shoulder to lead him towards the table. "But he'll be sore tomorrow. That was a nice throw."

Christine Knapp stood with Mellissa Bannister, shocked by the amount of blood on Matt's face and shirt. She couldn't help but start weeping when she saw how severe the gash on his head was.

"Come on back, you coward! I'll box your head off!" Hiram shouted in a drunken slur.

Truet answered, "No, you're coming with me. And if you try to hit Tim or me, I promise you may never see straight again because I won't hold back!" Truet grabbed him roughly and forced him towards the stairs.

"Matt, let me see your wound," the voice of Doctor Mitchell Ryland said. It only took a moment for him to look at the gash and shake his head. The gash went to the skull and was about two inches long above his left eye on the forehead at an upward angle. There were a few minor cuts around it, with the glass still embedded in his flesh. Doctor Ryland took a deep breath. "Yeah, you need to come to the office so I can suture that."

"Is he okay?" Christine was holding Matt's hand.

"Well…yeah. It's a superficial wound that needs to be sutured. I'll meet you in my office in about twenty minutes. Does that sound fair enough? You're not going to feel like dancing for the rest of the night, though."

Matt was embarrassed to have so much attention being brought to his wound while the large crowd gathered around to watch him bleed.

"He's not going to bleed to death, is he?" Billy Jo Fasana asked with concern for her cousin. Joe Thorn stood beside her with his arm lovingly around her shoulders.

Doctor Ryland answered, "No. The bleeding will stop. Head wounds bleed a lot by nature. He'll be okay. I'll see you at the office, Matt." The doctor squeezed Albert Bannister's bicep. "Albert, you seem like a stout man. Can I trouble you to help carry Mister King downstairs? We'll grab about four guys and see if we can borrow someone's wagon to take him home and bring him inside his house. He can't walk on that knee."

Albert answered, "Yeah, I can bring my coach around to the front and we'll put him in there."

Joe Thorn spoke, "I'll help. Let me grab my brother and friends and we'll carry him."

Billy Jo went to hug Matt but he stopped her. "You don't want blood on your dress, Billy Jo."

"Are you okay?"

"I'm fine." He called out to Joe Thorn as he walked away with Albert. "Joe," he got his attention. "Thank you for stopping me. I would have hurt him. And I apologize for coming at you."

Joe came back and shook Matt's hand. "I understand. No hard feelings. If you'll excuse me, I going to help Roger."

Annie Lenning carried a wet towel to Matt. "Let's get your face cleaned up."

Matt took the towel but held it. "Leave it be for now. I want to see what everyone else is looking at."

Annie narrowed her brow questionably. "Why? It's ugly. You're ugly. You look like you always do, just plain ugly."

A slight smirk lifted Matt's lips. "Probably."

Lee offered thoughtfully, "Do you know what you should do? You should go downstairs and have a photograph taken of you looking like that. People back east are hungry for real news out here and most have never seen your face but do know your name. We could sell the photo to the highest bidder. A photograph of your face and shirt covered in blood and pointing your pistol at the camera would be terrifying to them. Fear sells and you'd become a household name for your photograph. Seriously, we could make a lot of money with a photograph like that. I'd put a copy of it on my wall."

"Me too," Annie offered. "I'd tell my kids that's what's happens when their Uncle Matt smarts off."

"You're not serious, are you?" Mellissa Bannister asked, repulsed. "Matt needs to get to the doctor, not stand for a photograph. That's a bad cut and he probably doesn't want a picture of it."

Christine took the wet towel from Matt's hand and put it on the gash. He grimaced when she did. "I can't tell Matt what to do but this bleeding needs to stop. Let's go sit down for a little while before we go to see Doctor Ryland."

Lee lifted his hands questionably. "I'd pay for the photograph."

Matt held the towel in place and answered his brother, "Christine and I had our photograph taken earlier when we got here. That's the first photograph I've ever done and the only photograph I'm doing tonight."

"Lee," Regina came to him urgently. "I just got done talking to Martha and she asked me to finish the drawings. I need your help."

Matt sat down at the table where his family was and held the towel over his forehead. It stung as the bits of glass slivers were being pressed deeper into his flesh. They were too small to see in the faint lighting of the room.

Annie sat across the table staring at him like a disappointed parent in her child. "I could have set that picture on my mantle and told everyone I hit you. You're ruining my plans."

Matt chuckled. "I'm sorry, Annie. You could always throw another glass at me and open up the other side of my head."

She frowned sincerely. "How are you feeling?"

"I feel fine but it hurts a bit." He noticed quite a few of the people kept glancing towards him before uneasily looking away. "It must have looked bad?"

Annie nodded sadly. "Yeah, it does. You know I only give you a bad time because I love you, right?"

Matt noticed the slight watering of her eyes and chuckled. "I'm not dying. Who knew a little blood would make you cry like a girl?"

Annie raised her eyebrows daringly. "Do you want the other side of your head broken open? I thrive on making people bleed, especially you."

Matt grinned. "That sounds like my sister."

Billy Jo Fasana had watched Albert, Joe, Richie Thorn and Bruce Ellison carry Roger to the stairs and awkwardly maneuver him down the stairs and into Albert's carriage. Joe got into the carriage with Albert and the other men to take Roger and Martha home. She stood outside watching the carriage leave and was startled to see Wes Wasson standing behind her when she turned to go back inside.

"Wes! Oh, my word, you scared me," she said, clutching her chest in reaction.

"Sorry. I didn't mean to scare you." He was off his crutches and using a cane to help support his foot. He was moving around well and figured he'd feel well enough to walk without a cane in a month. He was dressed as a gentleman in a suit with a new derby hat.

"I didn't know you were here," she said uneasily.

She had ended a short romance a few weeks before and had not seen him since. She had feared he would tell Joe about them and ruin her relationship with Joe but he had not.

"I just got here a little bit ago. I wasn't going to come but hoped I'd see you and get a moment to talk. Do you want to go for a short little walk so we can talk?" he asked invitingly.

She shook her head with a fake smile. "No, I better not. Joe will be back pretty soon."

Wes smiled sadly. "What if Joe wasn't here? Would you then?"

"No. Not even then."

He spoke sincerely, "I miss you, Billy Jo. I know what we had was short but I never lied to you. I think I'm in love with you and would do whatever I could to spend my life with you. I know I was a bit upset when you ended it with me and I apologize. I won't harass you or cause you any problems with Joe. I respect you too much for that. If I could, I'd just like to be a friend and let any harsh feelings go."

She tilted her head sideways with surprise. Wes was a constant source of anxiety and to hear his words brought great relief. "We can be friends but nothing more," she agreed. "Joe and I are getting married, Wes. I've never been happier."

He nodded knowingly. "I saw him win the money for a ring. I can't argue with a man that gets that excited. I'm happy for you both. I really am." He smiled. "Congratulations."

"Thank you. I'm going inside to see my family. Thank you, Wes."

"You're welcome. Hey, are you still interested in renting your house?"

She grimaced hesitantly. "I'll get back to you on that. We may move into it before too long. I don't know yet."

He shrugged his shoulders uncaringly. "Either way. I just want to say maybe I was wrong about Joe. It sounds like he's changed. I wish you both a great future."

Her expression relaxed a bit. "Thank you."

"I know it may be a…well, like I said, I hope we can still be friends. Just friends."

She wiped her sweaty palms on her dress. "I hope so. It was nice talking to you, Wes. I'm going to get a piece of pie before joining my family. I'll see you later."

"You bet," he said and watched her walk into the community hall. He loved her and he would bide his time. She would end up with him eventually and he would love her like the treasure she was. Until then, he had to think of a way to stop her from marrying Joe Thorn. And he would think of something to get her to come back to him. For now, though, a piece of peach pie did sound good.

12

Truet Davis had locked Hiram Stewart in the marshal's office jail and then walked with Tim Wright over to his office to let his young deputy, Alan Garrison, know that he could take the rest of the night off and go to the dance. Tim opened the door and Alan was sitting at the sheriff's desk. He quickly laid a booklet down that he was reading.

Alan was surprised to see his boss. "Tim, what are you doing here?"

Tim's forehead wrinkled curiously. "I came to tell let you know you could go to the dance and enjoy some time with your lady friend. She came up to me and asked if you could. She is so dang cute, I couldn't tell her no. What are you reading?"

"Nothing," he answered quickly.

"Let me see that?" Tim picked up the booklet about twenty pages long and read the title. It was a dime novel titled: The fastest gun: The midnight fast draw between Wild Bill Hickock and Matt

Bannister. What the world doesn't know. Tim stared at it with a slow-growing grin. He handed it to Truet. "Alan, why are you reading this?"

Alan's face reddened with embarrassment. "I saw it at the Swindall Trading Post and thought I'd read it."

Truet chuckled. "What's it say?"

"The story says Matt and Wild Bill Hickock were best friends and one night, they argued over who was the fastest. Wild Bill suggested they use black powder revolvers without a ball to draw. Wild Bill won." He asked Truet, "Is there any truth to that?"

Truet snickered as he handed the booklet back to Alan. "No. And I wouldn't show Matt that book either."

"You don't think it's true?"

"No. But if you want to see Matt get irritated, just show him that. Where did you get it?"

"The trading post."

"Marcus Swindall is at it again?" Truet chuckled while shaking his head. He figured Matt would visit Marcus soon enough to end any book sales with his name on it. He moved over to the jail cells, passed the first cell where a lone young man was lying on the bottom bunk listening to the lawmen talk. Truet stopped in front of the second cell door where Elias Renner and Jude Maddox were. "Are you two men comfortable?"

Elias was lying on the bottom bunk. "Snug as a tick in a deer's ear," Elias answered bitterly.

"Good." Truet's attention shifted to Jude who sat on the edge of the top bunk with his cold gaze fixed on Truet. Truet spoke sincerely, "Jude, I wanted to tell you I had nothing against your little brother. He'd still be alive today if he had not come after me. I shot him in self-defense. He was not shot in the back."

Jude's head tilted while his eyes narrowed into sharp daggers that would gladly penetrate Truet's soul if they could. "Billy Marks and Tommy Yonker were both there that day and watched you shoot Farrian in the back. They said Farrian challenged you to a duel, the old-fashioned and honorable way. Back-to-back, someone counts ten steps and you turn and shoot." His lips twisted into a sneer. "You turned and fired into his back at the count of five. You murdered my little brother like a coward!"

Truet was troubled by the story he was hearing. "That's not true at all. We didn't have a duel and your brother fired at me first."

Jude raised his voice, "Farrian's friends say differently and they were there! They wouldn't lie to me but you would to make the reputation you have here. You ambushed AJ Thacker and his friends when they weren't expecting it!" He pressed his lips together tightly. "Have you ever had a fair fight or do you always find the most cowardly ways to kill someone? I don't have any problem with Matt; he'll look you in the eye and pull the trigger. I respect that. But you are a coward! And if I get out of here, I will make you fight me and I will kill you."

Truet took no pride in killing anyone but to have his integrity questioned in front of others irritated him. "Farrian was drunk when he pulled his gun and fired at me. He missed. I pulled mine and we fired about the same time and he missed again; I didn't. He died of a bullet in his chest, not his back. Go dig him up and check if you must. But don't think for a minute that I take the cowardly way out. If you ever do get out of jail and come after me, you'll find that out." The aggravation of being falsely accused of a cowardly act was revealed in the sharpness of his voice.

Jude hopped from the bed to the floor in his socks and neared the cell bars slowly. His lips were tight as he sneered. "I hope so. Elias and I came here to do honest work and earn a living but that ended for me when I heard you were here. I knew then that all I care about is putting you in the ground. And I will. I don't need to dig up Farrian to know what happened to him. His friends were there and watched you! I'm telling you now; you're not going to get away with killing my little brother."

Truet hesitated. "There's nothing I can say that will convince you his friends are lying to you, is there?"

"No."

Truet took a deep breath and exhaled. "Well, it doesn't matter. You're going to be in prison for a long time if not hung. I doubt I'll ever have to worry about you, after all. But if you ever do come for me, keep in mind, I'm not helpless."

"I'm not convicted of any crimes yet." Jude's jaw clenched. "But no matter what happens, I swear, before my dying day, I will kill you."

Truet held an even gaze to show no hint of intimidation or concern. "I'll see you two in court."

Jude watched the three lawmen walk out of the office and lock the door behind them. He jumped back on the top bunk and laid down to calm the fury that pounded in his chest.

The young man in the next cell asked, "When you say Farrian, were you talking about Farrian Maddox?" Jimmy Donnelly was no stranger to the jail and had been arrested for fighting at the pool hall. He had cracked a pool cue over a man's head when he lost a game and about ten dollars he could not afford to lose. Judge Meryle P. Jacoby had warned Jimmy after his last burglary arrest that one more arrest and he would be sent to prison rather than shown any mercy by the court. Judge Jacoby and Jimmy's grandfather were friends and often fished and hunted together. He had been given multiple warnings, chances and even spent a few stretches in jail. Still, the lure of easy money and the excitement of picking locks and sneaking into people's private lives without getting caught was excitement that he found nowhere else. Jimmy knew he was facing prison time and he was in no mindset of going. He had been arrested on Friday night and waited patiently for this moment when he had the time and opportunity to break out of jail.

"Farrian was my little brother," Jude answered dryly. "Did you know him?"

"No. I've just heard of him," Jimmy answered. "Do you know the Sperrys? Jack, Vince or Morton by chance?"

Jude was uninterested in any conversation. "No."

Elias Renner turned his head towards Jimmy. "Why does that name sound familiar?"

"The Sperry-Helms Gang. You two aren't from around here, are you?"

"No."

Jimmy sat up on the edge of his bed and asked, "Do you two want to see a magic trick? I'll bet I can unlock that door and get us out of here."

Jude sat up on the edge of the bed with interest. "How?"

"Watch." Jimmy untied his right boot and slipped it off, exposing his brown stocking. He picked up the boot and showed them the boot was empty. "Now watch this." He pulled the leather sole out of his boot and turned it over. Carved into the leather insole's bottom side were two warded lock picks that could be mistaken for skeleton keys. The two keys were facing opposite directions and fit snuggly into the leather. "Magic, huh?" he asked with a grin. "I'm getting out of here while I can. Do you want to come with me?"

"You have the key?" Elias asked, taking a sudden interest.

"My right boot has these warded keys. They'll open up most locks around here. My left boot has a hook and rake pick. I find it a challenge to pick any lock." He walked to his cell door and used the larger of the two ward keys to manipulate the lock until it opened. He returned the key in his insole and put it back in his boot before putting his boot on.

"Hurry up, get us out of here!" Elias said anxiously, afraid one of the deputies would come in before they could get away.

"Relax. Tonight's the Spring Fling. It'll go on until midnight and then everyone will go to a saloon or home. No one's not coming back here until tomorrow morning. Listen, I'll let you out but you need to know Matt Bannister is the marshal and he'll be coming after all of us. If you don't know who he is," he chuckled. "Good luck! They write dime novels and books about him."

"We know who Matt is. He's why we're in here," Elias said dryly. "Now, come on, open the door. We need to get back towards Idaho."

Jimmy snickered. "You two will be caught if you do that. You have to be smarter than running. Matt has made a career tracking people down and he'll track your horses all the way to your doorstep. Listen, I've been planning this since last night. The Spring Fling is a big event that draws people from all over the area. I say we take some horses from the stable and ride through town and mix our tracks with the numerous others that will cover ours up when the dance is over. And then, if your smart, you'll come with me and hide for a week or two where Matt can't find us."

"Where's that?" Jude asked curiously.

Jimmy was a medium height, skinny young man with straight brown hair that touched his shoulders. His acne-covered face was narrow and long. His eyes were a darker shade of blue and he had a hooked nose that appeared a bit too big for his face. He grinned. "I'm not saying where just in case we part ways and you get caught. I'm going to prison if I stay here and so are you, at best. You two will fit right in where I'm going but, the only thing is, I need to ask you to help me steal a horse from the stable because I don't have one."

Elias agreed. "Fine. Let us out of here and we'll go."

Once out of their jail cell, Elias and Jude grabbed their gun belts, saddlebags and rifles. Elias found his new brass-handled expanding knife in the desk drawer. They left the sheriff's office and quickly walked down Main Street towards the stable.

Old Gus Fread was a longtime resident of Branson and had known many of the county's early residents. He was an encyclopedia of the local history and talked about it with whoever he could. He had worked at the grist mill for much of the time and finally retired from a manager's position seven years before. Having never taken a wife, he worked the night shift at the stable more for something to do rather than as a need. It gave him a purpose and an excellent way to meet folks entering the town at night and an opportunity to tell a story or two about the city. He'd go home around six or seven, stop by Faye's Border House, eat breakfast, and then go to church on Sundays. After church, he'd mingle with friends and around three or four in the afternoon, he'd sleep and wake in time to go to work at ten. He didn't mind his hours of quietness in the office of the stable. It gave him time to write his memoir and put his living history on paper. He wasn't writing a book necessarily, he just wanted future folks to know where their county and town came from, little stories of individuals and the celebrations, and moments in his life that mattered to him.

"Let's just get saddled and get moving," Gus heard someone say. It took his attention off his memoir and he peered out the office window into the stable.

The Branson stable was large, by most standards, with six rows of stalls running ten deep under the covered building. There were uncovered stalls as well and four corrals and plenty of pasture. Above the stall was the loft where tons of straw for bedding, hay and barrels of grain were stored. Gus stood up and stepped out of the office. He was a friendly man and it showed in his grin. "Hello, gentlemen. Are you leaving the dance already?" He recognized Jimmy Donnelly and knew Jimmy had no horse or legitimate business in the stable.

The tallest man with dark hair and graying beard said, "You boys go saddle up the horses. I'll settle up with the stableman." He addressed Gus, "Hello, so how much do we owe?"

"Well, if you give me your names, then we can tally it up." There were too many boarded horses and mules to know them all. All were registered in a book that contained the number of days, feed, water and any extras that could be marked down and tallied for the total cost.

"Johnson and Brown." Elias lied.

"What part of the county are you folks from? I'm guessing northwards towards Hollister or Cold

Creek. You know the history of those cattle towns is quite interesting..."

Elias pulled his knife when Gus had his back to him while entering the stable office. Elias held the knife backward and pressed the lock pin and slid the spring to release the expanding blade of his knife. The blade flipped open. "What's this here?"

Gus turned around to see where the man was looking. A flash of movement and Gus was pierced in the abdomen. The blade caused pain to his heart. The last he could see was the wickedness of a stranger's cold and emotionless expression. It wasn't fear that Gus felt in his dying breaths. It was sorrow for the man who had such ruthless and cruel eyes. Gus knew where he was going; he couldn't say the same for the man stabbing him.

On the other end of the knife, Elias pulled the blade back and rammed it upwards at another angle to puncture whatever organs it could. He turned the edge upwards and pulled the small sword , slicing the flesh as it was pulled out. The body of Gus slumped to the ground. Elias cleaned the blade on the back of Gus's coat and folded the blade. He put the knife in its sheath and turned to look at his new friend, Jimmy. "I may never use a gun again. I love this dagger!" He laughed.

Jimmy stared at Gus's body, stunned to his core. "That was ole Gus. He never hurt anyone."

Elias spoke uncaringly. "He won't now either. Go pick out a horse. I'm going to drag him around the corner."

"I just wanted to steal a horse. Not kill Gus,"

Jimmy said. He was unable to take his eyes off the old man's body.

Elias shot a fierce glance at Jimmy. "We don't have time to stand around. Go get a horse, and let's get to wherever you're taking us!"

They rode up Main Street to the Branson Community Hall, where plenty of horses were tethered to rails, wagons and carriages. They turned around and followed on Main Street to the main road leaving Branson and turned toward the west. The wagons, horses and foot traffic from the folks leaving the dance would cover most of their tracks and make it nearly impossible to identify which tracks were theirs by morning light.

Elias asked, "Jimmy, where is it we're going? And are you sure we can hide out there?"

Jimmy was a thief but he had never killed anyone or witnessed anyone being killed. He had robbed old Gus' house before but he had never wished the old man any harm. He was feeling sick to his stomach from the pointless killing he had seen. Jimmy considered going back and pleading with Judge Jacoby for mercy and turn the two men in but it was too late now that they were riding together. Jimmy feared that he had made a big mistake leaving the jail with the two men. If he could escape the men, he could testify against them and maybe be forgiven his crimes. Stealing was one thing; the murder of an innocent and helpless old man was another. He answered quietly, "We're going to my friend's place in Natoma."

"How far is that?" Elias asked.

"About twenty-five miles."

Jude questioned, "We're going west. Where is the Big Z Ranch comparatively?"

Jimmy shrugged his shoulders. "I don't know. I've heard of it but I don't know where it is. My friends probably know, though."

"Who are your friends?"

"Jack and Vince Sperry. You know the Sperry-Helms Gang?"

"No, I don't know!" Jude answered shortly.

Elias chuckled. He removed his Stetson and swung it, hitting Jimmy's arm with the brim of his hat. "Jude and I will fit right in with them, huh? That's what you said." He laughed. "Well, it looks like we're going to get to know them, Jude."

13

Matt inspected the body of Gus Fread and sighed. It was the same stab wound that Dean McDowell and Felix Young had been killed with. The murder of Gus was the big news on this Sunday morning. He was a very respected man around town and the news of his needless murder was shocking. Gus had told Matt many stories about his two grandfathers, his father, aunts and uncles. He was a fascinating man with a story or two about everyone, it seemed. Sheriff Tim Wright held the register book in his hands. "It appears Jimmy Donnelly went with them. One horse is unaccounted for that belongs to Avery Wilson." Old Pete, the owner of the stable, was standing beside him. Old Pete was devastated about losing his friend.

Matt searched for a single track from any of the horses the men had ridden out of the stable. The stable floors were thick with sawdust from the sawmill and the stalls were layered with straw to keep the mud down. Multiple horses had come and left the stable throughout the night, making it impossible to tell which tracks were theirs. Quite a few men went to the stable to collect their horse after the dance, as indicated by a pile of change stacked on the office window seal when they couldn't find Gus to pay. The blood from the murder at the office door had been covered up with handfuls of sawdust.

"They couldn't have picked a better night to leave," Matt said with a hint of frustration in his voice. "Any idea how they got out of your jail?" He had already asked Tim that question earlier when he was notified that the three men had escaped. Gus' body had just been found buried in the pile of waste straw and manure.

Tim raised his hands questionably. "As I said, Jimmy is a living lock pick. I don't know how he unlocked the cell door. We searched him before we put him in jail. I don't know." He shrugged his shoulders questionably.

"I knew he was a thief but I thought he pried windows open. If he's good enough to pick a jail lock with no tools, then he may be the one who stole the gold from the Engberg and Penn Assayers Office too." He focused on Alan Garrison, the last deputy sheriff with them, before going to the dance. "Did any one of those men say anything that would help?"

Matt always made Alan nervous. "Nothing comes to mind, Marshal. Those two cowboys didn't talk to each other very much at all. I don't think Jimmy ever said a word to them."

Matt removed his hat and ran a hand through his hair. The white bandaging wrapped around his head, holding the gauze on his sutures, got in the way. He had received nine sutures to close the gash in his head. He walked to a large, open barn door and stepped outside, facing the north and took some time looking east then west thoughtfully.

"What are you thinking, Matt?" Tim asked, knowing he was in deep thought.

He pointed eastward. "Elias and Jude don't know this area but Jimmy is a local and stole a horse to leave with them. It would take four or five days to reach Boise City and there's a lot of open ground between here and there. They left late at night with little or no supplies. I don't see them doing that, knowing the law will be coming after them much better supplied than they are. So, the question is, where did Jimmy take them?" He paused. "I don't know Jimmy; I only know about him and who he is. What can you tell me about him, Tim?"

Tim raised his eyebrows while taking a deep breath. "He's a thief. We've arrested him multiple times. He can pick just about any lock and likes to steal money, jewelry and such. Small things, he never takes weapons or anything large or heavy, just small stuff that fits in his pockets. He's more of a pain in the buttocks than a physical threat. He's never been violent until just recently. He was in the billiards betting on a game and lost. He hit the other man over the head with a pool cue when he lost his money."

Matt asked, "Where does he sell the jewelry?"

"I have no idea. I've never found any of it at any of the stores around here."

"The trading post?"

Tim shook his head. "Nope, we looked. I've even searched Jimmy's parents' home multiple times and can't find any of it. It's hard to prove Jimmy stole something when you can't find it."

"So, he's smart?"

"He's clever."

Matt leaned on the door jamb of the open barn door and crossed his arms. "I'm betting Jimmy took those two men with him. He has nothing to gain from them, unless..." He glanced back at Gus' body. "It was to deal with Gus so he could steal a horse and leave town. They aren't going too far without supplies, so Jimmy must have a destination in mind. What relatives or friends does Jimmy have that he can hide out with?"

"I don't know if he has any," Tim replied.

Alan offered, "He was with Vince Sperry that night at the pool hall. I don't know if they are good friends or not but Vince was there with him."

Matt smiled. "I'll bet you they went to the Sperry farm. The Sperrys have a hiding box under their chicken coop and I'll bet you that's where we'll find them. If Jimmy had a place where they could hide, then that's where they'll be and that would explain why Jimmy needed to steal a horse. It won't surprise me if they're hunkering down for a day or two at the Sperry farm to figure out what they're going to do next."

"Are we going after them now?" Truet asked, standing back leaning against some stall boards. "By the time we got there, it would be near dark."

Matt tugged at the beard under his bottom lip thoughtfully. "I like to give them a day to relax. We'll leave in the morning. Tim, do you and your deputies want to come along since they broke out of your jail?"

Tim had no desire to ride to where Jed Clark was killed. The Sperry-Helms Gang scared him. "I'm going to have to decline. I'll send two of my deputies with you but someone needs to stay in town tomorrow."

Matt pointed to Alan Garrison. "Fine. I'll take Bob and Alan."

Tim agreed.

Matt peered at Alan sharply. "Have you ever shot a man before?" He already knew the answer.

"No, sir." Alan was in his late twenties and still inexperienced in the job of a lawman.

"Hopefully, you won't have to. Be up and ready to leave early tomorrow. Make sure to clean and oil your weapons tonight. I doubt you've used them in a while."

14

Jimmy Donnelly was grateful to the Sperry family for putting him and his two new friends up for a few days. Vince Sperry was a friend of his and bought his stolen goods. Every other Friday, Vince came into Branson to drink, have a good time, and meet up with Jimmy and buy whatever Jimmy had stolen. Vince then sold the items to the Gregory Hotel and Restaurant in Natoma, where the stagecoach stopped. It had become a good little business for Vince and Jimmy. Hitting a man with a pool stick turned out to be a bad decision because now their little business venture was over in Branson. Vince had told him a long time ago that they had a place to lay low if Jimmy ever needed to escape from the law. True to his word, Vince and his family gave them some food and put the three men in a small log cabin on the forested hill above the Sperry home. The cabin was not noticeable from the house, nor was the lean-to set back a bit from the cabin where their horses were tethered. The log cabin was just big enough for two straw-filled mattresses tossed on the floor, two wooden dining chairs, a small cabinet holding a few pots and dishes. The woodstove they could only use at night when the smoke would not be noticeable. The place had two windows on the front overlooking the house below the hill. There was no glass but both windows could be closed with hinged panels two inches thick that would latch at the top to keep any weather out or be dropped down to open the window.

The cabin was built as a hideaway and set back in the darkest part of the forest. The Sperry family planted blackberry briars along the hillside to help conceal the trails and cabin. The briars had grown wild and grew into a wall of thick thorns, vines and leaves. The family kept the trails and view from the cabin windows trimmed. Morton and his brothers decided long ago if they were going to build a cabin to hide in then, it needed escape routes if they were ever discovered and trapped inside. Each side had a full-sized door to exit quickly into the maze of briars. Before he was sent to prison, Alan Sperry liked the idea of hiding boxes buried in the ground and there were a few on the property. Alan's most ambitious idea was digging a four-foot-deep trench three feet wide from the back of the cabin up the hill twenty feet away. They constructed a wooden boxed tunnel in the channel and wrapped it in oil-soaked canvas to keep the rainwater from destroying the wood. The box tunnel was buried and grass and briars were planted over it, making the tunnel undetectable outside the cabin. Twenty feet away, behind a wall of briars twelve feet high and low limbed trees, was the escape hatch. To camouflage the escape route from any lawmen or anyone else who chanced upon a trap door in the woods, Alan bolted a broken old hand pump onto the wooden frame to make it look as though it was an old well. He doubted anyone would suspect anything other than a broken pump for the cabin if it were found. Inside the cabin, the tunnel was accessed through a three-foot-square door held closed with a hook. The idea had been genius, the labor had been extensive, but unfortunately, neither Alan nor his brothers had inherited their father's carpentry skills. Luckily for them, other men in the Sperry-Helms Gang knew something about carpentry and repaired the tunnel when and where it had failed.

Bo Crowe sat in a dining chair looking at Elias Renner and Jude Maddox, who were both hungover from a late night of drinking. The two men had arrived extremely late on Saturday night and then went to the Natoma Saloon with Bo and his cousins for a night of hard drinking on Sunday night. Bo didn't drink that much and felt fine. He watched Elias and Jude sit on their mattresses, leaning their heads against the wall or in their hands. Bo found it humorous how the two cowboys with spurs on their boots that jingled when they walked had talked such a tough talk the night before but, now, whined about how sick they were.

Bo said through an entertained grin, "You boys need to toughen up and handle your alcohol like men."

"Shut up," Elias Renner replied with no humor in his voice. He had heard of the Crowe Brothers and how ruthless they could be in the Central Oregon cattle territory where they roamed. The Crowe Brothers had made a notorious name for themselves among the ranchers and cowboys throughout the region. Elias had made the mistake of letting the alcohol get the better of him early in the evening and he made an ill-timed joke about Bo's left eye being cockeyed. It almost ended in a fist fight. Elias had no doubt that Bo was a man with blood on his hands and certainly able to defend himself but Elias would have liked to have flipped his knife open and drove the long blade deep up inside of Bo. The only thing that saved the younger Crowe brother was being in the company of his cousins and, particularly, Jannie Sperry. She had taken a liking to Elias and being the only woman in the saloon, Elias took a shining to her too. Unfortunately for Elias and Jannie, they were never left alone. Elias seemed to have a problem with the Sperry boys also, though. A few too many drinks and the tongue loosens. Elias fully expected to be hit in the mouth by at least one of the Sperry boys about some disparaging remarks he made about the youngest Sperry sister, Daisy. Whatever he was drinking had brought out some of the worst in him. He rolled his head along the wall to look at Bo. There was not much fire in his voice, "I don't know what your barkeep gave us towards the end but it's stronger than what we were drinking before. You could light a fire in a river with that stuff, I swear."

Bo was of average height and had a broad chest with neck-length straight black hair, a beard, dark eyes, and his left eye was cock-eyed. He chuckled. "That's some homemade shine. It'll take your breath away for sure and your common sense too. My cousins have a still and sell the shine to the saloon and hotel. The hotel sells it to travelers who want a little fire on the road. It is a good fire starter, by the way."

Elias's elbows rested on his knees while his hands covered his face. "I don't even remember walking back here. Did I make an ass out of myself with your cousin, Jannie?"

Bo chuckled. "You did. I have never seen a grown man on his knees crying while he begs a woman he just met to marry him before. She's probably down there planning your wedding as we speak. She did accept." He laughed.

"Oh," Elias groaned. "I never should have started drinking that stuff."

"That's why I don't drink it. Yeah, you're going to have an interesting day," Bo said with an expectant grin. "No one's ever asked Jannie to marry them before. As you were saying all night, 'love grows where Elias goes'. Good thing too, because those kids of hers need a papa. So congratulations!"

"I'm not marrying anyone," he answered solemnly.

"Tell that to her, not me. You were the one kissing all over on her."

Elias's expression turned to disgust. He was not attracted to Jannie at all before drinking. "Did you come up here just to remind me of that?"

Bo held his grin. "Yep. I wanted to be the first to welcome you to the family. Aunt Mattie is probably packing up those trouble-making kids of Jannie's and telling them about their new daddy."

Elias closed his eyes and shook his head wordlessly.

Bo shifted his attention towards Jude, "I was thinking, you and me both want Truet dead. You can kill Truet. I want Matt's brother, Adam. I want to put his head in a vice and squeeze it."

Jude slowly turned his head to gaze at Bo questionably. "What? You want to squeeze his head in a vice?"

"Yeah. And with Matt looking for you two way east of here, we could get away with it too."

"What are you talking about?" Jude asked sharply. He and Bo had gotten along well the night before with their mutual dislike for Truet. He was no mood for foolish talk now, though. He was hungry, his stomach was growling and he wasn't feeling good.

"I told you about Matt's brother, Adam, last night, remember? It took him and two others to squeeze my head between the cell bars when I was in Matt's jail. Remember? I want to squeeze his head for some payback. The three of us could ride to the Big Z Ranch and get our justice."

"I don't care about Matt's brother," Jude said through a scowl.

"I want his brother and you want Truet. Truet's woman lives there. You can hurt him as he hurt you," Bo suggested. "She's a pretty woman and all alone."

Jude exhaled tiredly. "That's Matt Bannister's sister. If you touched her in any way, shape or form, he'd track you down until there's nowhere else to hide and I doubt he'd give you an option to surrender, even if you wanted to."

Bo exclaimed, "Not if he's dead! A bullet will kill him just as easily as anyone. I don't know why no one dares to stand up against him. He's just a man. My cousins don't want any trouble with him or his family either but I'm no slouch with my guns. With your help, we can wipe that ranch out and be gone before anyone knows."

Elias glanced at Bo through his fingers. "Good luck. Tomorrow morning rain or shine, Jude and I are heading to Walla Walla and back through Lewiston to where we belong. We plan on avoiding the marshal."

Bo leaned the chair forward towards Elias. "And you think he's just going to forget about you killing three men in Branson and let you go back home? If he doesn't find you, he'll send out wanted posters with a high reward. You can't outrun those posters, believe me, I tried. You'll have bounty hunters coming after you. The only way to stay free isn't through running. It's having friends and family that will threaten the witnesses and jury members when you are arrested. You two should stay here and join my family and we'll keep you safe. You might be arrested but you won't be convicted because not one witness will have the courage to testify. Trust me. Between my cousins, my brothers and our friends, we could wipe out the entire Big Z Ranch and get away with it."

"Bull. Do you know how many cowhands they have?" Elias asked cynically.

Bo shrugged his shoulders. "Who cares? The beauty is it doesn't matter. We'll still get away with it."

"They're hiring. They just hired an old cowhand named Marvin. He's no greenhorn. But you must be crazy if you think you can just waltz onto a ranch and get away with whatever you think you might do. You can count me out. What about you, Jude?"

Jude spoke softly, "He might be right about staying here, Elias."

"How so?" Elias asked.

Jude explained, "We'd be arrested if we went back where we're known. Killing those men in Branson turned the tide against us and bounties kill friendships. We're doomed no matter where we go. Unless we join up with the Sperry family and Crowe Brothers and hope for the best, if they can do as Bo was saying, then we have it made. We'd never be convicted."

Elias took a deep breath. "I wanted to go straight and make an honest living cowboying."

Jude laughed. "Says the man who killed a kid for a knife."

Elias nodded. "Yeah, and I'd do it again."

Jude continued with a serious tone, "I don't see that we have a choice now but to join up with these folks. We don't have many choices anymore." Jude spoke to Bo, "It looks like you all might have two new hands. Can your family keep us out of jail, as you said?"

"We always do. I'll talk to the family and let them know you two want to join us. We can always use trustworthy and capable men."

The sound of the Sperry's dogs barking sent the alarm that someone was approaching and brought Bo to his feet. He unhooked a window panel and let it drop, allowing the bright sunlight to shine in. He stared out the window, fearless of being seen. He watched as Matt Bannister, Truet Davis, the Natoma Sheriff, Zeke Jones and the Willow Falls Sheriff, Tom Smith, stopped their horses in front of the porch. Bo could see four more riders back from the house keeping watch but Bo couldn't see who they were through the trees and brush.

Bo turned to Jude with a growing grin. "They sent a whole posse after you two. Truet's sitting right down there waiting for you. Here's your chance, buddy."

Jude stood up quickly and grabbed his rifle and joined Bo at the window. Elias as well crowded them, trying to see.

Bo cursed irritably. "There's another window! I'll be over here." He opened the other window and watched down below. He didn't have his rifle but he was wearing his gun belt.

"Don't shoot. They might leave," Elias said nervously.

Bo spoke, "I say we kill them all and bury them

in the woods, make jerky of their horses and sell the horse hides to the tannery. It wouldn't be the first time and we always get away with it." Bo pulled his revolver and aimed it downhill.

Jude raised his rifle and aimed at Truet, but it was hard to see clearly with the bright rays of sunlight that cut down through the trees into his line of sight. His hands shook from the night of alcohol in his system and not eating any nourishment for a day. A heavier man on a horse was blocking a clear shot at Truet. "This isn't how I planned on killing him but let's end it. You shoot Matt and I'll kill Truet."

"You got it," Bo said. "Elias, you just start shooting at whoever is in the open. Let's take them out and rule this county."

15

Matt and his two deputies Truet and Nate, had left Branson with two of Sheriff Tim Wright's deputies, Bob Ewing, the most experienced lawmen, and Deputy Alan Garrison. They rode to Willow Falls and picked up the Willow Falls Sheriff, Tom Smith and his deputy, Johnny Barso. Together, they rode into Natoma and forced the Natoma Sheriff, Zeke Jones, to go along as well.

Matt could not forget the last time he had gone to the Sperry farm and his deputy Jed Clark had been gunned down unexpectedly by gang member Charlie Walker. Charlie was now dead but there were other family and gang members that might be a bit touchy when Matt's posse of lawmen showed up. There was a good chance that Matt was wrong and the men they were looking for were not there. But he was not going to take a chance on losing anyone blindly again. No one would come sneaking along the side of the house this time without being seen. He hoped there would be no weapons discharged and he could take the men back to jail if they were there but, if gunfire did erupt, he wanted there to be a lot of guns shooting back.

Matt stopped at the last curve on the road leading to the Sperry farm. "Zeke, Tom, Truet and I will ride forward to the porch and talk to the family. I want you four to spread out and stay back about twenty yards or so to watch the property. If you see anything, call it out. This is where Jed lost his life and I want all of us going home tonight. If things go bad, get to cover and let the bullets fly but aim well because there are women and children in that house. If you have never shot a man before and you can't do it, turn in your badge when this is over because you'll never do any of us any good."

Nate Robertson was more nervous than any others which was expected since Nate was beside Jed when he was murdered. Going back to the same place brought some anxiety with it. Matt would be lying if he said he wasn't feeling some of the same.

The two dogs barked and nipped at the horses' heels as the four men rode forward and came to a stop in front of the porch. As expected, the door opened and Henry Sperry was the first outside. He was unarmed. "Marshal Bannister, Zeke." He nodded at Truet and Tom. His younger brother Jack stepped outside to listen; he was also unarmed.

Their mother, Mattie, walked out on the porch carrying a child in her arms. She spoke, "Marshal, I see you got bonked on the head and brought a posse. You're not looking for Bo or my boys, are you?"

Matt kept his hands on the saddle horn, although his coat was pulled back over his revolver if he needed to grab it. He gave a slightly embarrassed, lopsided grin. He knew the white bandaging around his head looked funny and had been teased by Tom since leaving Willow Falls. He could hear his old friend, Tom, snickering. "No, Ma'am. Bo is free and clear and so are all your boys. I'm looking for three men that I suspect might be here, a friend of Vince's named Jimmy Donnelly, who is with two other men. Missus Sperry, they are not the kind of men you would want around your grandchildren. So, I'm going to ask, have you seen them? Before you answer," he added quickly, "I remember being lied to the last time I was here and I lost a man. If you lie this time, I'll arrest you for harboring fugitives. Guaranteed."

She hesitated just a little too much for Matt not to notice the alarm flash through her expression. It was only momentary before her eyes hardened again.

Morton Sperry came out of the house before Missus Sperry could answer. "What's going on, Matt?"

"I'm looking for three fugitives that broke out of the Branson jail…"

Vince Sperry shoved his way out of the door and spoke sharply, "They're not here!"

"Shut up, Vince!" Mattie exclaimed with a nasty scowl. "I'm not going to jail for fools I don't know."

Morton Sperry pointed up on the hill. "They're up there."

A rifle sounded and a bullet whizzed past Tom's head, barely skimming past Truet and hit Matt's horse in the neck. The horse reared up as Matt instinctively kicked his leg over the horse's rump and held the reins trying to keep the horse between him and the line of fire. He tried to pull his rifle out of its scabbard, but he couldn't grasp it with the horse rearing, bucking and trying to break free as more shots were fired from up on the hill.

Truet leaped out of the saddle and pulled his rifle from the scabbard before allowing his mare to run free. With a glance towards the hill, he could see nothing except the dark forest beyond the first layer of trees and underbrush. He ran to the corner of the house to take cover behind a Conestoga wagon parked on the access road to the barn. Bullets were being shot through the canvas cover directed at him. He stayed low behind the wheel for the protection it offered.

Matt got his horse to settle down just enough to reach his rifle when his horse collapsed to the ground with a well-placed round to its head. The horse's body fell towards him and he sprawled back before his saddle hit him in the knees. His rifle was pinned under the weight of the horse. Now openly exposed, Matt ran towards the opposite side of the house from Truet and dove to the ground.

Tom Smith had turned his frightened horse towards the base of the hill and jumped off with his Winchester in his hands. He laid at the bottom of the mountain, looking for the shooters. Sheriff Zeke Jones was bucked out of his saddle when his mare took off crow hopping and threw him along the way. He laid on the ground where he landed, reaching for his lower back and groaning painfully.

No one was shooting at him, though; the bullets were focused on Truet and Matt.

The four deputies away from the house were numbed by the sudden shock of watching their four leading riders scrambled like mice in a granary.

Bob Ewing shouted alertly to the younger deputies, "Up on the hill. Go!" he was already dismounted and carrying his rifle. He was quickly followed by Johnny Barso and, more reluctantly, Alan Garrison and Nate.

Matt peeked around the corner and a bullet zipped past his head by mere inches. He watched Henry Sperry run out from the porch into the open with his hands waving frantically. "Stop shooting!" he screamed. "Stop shooting!"

A bullet from a rifle sent Henry spinning to the ground crying out in pain. They could hear a loud shout in the distance and then the sound of a revolver being fired followed by two quick rifle percussions that were not directed towards the house. Henry's three brothers Jack, Vince and Morton, ran out to him followed quickly by his mother. It had grown silent except for the Sperry brothers carrying Henry into the house and the sound of Mattie and Henry's wife wailing with the unmistakable sound of panic.

Vince Sperry stormed out of the house and yelled towards the hill, "You shot my brother!"

Elias Redding had killed Matt's horse with a Spencer rifle. Bo had complimented Elias while he aimed and fired his Colt .44, barely missing as Matt dove behind the house. He cursed in frustration. He wanted to be the one who killed Matt Bannister. It would be a nice addition to his reputation among his lawless family and friends.

Elias was shooting at anyone who moved while Jude was single-minded and kept his weapon firing at Truet but the angle of the wagon from his window was too narrow and he couldn't get a good line of sight. Jude cursed and moved back from the window he shared with Elias and stepped towards Bo's window when Henry Sperry had run out into the open, waving his arms for them to stop shooting.

"Don't shoot!" Bo demanded quickly just as Elias pulled the trigger. Bo watched Henry fall to the ground. In a furious reaction, Bo spun his revolver around and pulled the trigger. The bullet ripped into Elias's thigh.

Seeing his best friend getting shot, Jude fired his Winchester rifle at close range into Bo's gut. Jude ejected the spent casing with the lever-action and fired again mercilessly, sending a second bullet through Bo's abdomen. Bo dropped his revolver and slid down the wall leaving a blood-smeared trail. He held his stomach and stared wide-eyed at the blood on his hands.

"You shouldn't have shot my friend!" Jude exclaimed and kicked Bo's revolver across the floor. He glared at Elias angrily. "The whole family is going to be coming after us now. We have to go!" He grabbed his gun belt and quickly fastened it around him. He peered out the window. He could see movement coming closer from the right side of the hill. It was the part of the posse that they couldn't see through the brush. "Close that window. We have company coming up the mountain."

"My leg. He shot my leg!" Elias shouted out in pain. He was watching the blood trickle down his pant leg. He glared at Bo with a pair of wild eyes and raised his rifle. "Die, you son of a..."

"Don't!" Jude hissed, trying to keep his voice down. He grabbed the barrel and pushed it to the side as Elias pulled the trigger. The bullet splintered the wood not far from Bo's head. "Let him suffer!" Jude snapped. Jude raised his rifle and fired two quick shots towards the deputies coming up the hill before he was out of ammunition. He shouted outside, "Stay back! We'll open fire on you!" He then closed the wooden panel over the window. He repeated to his friend. "Elias, close that window! And lock that door."

Elias did as he was told. "I'm not letting him suffer. He shot me," Elias said, glaring at Bo with murder in his eyes.

Jude pulled the escape tunnel's door open and got down on his hands and knees to crawl through it. "He'll slow them down if he's left alive. Elias, leave your crap and let's go!" he shouted impatiently.

Elias groaned as he bent his leg to get on his hands and knees. "I don't know if I can do this! I'm not going to be able to keep up. We need our horses."

Jude knew the dire situation they were in and there was no time for whining. He shouted, "Toughen up! We don't have time to get the horses or time for pain! We have to run. When we get to good cover, we can fight, but you need to run!"

16

Matt peeked around the corner and saw his horse lying dead. All the other horses had run off. He was hesitant to step out from the corner because whoever had been aiming at him was a good shot. It had happened too fast to count how many shots were fired but he guessed somewhere in the range of twenty from three weapons. The shooters might have been playing possum and waiting for him and the others to step into the open. So far, no one had.

Morton Sperry came walking out of the house, dragging Jimmy Donnelly by the hair with his blood-covered hand. Jimmy's face was bloody and his large, hooked nose was broken. Morton was enraged and glanced at Matt harshly. "Here is one of them! The other two are up on the hill." He turned towards the hill and yelled, "If you fire one more time, you're dead! Bo, get your ass down here! Henry's been hit!" He explained to Matt. "My brother's been hit in the neck. I don't think it's that bad but it might be. My sister's going to get Tillie. She's the closest we have to a doctor around here. So, if you see Daisey ride off, that's where she's going!" He pointed at Jimmy. "And you! If I ever see you come around here again, I'll kill you myself!" he shouted.

"Is Bo up there with those men?" Matt asked, watching the dark forest trying to spot them.

Morton appeared ferocious with an untamed appearance in his hard green eyes. His neck-length brown hair and thick brown goatee gave him the menacing expression that he was notorious for having. "He is." He hollered back up the hill. "Bo! You better not have been shooting at the Marshal! Now get down here!" He listened and there was no response. Concern began to grow in his expression as the silence remained. "Bo!" he yelled again and listened. He turned to Matt with more concern. "I'll be right back and then you come with me." He went back inside and came back out, tightening his gun belt around his waist. "Bo's not answering and I don't know those men. Are they killers?" he asked.

"They are. They killed a young gambler named Dean McDowell, the bartender Felix Young, and Gus Fread all with the same knife."

Morton paused and narrowed his brow questionably. "Gus? They killed Gus and Felix?"

"They did."

They could hear Bob Ewing's voice ordering the men to come out of the cabin unarmed. Morton spoke irritably, "It sounds like your deputies have them cornered. I'll go in and bring them out."

Truet walked up the hill with them on a trail

concealed by blackberry briars. It was a steep hill to climb, but they found Bob and the three others taking cover behind a fallen log and trees with their rifles pointed at the cabin.

Bob spoke, "They're in there. They saw us coming and took a couple of shots before closing the windows. They ain't saying much but they're in there."

Morton walked past them to the door and spoke loudly, "It's Morton. I'm coming in!" He tried to open the door but it was locked. He kicked the door open and saw his young cousin sitting against the wall. Bo was in shock and holding his bloody stomach. "Bo!"

Matt went inside and found Morton leaning over Bo, talking frantically, "Bo, you're going to be okay. I'm taking you to the house. Tillie will be here soon."

Bo raised a bloody hand and pointed towards the tunnel door going out the back. "Jude…"

Morton spoke as he grabbed a blanket off the other bed, "I'll track him down and kill him. Let's get you home." His voice was cracking with emotion.

Matt noticed the spotted blood trail leading to the tunnel hatch.

Bo stared at Morton. "I'm…scared."

Truet spoke softly to Matt as he entered, "Their horses are here, so they didn't get too far."

Matt answered, "Go tell the others to gather the horses. . One of them is injured. There should be a blood trail for us to follow."

"This is going to hurt, Bo. We're going to carry you down." Morton said and tried to move Bo onto a blanket. He gazed at Matt desperately. "Are you going to help me or not!" he shouted.

Matt spoke with as much compassion as he could, "He's not going to make it, Morton. He's been shot twice at close range and both shots went through him. He's bleeding to death as we speak. He'll be dead by the time we got him downhill."

Morton's expression twitched multiple times as he realized that Matt was right. He could see the blood smeared down the wall and the blood soaking into the mattress Bo was on. There were two bullet holes in the wall where the blood trail started. Morton held Bo's hand tightly. He squeezed his lips together, fighting a rage that was taking him over. His breathing grew heavy as he clenched his jaw tightly.

Tears slipped out of Bo's eyes. "I'm scared...Mort."

Morton sniffled, not knowing what to say. He shook his head and yelled in rage. He abruptly stood and stormed out of the cabin.

Bo spoke as loud as he could, calling after Morton, "Don't leave me! I don't want to be alone." He began to sob, terrified of dying alone.

Matt moved forward and knelt beside the dying man. He took hold of his hand. "Bo, in my jail, there was a Bible on the bed. Did you read any of it?"

Bo gazed at him with lost desperation. "I'm scared..."

Matt spoke softly, "You're about to meet the Lord, Bo. You need to ask him for his forgiveness of your sins. Jesus offers the gift of salvation and all you have to do is accept it. Accept Jesus as your Savior and you won't have any reason to be afraid anymore. You'll be welcomed into heaven. Time's running out and you're getting weaker. You don't have to speak anymore but you must pray and ask Jesus to forgive your sins and accept his gift of salvation before you meet him."

Bo was listening but fading fast as the blood poured out of his body.

"Bo, squeeze my hand if you want Jesus to save you."

Bo's fingers curled around Matt's with a touch of pressure but it was all Bo had left. Bo stared into Matt's eyes and the fear dwindled away as his life came to an end.

Matt sighed and lowered his head as he held Bo's hand in his. What had been chaos moments before was now totally silent with no sound coming from the house below or the mountain above. "Jesus, Bo squeezed my hand with what little strength he had left. You were willing to save the thief on the cross and I know you are just as willing to save Bo. Thank you for a love so strong that you are willing to look past the right and wrongs of us all, right into the deepest parts of our wicked hearts and still want to save anyone who asks. You are truly amazing. Thank you, Jesus."

Matt walked out of the cabin down to the house. If there was any part about his profession that he hated, it was telling a family that their loved one was dead. He walked down the steep hill on a trail cut through the blackberry bushes and, towards the bottom, he stopped Jannie Sperry who walked hurriedly up the hill. She tried to ignore Matt but he grabbed her arm to stop her.

"Get your hand off me!" She smacked his hand. Jannie was unattractive to begin with, even though she had brushed her long brown hair and touched her cheeks up with some pink rouge. The bitterness in her green eyes and sour expression certainly didn't make her more appealing.

Matt spoke gently, "Sorry, Miss. I need you to come down to the house with me."

"I'm going up to see Elias. Get out of my way." She tried to shove him away from her.

He raised his voice firmly, "Elias is not there! I need you to come to the house, now."

Jannie was taken back by his authoritative tone. She was beginning to understand something was wrong and fear broke through her rough exterior. "Where's Morton? Where's Bo?" Tears clouded her eyes and her voice broke, "What did you do?"

"I didn't do anything. Morton went after Elias and Jude up on the mountain somewhere."

"And Bo?" she asked anxiously.

"I'm afraid that's what I need to talk to the family about. Please, come down to the house with me."

She was filled with dread while Matt guided her down the trail and off the hill to the house. Jannie had walked like a stunned zombie into the house and began to sob, "Bo's dead!" She grabbed hold of brother Vince and wailed.

Vince Sperry stunned, looked at Matt. "Is Bo dead? Did those men kill Bo ? Where's Morton?"

"Marshal, where's my boy?" Mattie asked anxiously, with tears welling in her aging eyes.

"Missus Sperry, please sit down. When Morton and I went up there, Jude and Elias were already gone. They shot Bo twice in the abdomen. Morton went after those two and I stayed with Bo until he passed away."

"Bo's dead?" Daisy, the youngest Sperry, shouted emotionally while bringing her hands up to her face in horror. She began to sob.

Vince Sperry stood with tight lips and breathing heavily. "What way did they go? Did they take the tunnel?"

Matt nodded. "They went out a small door out the back. I believe Bo shot one of them before they got him."

"Whoever shot Henry is the hurt one," Vince said. "Come on, Jack, let's go hunting!"

"I hope you don't mind, Marshal, but we're leaving. No one knows that mountain better than we do," Jack said while getting his weapons.

Matt spoke, "Jack and Vince, I'll be outside." He paused to look at a small elderly Chinese woman tending to Henry's neck wound. "How's he doing?" he asked.

"He'll be fine," she answered without looking at Matt. The bullet had grazed the side of Henry's neck, leaving a gash but not deep enough to cause much harm.

He spoke sincerely, "Missus Sperry, my condolences to you and the rest of the family."

"Did Bo say anything?" she asked with a somber expression on her weathered face.

"He didn't have much time left. He didn't want to be alone, so I stayed with him."

Jannie shouted through her tears, "You should have brought him down here!"

Matt frowned compassionately. "There was no time. His wounds were quite severe. I'll have my deputies bring him down now. If you want, we can take him back to Branson to the funeral parlor. And you all can make funeral arrangements in a day or two."

"No," Mattie answered. "I will wire his mother. Thank you for staying with him. Was he scared?"

Matt hesitated. "Only until we prayed. He wasn't afraid in the end. I introduced him to Jesus."

"Oh, praise the Lord," Henry's wife, Bernice said with a sense of relief.

17

Morton Sperry had run to the broken well pump to see if Jude and Elias had come out of the tunnel. The cover was open and the hand pump was on its side. He searched for drops of blood on the trail through the thick foliage and followed the sporadic drops uphill for about thirty feet until he was satisfied that the two men were running towards the top of the mountain. Morton had no intention of tracking them on foot and ran back to the lean-to where both men's horses were tethered. He grabbed a bridle off a saddle and removed the halter rope to slip on the bridle. He set the saddle on the horse's back and tightened it securely. Stepping into the stirrup, he swung his leg over the rump, pulled the split reins to the right, and kicked the bay gelding. He rode to where he had seen the drops of blood on the trail. He figured the two men had a twenty-minute head start up the mountain's side. The scabbard was empty which was a reminder that he was going after two armed men who had the advantage of being on foot and could take cover behind any bush, tree or fallen log. Although he was tempted to ride fast and hard to catch up with the two men, the woods were thick and common sense told him to remain calm and keep a careful watch. He could be blown out of the saddle and gut shot just as quickly as Bo had been.

He slowed to a steady walk while he scanned ahead for signs of movement, colors out of place or glints of sunshine reflecting off any metal surfaces. He listened for the sound of rustling leaves, snapping twigs or the sound of their voices. The woods were silent except for the gelding's hooves softly touching the ground and occasionally snapping a twig. Even at a slow pace, Morton knew he'd catch up to them. The steep terrain would exhaust a man on foot before it would exhaust a horse. He pulled his revolver and held it ready to react in an instant. The woods, a mixture of various leaf, pine, spruce and fir trees, were heavy with shadows and glints of sunlight that could blind his vision momentarily. Fear wasn't something that Morton felt often but, while he rode further from the cabin and drew closer to two desperate men running for their lives, he began to wonder if he was wise to come running after them alone. If the two men had known the property, they might've known they had run right by a hiding box buried in the ground. It was marked by a notch carved in the face of a tree.

Morton pulled the reins to a stop and smirked just a touch. The two men continued to run straight up the mountain, not knowing where they were going or what was ahead of them. The Sperry farm was at the base of the Blue Mountains and, since the mountain on their property also stretched to the edge of Natoma, the two men might've thought they'd get to town by crossing over the mountain. Nothing could be further from the truth. The mountain was a curved finger that reached out towards the valley. The men were running deeper into the mountains. Once they ran down the other side of the mountain, they would be stopped by a deep gully that they would be forced to either go down into or try to walk around. The gully stretched for eight miles, draining the east side of the Blues in a flowing stream of cold water called Wendling Creek. It wasn't as large as Heather Creek, which ran through Natoma, but Wendling Creek flowed for forty miles down the mountain before entering the gully and ending in a deep pond four miles from Natoma. The stream continued for another five miles before connecting with the Modoc River.

Morton didn't have to hurry but he did need to be cautious. The men were running towards a trap they knew nothing about. The gully was about a hundred feet deep with near-vertical banks covered in foliage, small trees, some larger trees, bushes of various kinds and thick with poison oak. It was early spring and the poison oak was just beginning to sprout leaves. The stalks and vines were a cinnamon color and, whether they had leaves or not, they still contained the oil that could make a man's life unbearable. Morton doubted the two men would recognize the barren stalks as poison oak. If the two men ventured down into the gully, they'd come crawling out of there in a day or two, scratching themselves like a flea-infested dog.

Morton nudged the gelding to keep moving uphill. He rode past trees and pulled the reins to a stop. He listened and heard a distant voice from the other side of the ridge. Morton urged the gelding forward and had his revolver at the ready. Cautiously, he crested the ridge and was able to peer down the other side. He saw Elias hobbling painfully downhill as fast as he could. He was about halfway down, calling for Jude to wait for him.

Jude was nearing the gully and turned around to encourage his friend. He tried to keep his voice down but shouted loud enough to be heard, "Hurry up!"

"We gotta hide. My leg's killing me. Jude, I can't keep up," Elias complained while coming to an exhausted stop. He rested a hand on a tree to catch his breath.

Morton's lips tightened into a sneer and he pulled the hammer of his revolver back until it clicked. He kicked the gelding hard to run down through the forest. "Y'all!" he shouted, guiding the reins with his left hand and taking aim as he neared Elias with his right hand.

Elias turned around and his eyes widened in horror when they saw Morton racing towards him. Elias stumbled backward and fell to his back before scrambling to his hands and knees, leaving his rifle on the ground behind him. Elias began to hobble helplessly downhill. "Jude!" he yelled. Elias could hear the hooves of his horse approaching fast and knew he was caught. He faced Morton and raised his hands to surrender. "I give up! I surrender."

Morton came to a sharp halt and aimed his revolver at Elias with a bitter scowl on his face. He pulled the trigger. The percussion of the .44 brought the gun upwards and Morton pulled the hammer back with his thumb as the revolver fell and he fired a second shot into Elias's chest. Elias fell to his back, gasping for air. Morton raised his pistol downhill towards Jude and pulled the trigger.

Jude watched Elias try to surrender and Morton kill him without any remorse. Jude had his rifle but it had happened so unexpectedly that he didn't have time to shoot. Jude took cover behind a nearby tree as two quick bullets flew past him and then there was silence. To Jude, Morton had made it clear that there was no option to surrender. It was going to be a fight to the death. Jude peeked around the corner and saw Morton had wisely moved Elias's bay gelding behind a large fir tree while reloading his spent shells in his revolver.

Jude raised his rifle, intending to kill Elias' horse out from under Morton. He aimed at the gelding's exposed head then paused. He could hear other riders coming over the mountain towards them. Jude lowered his weapon and began to run downhill towards a gully and stopped at the edge of it under the branches of a pine tree. He looked around, frantic to find someplace to hide, but there was nowhere else for him to go except down into the deep ravine that didn't appear very welcoming.

Jude had listened to his spurs jingling with every step he had taken and known they would betray him if someone got close to him. He had put the spurs on when he bought the boots, now two years later, the straps were too tight and corroded to take off. He set his rifle against the tree and used his knife to cut the straps off both spurs. With time running out, he ran and jumped over the gully's edge. He tried to land on his feet but the steep grade left no room for footing and he tumbled through grass, brush and came to a sudden stop against a three-inch alder tree unmoved by his body hitting it. He got to his feet and retrieved his rifle before making his way into the knee-deep water that flowed steadily out of the mountains. The cold water filling his boots sent a chill up his spine and, for a moment, he felt frozen in place while his body tried to adjust to the shock of the temperature change. He took a deep breath and began moving forward. The ravine was full of thick brush and trees, giving him plenty of cover while he sloshed through the creek. He could not outrun a horse but he doubted anyone would be dumb enough to risk injuring their horse trying to bring it down into the gully. Jude ran, stumbled over unseen rocks in the water and kept running. He didn't know where he was going or what was ahead but he had to keep moving.

18

Matt could not leave Bo Crowe to die alone in good conscious nor did he believe it was right to let the Sperry family find him like that. It was only right to let the family know as gently as he could. The body had been wrapped in a blanket and brought to the house to be cleaned up. Vince and Jack Sperry were told to wait for Matt before they left to join Morton but they saddled their horses and left as quickly as possible.

Matt discovered that Zeke Jones had hurt his back severely when he was thrown from his horse. He was in great pain and stooped over, unable to straighten his back. Jimmy Donnelly held him upright while the Chinese woman that doctored Henry Sperry's neck massaged Zeke's back with her pointy elbow. Zeke grunted and groaned with discomfort but shortly could straighten a little more. Matt assisted Zeke into his saddle with the orders to lock Jimmy in the Natoma jail. Jimmy was in physical distress with a broken nose that made his breathing difficult and had swollen his eyes nearly shut. The Chinese woman stated she'd straighten his nose at the jail. With a firm warning to Jimmy to stay put, Matt put his attention on the task at hand.

Tom Smith and Johnny Barso were waiting for Matt. The two of them had taken the other horse from the cabin's lean-to, a buckskin gelding and fit Matt's saddle on it while Matt was with the Sperry family. Matt pulled his Winchester out of the scabbard and checked the sight for damages. He wasn't concerned about his Parker shotgun but the Winchester's sights were more likely to get damaged by the horse's weight collapsing on it. He thanked Tom for saddling the horse for him to use. The gelding belonged to one of the two cowboys they were looking for because the horse Jimmy had stolen was in the Sperry barn. Matt took a moment to pet the buckskin's neck with long strokes and spoke softly while looking into its amber-colored eyes to get acquainted. He stepped into the saddle and softly nudged the handsome gelding with his heels and followed the fresh tracks left by Vince and Jack. They rode quickly to make up time and, as they neared the top, they began hearing gunshots one after another every three seconds or so coming from the other side of the ridge. After six shots were fired, they found Vince Sperry standing over Elias Redding's corpse reloading his revolver. He kicked the corpse and cursed it for what happened to Bo.

"Vince!" Matt yelled furiously as he quickly rode down the hill. "Are you stupid? We are on a man hunt and you're shooting a corpse? Those gun shots are telling Truet, your brother and the others to come back because Jude's here. Now Jude will get further away!"

Vince was angry. "They shouldn't have shot Bo and my brother then! I'm not part of your posse, so don't tell me what to do!"

Matt jumped out of the saddle and neared Vince quickly. Vince began to raise his revolver towards him.

Matt quickly pulled his Single Action Colt .45 with cherrywood grips and leveled it at Vince and pulled the hammer back while he continued forward. "Drop it!" he yelled viciously. His eyes were hard as stone and his finger was on the trigger.

Vince's angry expression lost its fire and his mouth opened with concern. He had not expected the speed and fury that Matt displayed. His revolver dropped to the ground. Matt drove the barrel of his revolver under Vince's chin while his left hand grabbed the back of Vince's hair and yanked his head back while the barrel dug deeper under his chin. "Listen to me and listen good because I won't repeat it. You have a choice; do as I say and only as I say or go home. Because if you do not and I get one man killed because of your stupidity, I will drop you out of the saddle! I do not care who you think you are or how tough you think and your brothers are. This is my hunt, my responsibility. I won't risk a fool being a part of it. I want Jude brought in alive. If Jude surrenders and you take it upon yourself to shoot him, I'll hang you for murder. Do you understand me?"

"Yes," Vince spoke through gritted teeth and a wince of pain.

Jack Sperry simmered in his stew of anger, watching his brother being humiliated by the Marshal, but he was provoked to action when he heard Jude was going to be taken alive. He had every intention of killing Jude and there was no other acceptable outcome he would agree to. Jack reached for his revolver but the sound of Tom Smith's voice and the unmistakable sound of a hammer clicking and one trigger pull from falling sent a wave of cold fear through his spine. "I wouldn't," Tom said.

Johnny Barso also held his revolver on Jack. "Bad idea."

Matt glanced towards Jack and he increased the pressure on the barrel under Vince's chin. "If either of you ever raises a gun towards me again, I will kill you! Do you understand that?" Matt emphasized to Vince with snarled lips.

"Yes!" Vince answered louder than he had before. His eyes watered from the discomfort of having to talk with the barrel digging into his chin.

"What about you, Jack?" Matt asked sharply.

"Yes, sir," he replied. He didn't sound as convincing as his brother.

Matt released his grip on Vince and holstered his revolver. "I hope you do, Jack, or you better be damned well ready to die."

They had ridden the short distance to the edge of the gully when they heard a group of horses approaching quickly. Vince lowered his head. Truet, Morton, Bob, Alan and Nate pulled the reins to bring their mounts to a stop. Their horses breathed heavily from the burst of swift running. "We heard the shots," Truet spoke curiously.

Matt was aggravated. "Yeah. Vince thought he'd take his anger out on Elias."

Truet, Bob and Alan all looked at him with frustration. Morton was a bit more verbal towards his younger brother, "You dumb son of a..."

"I'm sorry, okay! I didn't think about you all," Vince admitted sharply. He was in his mid-twenties and just under six feet tall and well over two hundred pounds. He had the Sperry green eyes and straight brown hair that fell below his ears. Vince had shaved his round face clean in recent days and reminded Matt of a pouting child under the piercing eyes of his older brother.

"We could have been this close to him," Morton emphasized by putting his fingers close together. "Now, Jude's probably escaped out of the gully! You and Jack head south to the canyon. He may be going that way. We don't know. If you see him, fire some shots in the air to let us know. But you better be damn sure it's Jude you see and not one of these men! Now get going."

"What if we don't see him?" Jack Sperry asked, not wanting to be left out. He was the youngest Sperry brother at twenty-three but the biggest of his brothers at six feet even and close to two hundred pounds of muscle. He had dark brown hair that barely covered his ears and was usually unbrushed and had a slight curl at the ends. He had a round face with thick eyebrows and the Sperry green eyes. He had a full-faced short dark brown beard and mustache.

"How are we going to know if you all get him?" Vince asked quickly.

Morton shouted impatiently, "You'll hear shooting! Anything else?"

Jack ran his tongue irritably against his cheek. "Yeah, what if I see that big buck and have a shot? Should I take it?" He asked sarcastically, merely to irritate Morton.

Morton didn't have time for jokes. "No shooting period unless it's at Jude." He questioned Matt, "Does that sound about right to you?"

"I want him alive. No matter who finds Jude, fire shots in the air and we will surround him. If he shoots at you, return fire. But if he surrenders, do not kill him. Morton, I'm assuming you killed Elias. I saw the two shots in his chest; he wasn't surrendering, was he?"

Morton maintained eye contact as he answered, "You probably heard the shooting. They weren't giving up. I killed Elias before he could shoot me and the other one jumped into the gully."

Matt looked down into the gully. "Has anyone gone down in there?"

"No," Truet answered. "Morton said we could head him off down stream somewhere."

Matt stepped out of the saddle. "Where does this

gully lead?" he asked Morton.

"This is Wendling Creek. The gully ends at a beaver pond about two miles downstream as it enters the valley," Morton answered.

Matt addressed the others, "Morton knows this area better than we do, so you all ride down there about half a mile and then Morton, start staggering them around the gully and pond where you think best. Whoever sees or finds a trail, fire three shots and we'll meet you there. I'm going down into the gully, so make darn sure you're shooting at him and not me. Are we all in agreement?"

Tom Smith couldn't resist one last jab at Matt's expense, "You'll know it's Matt by the white band around his head. He's a lot like a skunk, that way." He chuckled.

Matt grinned at his friends good naturedly but it brought up a solid point he hadn't considered. The white bandaging would stand out like a red flag in the dim light and foliage of the gully. "Good point, Tom. It would make an easy target." He unwrapped the bandaging and pulled the gauze carefully off the sutures that held his flesh together."

"What happened?" Morton asked, looking at the sutured gash with a distasteful expression.

"I got hit by a drinking glass Saturday night."

"Did you kill whoever did it?"

"No," Matt said as he grabbed his Winchester rifle out of his scabbard.

Truet added, "He would have if it weren't broken up. All Matt saw was red and it wasn't just blood."

Morton turned his horse. "I bet. Matt, we'll see

you downstream."

Nate had tethered the buckskin gelding to his horse and followed the others while Matt walked to where Jude's spurs were and carefully descended the steep bank. He reached the bottom, nearly slipping himself. He stepped into the water and shivered as it filled his boots. It only seemed reasonable that Jude would go with the water flow towards the valley. Matt put a bullet in the chamber of his rifle and walked through the water keeping his eye out for any boot tracks along the edge of the creek, freshly laid down grass or broken limbs. He was wary of the thick brush and vegetation on both sides of the gully and the number of trees Jude could hide behind. If Jude were in the ravine and heard Matt's moving through the water, it would give Jude the advantage of least taking one unhurried shot before Matt could react. One shot was all it took to kill a man. Matt had plenty of reason to be cautious and quick to respond to anything.

19

Running through the knee-deep water was more challenging than it appeared. Jude Maddox came to a stop and bent over to catch his breath. Jude had always been quick with his hands and feet and in good physical condition, he thought. Plowing through the frigid creek was wearing him out fast. Not eating for almost twenty-four hours didn't help nor being dehydrated from a night of drinking. He laid his rifle on the ground and cupped his hands and dipped them into the creek for a drink of fresh water. The best water is always the first drink that quenches a dry throat. He got another drink. He scanned the thickets of alder, birch and the occasional spruce and fir trees that lined the gully walls. The trees' height and width concealed the bottom of the gully with branches reaching out overhead creating a tunnel of shadows. He was thankful for the foliage that concealed his presence from the men searching along the edge of the gully.

Tall thistles, stinging nettles, ferns and multiple vines and bushes grew thick along the steep bank, leaving no room along the edges for him to walk on dry ground without his feet getting tangled in vines or thorns.

He picked up his rifle and sloshed forward, listening for the sound of approaching horses, but all he could hear was his legs pushing through the water. He kneeled behind a thicket of alder trees along the creek's edge and listened. When he didn't hear anyone , he darted forward again to the next good place to kneel and listen. Though he tried to run as fast as he could, he felt like a slug sliding away from a child with a can of salt. Jude heard several horses coming towards him at a run. He crouched closer to the green vines and hoped he wouldn't be spotted through small openings between the leaves. The horses passed by without the men bothering to slow down to look for him. He listened until he could no longer hear the horses. He didn't know where the gully led or where the riders were hurrying to cut him off. The idea of being boxed in like a rat in a grain barrel scared him. Jude could feel the restlessness and pressure to get out of the gully. He held his rifle tightly, knowing time was running out. He moved through the water alert for any sign of an ambush.

His hands shook primarily due to the icy water saturating his boots but he was also hung over and hungry. He regretted not taking the time to saddle their horses and escape the cabin. Elias would still be alive if they had. He had panicked, expecting

Matt Bannister, the Sperry brothers and several deputies to be right on their heels. As it turned out, they had a half-hour head start and if they had taken those few moments to get their horses, he wouldn't be walking blindly in a deep gully while the enemy positioned themselves somewhere up ahead.

A gunshot sounded from behind him. It was followed by three more shots from the same gun and then silence. Jude squatted down behind some brush and listened. He knew there were at least eight lawmen and two or three Sperry brothers looking for him and maybe more coming from town. He was growing uneasy, wondering if the shots meant something that he could not decipher. It only took a few minutes until Jude heard the four or five horses galloping towards the sound of the gunshots passing by him once again without bothering to look for him. Jude ran as hard as he could through the water, looking for the nearest escape route out of the deep gully before he ran out of energy to make the climb. He could scale the steep bank at any point but he was afraid of two things, one was being caught halfway up a bank and the other was leaving a noticeable trail. He had trailed enough cattle to know an obvious track led right to the cow. He was more intelligent than a cow but he had to think quick to outwit very experienced men in their own backyard. He did not want to leave a trail for the men to follow and while in the creek, he wasn't, but he would leave a noticeable trail if he climbed up the side of the gully.

A hundred yards ahead, an old spruce tree had

fallen across the gorge from the top of the opposite bank and landed midway up the left bank. The fallen tree created a natural bridge out of the gully. All the needles had long since fallen off the limbs that stuck out like a pin cushion in various directions. Jude smiled upon his luck as it occurred to him that this is where the lawmen were waiting to ambush him. He was tired from running but the urgency to escape the death trap of the gully overrode the fatigue that was setting in. Jude ran, determined to get across the tree before the lawmen returned.

Jude climbed halfway up the bank and stepped onto the tree and glanced around. Not seeing anyone, he began the work of maneuvering around limbs that stuck up and in various angles to work his way across the creek that ran smoothly below him. Being aware that his wet boots made the deteriorating bark left on the tree slippery, he stepped carefully and kept a hold of the limbs as he worked his way over the creek. The steep angle of the tree made the climb more difficult but, limb by limb and step by step, he proceeded. He wasn't afraid of heights but he was preoccupied with a continuous need to pause and look for any sign of the lawmen returning. He did not want to be caught in the open standing on an uneven log high above a shallow creek. Jude used his left hand to hold onto branches as he stepped carefully and tried not to lose his balance while his right hand clung to his Winchester rifle with an iron grip. He fought to control a growing feeling of alarm, knowing he was taking too long to cross the log and the others could return at any time. He came to a stout limb that stood upright in the center of the tree's trunk at the midway point across the creek. So far, he had been able to squeeze around the limbs that were angled one way or the other but he would have to swing his whole body around this one with very little space to do so. Jude hooked the thick limb with the crook of his elbow to hold himself close to it. He supported his entire body weight on the branch while he stepped around it with his right foot and switched his weight onto his right foot to complete his swing around the limb. The bark he stood on broke loose and he lost his footing and balance as the bark fell to the creek. Jude clenched his elbow tighter around the limb to hold himself on the log but his weight was pulling him backward off the tree. In a panic, Jude released his rifle and grasped the branch with his right hand as well and pulled himself against the stout branch. He watched his Winchester fall thirty feet and land in the creek with a splash. Infuriated, he cursed. He could see the rifle under the water and was tempted to get it but the risk of being caught wasn't worth the risk. Jude found it easier to climb up the dead tree using both hands to steady him and reached the top.

Jude jumped onto the grass and began running away from the gully deeper into the forest. The ground was a mixture of needles, pinecones, broken limbs, ferns, patches of grass and bushes. The trees were tall and thick with branches of green needles. He ran until he could run no more. He bent over to catch his breath, glanced behind him and cursed.

He was extending off his toes as he ran and leaving a small divot in the soft needles for someone to follow. Small drips of water also marked his way from his wet pants and boots. He had not taken the time to remove his boots and drain the water out of them and he still didn't have time to do so. What he could do was grab handfuls of needles and dirt and rub it on his pantlegs and boots to soak up any extra moisture and slow the dripping. That solved the wetness temporarily but it didn't solve his toe from leaving divots when he ran. He forced himself to stay calm and step lightly as he walked, using care to leave a lighter track. He studied his back trail and could not see a noticeable print in the bed of needles. He turned his direction back towards the mountain and, although his every impulse was to run like hell, he reminded himself to step softly and as flat as possible. From the direction of the gully, he could make out the sound of one man shouting to another. Jude knew they were getting close but he could not afford to panic.

He located a small stream no more significant than two feet wide, draining some portion of the mountain of its clear melting snow towards the gully. Jude reached down and cupped his hands to get a drink and then another. The stream had a fine gravel bedding inviting Jude to step into the water and follow it upstream. He was careful to step in the center, where it barely came above his ankles. The stream led him through the woods to an open meadow. A few deer raised their heads from eating and stared at him standing in the shadows of the woods. They began to skip away, which told him the deer had not noticed anyone else.

Finally, with a view of the sky, he was discouraged to see dark storm clouds coming in the distance and he could already feel the temperature cooling as the storm drew closer. Needing to find some cover, he ran through the stream across the vast meadow and into another thick wall of tall spruce and fir trees. He continued up the creek a reasonable distance before stepping on a good-sized rock to leave the stream and then carefully stepped on broken branches when possible and needles as he went deeper into the forest.

Jude had done his best to lose the posse that was tracking him. He wasn't overly confident that he had but he had given it his best try. He looked up into the trees and could not see past a certain height. However, the least likely tree anyone would suspect him to be in seemed impossible to climb. The tree's lowest branches were near eight feet off the ground and out of his reach. He searched in the waning light and found a strong stick about two inches thick and five feet long and after a few jumps, Jude used it as a crossbar. It took near all the strength to pull himself up to the first two branches. He sat on the lower branch for a moment to catch his breath and then carefully stood. He tossed the stick as far as possible and then began to climb the limbs above the first layers of cover until he felt secure that he wouldn't be noticed from the ground. It was uncomfortable but he wedged himself between four branches close enough together to make a place to rest without worrying about slipping out of the tree.

There was nothing more he could do until darkness came except curse himself for not grabbing his duster and tighten his arms around his chest to try to stay warm and hope they didn't find him.

20

Matt alertly scanned everything around him as he walked in the creek. The foliage and growing shadows created many potential places to set an ambush and the thought of it put Matt on guard. His toes were numb from the frigid water but he moved at a steady pace trying not to slosh through the water to keep the noise down. He walked about a half-mile without seeing a whole lot of signs. There were a few places where Jude had kneeled behind bushes leaving knee prints in the compressed vines and grass. He saw a handprint in soft mud where he might have hidden behind some brush but Jude hadn't left much of a trail. Matt walked for another half mile and then stopped. A large spruce tree had fallen from the right-side bank down across the creek and landed midway up the left-side bank spanning over the creek. The tree offered an escape route that anyone would take. There were places where pieces of the bark had come off the tree trunk, but none were as fresh as the one in the middle of the tree where a large limb pointed skyward. Matt grinned when he saw Nate Robertson sitting on his horse at the top of the left side of the gully, watching him. Nate had Jude's gelding tethered for Matt to use. Matt pointed at the fallen tree as he left the creek and started climbing the bank. "This is where he crossed," he shouted up at Nate.

"What?" Nate shouted.

Matt shouted louder, "This is where he crossed over to up there." He pointed across the gully.

Nate shouted down, "Morton said he might cross here. He's on the other side looking for Jude's trail now."

Matt was irritated by the foreknowledge Morton had of the fallen tree and had neglected to mention it. "He better not be messing up any tracks!" Matt shouted angrily while he climbed the bank and worked his way to the end of the tree. He stepped onto the log and worked his way around the barren branches. If the tree had been level, it would have been easy enough, but at a relative thirty-degree incline on a round surface with brittle branches and fragile bark made it a bit uncanny thirty feet above a two-foot-deep stream. He reached the middle of the creek where the large vertical limb blocked any easy access around it and where the bark had broken off. Glancing down, he caught the glint of brass and saw the rifle lying underwater. He searched downstream for Jude's body. If he had fallen from the tree, the fall could have severely injured or killed him. The water was at a steady flow and relatively strong with the potential to carry a body downstream quite a way before getting tangled up in the brush somewhere. Matt hollered to Nate. "He might have fallen in. His rifle's down there." He pointed towards the water.

"What?" Nate yelled back.

Morton Sperry appeared on horseback near the roots of the tree. "He came this way, Matt. I followed his trail for a bit."

Matt questioned sharply, "You knew he would cross over here, didn't you?"

Morton answered honestly, "No, I didn't know. Some men are afraid of heights and no one afraid of heights will cross that log. We needed to check the gully and surround the beaver pond. There are more fallen trees the further you go and the gully gets shallower, so he could have come out anywhere from this point on. I wasn't trying to do you wrong, Matt."

Matt crossed the log and jumped onto the grass near Morton. "He lost his rifle in the creek."

"Where?" Morton asked.

"See that vertical limb? His rifle's straight down from there. How far did you track him?"

"Half a mile east and then the trail goes cold."

Matt yelled to Nate. "Come around and bring everyone with you!" He had noticed the air had changed since leaving the depths of the gully. He focused on the southwest, where the sky was filled with dark clouds coming their way. "We have some bad weather coming."

Morton glanced at the clouds but his mind was

on finding Jude. "I'll show you where his trail ends."

It didn't take long for Matt and Morton to walk the half-mile through the woods following the toe divots from Jude's boots. The divots came to a stop and Matt peered up through the trees to the sky. The daylight was fading as the storm got closer, making it harder to see any fine details. The sound of thunder was growing louder with each flash of lightning in the distance. It began to sprinkle, warning of heavy rain. The trail had not disappeared but Jude had gotten wiser about the divots.

"See?" Morton asked. "It ends. I looked in the trees, wondering if that's where he is, but I didn't see anything."

Matt watched the ground and took a few steps. "Jude noticed he was leaving a trail and took more care to hide it. We can't trail him in the dark."

"I can have the boys run to the house and get some lanterns," Morton suggested.

"Let's see where he's going while we can." Matt kept his attention on the ground to make out any compressed spruce needles every twenty-eight inches, which was an estimated distance of Jude's walk from heel to heel. Morton walked beside Matt leading his horse and trying to recognize what Matt was seeing. "He's trying to avoid extending off his toes but look here," he knelt and pointed at a barely noticeable divot in the needles. "You can see where the ground is exposed from the tip of his boot." He gave a knowing grin to Morton. "He can try to walk flatfooted but naturally extends off his toe when he walks. He isn't outsmarting us but the darker it gets the harder it's going to be to see. He's intentionally going deeper in the mountains to throw us off his trail."

"We can get lanterns," Morton offered again, not wanting to quit searching until Jude was as dead as Elias Redding.

"No. We're not tracking an unarmed man and you don't want to use a lantern or you'll become an easy target. The only cover that I know of out here is under a tree and with a thunderstorm coming, that's the last place he'll want to be." Matt hesitated and stared thoughtfully in the direction Jude's trail led. "How far is the valley from here?"

"Two miles."

Matt spoke thoughtfully, "He's not going back towards town right now but he will seek shelter at a homestead before morning. We need to send everyone to warn the homesteads in a five-mile radius that there is an armed fugitive loose. When the fellas get here, we will split them up into groups of two and I need your help to send them in the right directions. I want every house in Natoma and every homestead notified because that's where Jude will be going. And in the morning, I want every homestead nearby here searched."

Morton acknowledged Matt's words but was disappointed. "I wanted him today. You don't mind if I keep looking after you send everyone away, do you?"

Matt sighed. "Right now, notifying the folks around here to lock their doors and keep their family inside is our highest priority. We'll get him tomorrow."

21

Matt offered to pay for a room at the Gregory Hotel for Tom Smith and Johnny Barso to share for the night but they wanted to go back to Willow Falls and be with their families. After knocking on doors and warning people of a fugitive on the loose in the area, they did not feel secure about their own homes only seven miles from where they last left Jude's known location. Matt understood perfectly and shook their hands and sent them on their way after a hearty meal at the restaurant. Matt talked to the owner of the Natoma livery stable and convinced him to put padlocks on all the doors overnight as a precaution. Matt was concerned that Jude might sneak into town and take his horse during the night.

After dinner, Bob, Alan, Nate, and Truet went to the local saloon for a drink to get out of the hotel. Matt was the only one with a room to himself and enjoyed the solitude after a long day. After the others left the hotel, he walked downstairs and found Mister Jay Gregory in a small room close to the front counter used as hotel check-in and to pay for the restaurant bill. The small room had a carved wooden sign above it that stated simply, store. The room had been closed off with a red drape earlier. Matt entered the small room and glanced at the shelves of miscellaneous merchandise and reading material. The Gregory Hotel was the main stop for the stagecoaches to rest as they traveled through Jessup Valley. Sometimes, the stage stopped for the night and, other times, it stopped for a meal and allowed the travelers to stretch their legs. The store was set up conveniently for travelers. It contained liquor, medicines, blankets, books, newspapers, earmuffs, footmuffs and gloves made at the Natoma Glove Company, along with other things to make traveling a bit more comfortable. Jay Gregory was behind a display case with a glass front. Behind the glass was a collection of jewelry of various types, pocket watches, jackknives, small ceramic figurines, beautiful hair combs of good quality. Some of the rings appeared to be far too expensive for a small-town hotel owner to buy and sell at a much lower price.

On top of the counter was Elias Redding's knife with an ornamental handle in a cheap leather sheath with a five-dollar price tag fastened on it. Jay was making room in his case for the knife. Matt held the knife and pulled it out of the sheath exposing the seven-inch narrow blade and sharp tip. It was quickly recognized as the same knife Matt and Tim Wright took off Elias when they arrested him. Matt knew the blade flipped out, expanding the blade, but he wasn't about to demonstrate it to Jay. The knife had mysteriously disappeared from Elias' body when they went back and took his body to the livery stable for the night. "What's this?" Matt asked curiously.

Jay was startled by his voice. "Oh! Marshal, I didn't hear you come in. That's a…" he hesitated to think about it. "I'd say it's more of a paring or filleting knife by the thin blade. It has an oversized and decorative handle and ought to sell okay. This is our store we open when the stage comes. You'd be surprised how many folks tired from traveling are willing to buy something new on a long trip. Look around, maybe you'll find something that you can't do without."

Matt ran his thumb across the blade to feel the sharpness. "I'm about half tempted to buy this knife. May I ask where you got it from?"

Jay answered honestly, "I just bought it this evening from Vince Sperry. He took it in trade for some work and preferred to have the money. I gave him a few dollars for it. I think it's worth five just for the quality of it." He paused to look at Matt with a sideways grin. "Or are you thinking that's priced too high?"

Matt bit his lower lip, undecided. "Five dollars is two day's work for most people and for a paring knife? It has a good handle but it's still a kitchen knife, right?"

"Yeah, but do you feel the width and weight of

that handle? It would be great for some old lady with arthritic hands to hold and peel apples or potatoes. Some wealthy woman with arthritic hands will consider this paring knife is as good as gold."

"I see," Matt said. "Is that a wedding ring? Is that a diamond ring with the red garnets or something around it?"

Jay pulled the ring out of the case to show Matt. It was in a small tin box with gray velvet covering a small pillow of cotton. "No, sir. Those are not garnets; they are rubies. This is one of my best rings. I have it priced at thirty dollars and you won't beat that price anywhere for a ring of that quality."

"You're probably right about that."

"It is a size seven. I've sized every ring and the size is written on the tag in case you're looking for one," Jay offered.

Matt held the ring in his fingers, looking at it with interest. "Can I ask how much you paid for it? I'd hate to buy a ring and think I got a great deal and find out it's fake. My fiancé already thinks I'm cheap and if I got her a fake diamond, trust me, I may not have a fiancé anymore." Matt grinned.

Jay laughed. "Matt, before I bought this place, I worked for a jeweler and learned a lot about diamonds. I assure you it's worth three times what I'm asking but I won't get that kind of money for it around here. I'll make you a deal, purchase it, take it to a jeweler, and get it appraised and if you're not satisfied, return it and I'll give you your money back."

"How did you come across this ring?" Matt asked, already having a good idea where it came from.

"A lady came through here a few months ago and sold it to me. She left her husband and needed some money, so she sold it to me for twenty dollars. It's real, though."

"It's a little spendy for me. But what the heck, can you add the ring and knife to my bill and we'll settle up tomorrow?"

"Absolutely," Jay answered with a touch of excitement in his voice.

The sheriff's office was locked and Matt found the town sheriff, Zeke Jones, at home in bed with a bad back and unable to sleep on the jail cot. Zeke had left Jimmy Donnelly in the jail with no one to keep the fire lit or stop him from escaping again. Matt got the door keys and returned to the jail.

Matt placed the desk chair backward by the jail cell and sat facing Jimmy. He rested his arms on the back of the chair and sternly looked at the young man. His nose had been straightened but his eyes were swollen and black and blue. Jimmy was quite nervous under Matt's gaze. Matt asked, "Do you know who I am?"

"Yes, sir," he answered respectfully.

"You do understand that Bo Crowe was killed today. He is the cousin of the Sperry and Helms boys. They blame you. You'll notice the sheriff isn't here? He's expecting you to be lynched tonight and so I'm here. But I'm leaving and I may or may not leave one of my men here to protect you. I already did some questioning around here and know some things." He was bluffing like his cousin, William, did at the poker table. Sometimes fear could motivate the truth out of a liar better than asking for an honest answer.

Matt continued, "I'm going to ask you a few questions and you better tell me the truth. Because if you don't, you won't give me a reason to save you. Understood?"

Jimmy swallowed hard and stared at Matt with concern on his face. "Yes, sir."

Matt pulled the tin box out of his pocket and revealed the diamond wedding ring with tiny rubies set beside the diamond. "Have you seen this ring before?"

Jimmy took hold of the ring. "No, Sir." He handed it back to Matt. "It's a nice one, though."

Matt frowned. He had hoped to catch Jay Gregory in a lie about where he got the ring. "If you had stolen this ring, what would you do with it?"

"Well, if I had a sweetheart, I'd give it to her. That's a nice one."

"What do you do with the jewelry you take?" Matt asked bluntly.

"I didn't take any jewelry."

Matt stood up and sighed. "What Morton did to you earlier today was a quick beating before he learned that his cousin was dead. He'll be coming into town with the rest of Sperry-Helms Gang in a couple of hours. The sheriff asked me to leave the door unlocked so he doesn't have to replace the door. Have a good evening." Matt picked up the chair to replace it behind the desk and leave. "Here are the jail keys," Matt said, dropped the keys on the desk and walked for the door.

Jimmy held the bars and answered quickly, "Vince Sperry buys it all from me! Please, Marshal, don't leave me alone. I didn't kill their cousin!"

Matt paused at the door. "No, but you did bring the men here that did. In their view, it's the same thing."

Jimmy's chest rose and fell with his heavy breathing. "Marshal...I'll tell you anything you want to know. Please, don't let them kill me!" The tears of desperation in the young man's eyes revealed that he was ready to answer some questions.

Matt replaced the chair and sat. "I'll give you another shot at telling the truth. Question number two. What does Vince do with the stuff he buys?"

Jimmy swallowed. "Keeps what he wants and sells the rest."

"To the Garrison Hotel?" Matt asked knowingly.

Jimmy nodded.

"Does Jay Gregory know where Vince gets the stuff? Are you all in it together?"

Jimmy's hand shook. "I've never met him. That's between him and Vince; I don't know."

"But you didn't steal this ring?"

He shook his head. "No, sir."

Matt observed Jimmy carefully. "Another question. How do you open a locked safe?"

Jimmy lowered his brow questionably. "I don't know. I never have."

Matt hesitated. "You didn't make keys to unlock the Engberg and Penn Assayers Office a few weeks ago?"

He stared at Matt with a blank expression. "No, sir. I don't make keys. I pick locks. But safe's, I don't know unless they have a key lock."

"What about combination locks?"

"No, sir. I can pick key locks. That's all."

Matt took a deep breath. "How did you get out of the sheriff's jail?"

Jimmy closed his eyes and sighed. He raised his index finger to indicate waiting a moment and removed his boot and pulled the insole out before pulling the two ward keys from of his insole. He handed them to Matt. "They were in my boot."

Matt held the ward keys and admired the carved-out settings for them in the insole. "Very clever. Let me see your other boot." When Matt had all four of the lock picking tools from Jimmy's boots, he said, "You're a bright guy, Jimmy. It's too bad you use your intelligence to be a criminal element in society. Just imagine how nice it would be if you used that brightness to make an honest living for yourself. You wouldn't have to worry about someone like me looking for you or worrying about a long jail or prison sentence. You wouldn't have to worry about getting involved with bad men or facing the consequences like the Sperry-Helms Gang wanting you dead because of those bad characters. Since you broke out of the Branson city jail and left town, that makes you my prisoner. I don't have to leave anyone in here tonight but if I decide to have Nate stay here overnight, tomorrow you're going to the hotel and collect every item you have stolen. We'll be taking that stuff back to my office and returning it to the owners. You're going to apologize to every one of them and as repreparations for what you've done, you're going to offer two to three days of free hard labor. And if they tell me you shirked a task, we'll add two more days. If you can do that and work your butt off and prove to me that you want to change, I'll talk to Judge Jacoby on your behalf. If not, you're on your own tonight. Agreed?"

"Yes, sir."

"There's no honor in being a thief, Jimmy. If you can't be an honorable man, then what kind of a man are you? If you don't like the answer, change it. You're the only one that can."

"Marshal Bannister," Jimmy said softly. "Are you going to have someone come stay here tonight? And what if they can't stop the Sperry-Helms Gang? They're bad men, Marshal."

"I'll have Nate spend the night in here. The Sperry-Helms Gang won't do anything if Nate is here. Some folks need free labor back in Branson and you're just the guy to volunteer to do it. Aren't you?" Matt asked.

"Yes, sir," Jimmy said with a sense of relief. "I'll do whatever it takes to make things right."

The rain poured down and flashes of lightning brightened the sky as a loud crack of thunder rumbled through the valley. Matt walked to the Heather Creek Tannery, where many folks brought their livestock and game hides to sell. He found the small shed that Jay had directed him to. It was no larger than a chicken coop with two small windows covered with black curtains. He could see a faint hint of light through the black material. He knocked on the rough-hewn board door.

A female voice asked curtly with a heavy Chinese accent, "What do you want? It's late at night."

Matt grinned. It was still early, being just after seven-thirty in the evening. "My name is Matt Bannister. I'm the United States Marshal. Can I speak with you for a moment?"

"What do you want?"

"I would like to speak with you if I could."

The door opened just far enough for the small Chinese lady to peek out while blocking the door with her body. Matt doubted there was enough weight on her to stop the door if a gust of wind blew against it. "Oh, you're hurt, come in," she said, noticing the sutures in his forehead. She pulled the door open to let him step inside. "Sit there." She pointed at a wooden chair across from another chair beside her low bed. He removed his hat and wet coat and set them by the door where she motioned for him to set them down. "Sit, sit," she waved at the chair while she opened a wood cabinet on her wall and pulled a roll of gauze down and scissors and cream of some sort in a small jar. Matt sat and looked around the cabin while she searched through her cabinet. The shack was cluttered with a wide variety of papers, cloth material, pinecones and a shelf of powders and herbs. In the corner, a small cookstove heated the shack a little too well as it was quite warm. She sat down and scooted her chair closer in front of him.

She reached her finger into the jar of ointment and rubbed it on his sutures.

He didn't know what she was putting on him but she had treated Henry Sperry and Jimmy Donnelly. "Thank you but I didn't come here for that."

"Why are you here then?" she asked him curiously. She wiped her finger on her pants and reached for the roll of gauze and scissors. Tillie was a small lady dressed in homemade black flannel pants and a red and black checkered flannel long sleeved shirt that pulled over her head. Thick wool gray stockings were on her feet. Her square shaped face was wrinkled and her gray hair was tied in a tight bun against the back of her head. Her narrow dark eyes were intelligent and lively having probably never known a lazy day in her sixty some years.

"I came here because you speak English. You can speak Chinese too, right?"

She sat on the chair facing him and sighed heavily. "Of course, I am Chinese! Let me finish, please." She began wrapping the gauze around his head without a gauze pad.

Matt chuckled at her response. "You speak English very well."

"I speak English every day."

"Can I ask you, this past fall, did you write a letter in Chinese for Morton Sperry?" Matt neglected to say any more about where or how it was used.

She narrowed her brow thoughtfully while she cut the gauze and tied it behind his head. "Yes. Who are you and why are you here if not to fix your wound? It's late and I must work in the morning."

She held out her hand. "Two dimes, please."

Matt laughed lightly. He stood and reached into his pocket for his pocketbook. He handed her a silver dollar. "I apologize. My name is Matt Bannister. I am the United States Marshal." He pointed to the badge on his left breast. "You're Tillie, right?" He put his hand out to shake hers.

"Tillie, yes," she responded, turning her back to him to open a small drawer on a four-drawer jewelry box with an extended top with a mirror. She counted out the change and handed him a handful of change that he put in his pocket. "Who are you?" she asked, putting her attention on him.

"I'm a U.S. Marshal. Is Tillie your Chinese name?"

"No," her voice began to quiver with sudden nervousness.

"What is your Chinese name?" Matt asked with interest.

Tillie's face suddenly lowered and then lifted with worry filling in her aging eyes. "I came here twenty-five years ago with my husband. We worked hard and minded our own business. My husband died ten years ago and is buried here. This is my home and I must stay here and live here. I work hard and ask nothing of no one. You cannot send me back to China, please." Her fear of being deported due to the Chinese Exclusion Act was plain to see. She had no family left in China and being sent back would be a death sentence from starvation and exposure if the trip back didn't kill her first. She had made a home in Natoma and worked at the tannery. She was a welcomed member of the community and loved the people in her town.

Matt held up his hands and waved them. "No. I'm not here to send you back to China. You have nothing to fear about that. I came here to ask if you know Wu-Pen Tseng over in Branson?"

"I have no reason to be in Branson. All I need is here. You won't send me back to China?" Her concern needed to be validated.

"No. And no one else will either. I promise you that," Matt said sincerely. "Have you ever heard of Wu-Pen Tseng?"

She was relieved to know she wasn't being taken from her home. "No."

"Do you know any Chinese people that live and work there?"

She shook her head. "No. I only know the Chinese that live and work here. Now, what do you want? I must get to sleep, so you must go."

"I don't want anything else. Thank you for bandaging my head."

"Keep it dry. The lotion will help."

Matt left and chuckled when he realized she had not given him her Chinese name.

22

Jude Maddox waited until after dark before he climbed out of the tree. He was wet and the rain continued in a heavy downpour. The lightning flashed violently, brightening the forest for a few seconds at a time. The flash of light was followed by a sharp crack of thunder that roared through the valley. For Jude, it would be easy to run towards town and not worry about anything except finding cover but it wasn't that easy when there was a posse of experienced killers looking for him. He avoided trees and water sources while he hurried to get to lower ground and find a source of cover. There was no safe place while in a lightning storm and the fear of being struck by lightning overrode his concern about leaving a trail for the lawmen to follow. If the lightning hit the trees above him, it could splinter the tree and the falling debris could kill him just as quickly as the lightning. He bent over, knowing the height of an object determined what was most likely to be struck. Running through the open meadow, he was the tallest object and, this time, he made sure he was not running in the stream. His clothes were saturated with rain but he didn't want to be standing in ankle-deep water if he was unlucky enough to be hit by lightning. Every flash of light and immediate crack of thunder that vibrated through his body like a train shaking an unstable trestle terrified him. He made it across the meadow and ran into the forest he had so carefully tried to hide his tracks in earlier. He quickly learned it was a bad idea to run in the woods at night when a small limb connected with his eye. The shock of being gouged in the eye hit him like a bolt of lightning would and stopped him immediately, followed by a few loud curses. Jude covered the eye, hoping there was no severe damage done. The searing pain couldn't be ignored and he could not open his eye as his body naturally fought to protect itself. His eye watered and, with some effort, he could open and close the eye and he did numerous times to clear it of any debris.

At a much slower pace, he worked his way through the forest and eventually down a steep wooded hill. He knew he had to be getting close to the valley but the woods continued until he saw a clearing and could make out a fence post through a flash of lightning. If there was one thing, he hated it was fencing, especially barbed wire, but it was the most welcome of sights. A fence meant a homestead was nearby and that filled him with the hope of finding a warm fire, dry clothes and some food for his empty stomach. He felt for the barbed wires and pushed the top wire down but it was too tight to lower enough to step over. Whoever had made the fence had built a two-strand fence and set the posts close enough together to keep the barbed wire tighter than other fences he had crossed in the past. Frustrated, he went to a post and stepped on the wire and using the post as a pendulum, hopped over it. It would be an easy run across the pasture towards the light of a house in the distance. The desire to get out of his wet clothes and have a hot meal beckoned him like the warm embrace of a mother's arms to a scared child. He ran towards the homestead expecting to be welcomed inside and out of the thunderstorm.

He saw the post's outline too late and felt his legs run straight into two strands of tight barbed wire that dug through his jeans and pierced his skin and tore his flesh while his momentum carried him over the top wire. The barbs tore his pants while he flipped over the fence, landing parallel on his back. He cursed loudly from the deep scratches' searing pain and cuts on his legs the barbed wire had caused. His right leg was stuck pointing skyward from the torn material of his pants snagged on the barbs of the top wire. Jude grasped his pants and ripped the fabric off the fence. Jude hated barbed wire and would not quarrel about shooting the man who built the fence.

Jude stepped onto a road that went along the fence line and figured it was the main road to Natoma. The lighted windows of a house across the road drew him like a moth to a fire. He limped along the road a short distance until he reached the small homestead and banged on the door.

"Who is it?" a man's voice answered from the other side of the door.

Jude stood with his hands wrapped around his shoulders, shivering. "Sir, I got lost in the woods. I'm hurt and freezing. Can I come in and warm up? Maybe get some food, please?"

The man's tone was harsh, "Go away! No one's going to help you around here and if you go towards my barn, there's four of us with rifles and we won't hesitate to kill you long before the Marshal can string you up!"

Jude was stunned by the hostility in the man's voice. He could feel the hope of being helped fade like a stone being tossed from a bridge. "Sir, I haven't done anything wrong. If you won't let me in, then do you have a coat or blanket I could have, please? Some bread if nothing else?" It occurred to him that Matt and the deputies must have notified the locals about him. "I need help," Jude shouted irately, hoping they might have compassion on him. The thought of being rejected everywhere he went frightened him.

The man's voice was most unfriendly, "Get off my property before I put a fifty-caliber ball through my door!"

"I'm not meaning you, folks, any harm," he pleaded. "I just need to get warm and maybe purchase a meal from you. I have money," he lied.

"I'm counting to three!"

"I'm leaving!" Jude shouted and drove his fist into the door in anger. A fifty-caliber ball exploded through the door splintering the wood with a loud percussion. It missed Jude by an inch or two at chest level. Jude ran as fast as he could off the property, terrified of being shot in the back. He ran to the road and dove into the mud when he heard the front door of the house open. A man stepped out onto the small porch holding a black powder fifty caliber musket. Jude, fearing his white skin would be visible even at the thirty-yard distance, grabbed a handful of mud with his left hand and smeared it over his face to darken his features. His right hand pulled his revolver out of the holster to be ready if the man spotted him. A teenage boy stepped out behind his father; the boy held a repeating rifle.

"Anything out back, John?" the father shouted.

"Nope," came a voice from the back of the house. "He must've left, Pa."

"Darryl, you and Josh stay with your Ma. John and I will check the barn."

"Which way did he go, Pa?"

"I don't know. He may still be here. Don't hesitate to shoot him if you see him. John and I are going to get the Marshal."

Jude's blood ran cold. He stood hunched over low and began moving along the road for a reasonable distance to be sure he couldn't be seen in the darkness. Jude ran to put as much space between him and the house as possible. In the time it would take them to get their horses saddled, get to town and for the Marshal to return to the homestead, Jude hoped to find cover. The longer the distance to town, the more time he had, but Jude had no idea how close to Natoma he was. Nature offered no protection from the elements and it was pure bad luck to be on the run on such a stormy night. The man behind the door was not lying one bit nor willing to risk a moment's worth of charity. If the marshal and the deputies went from house to house, it would be a long night unless Jude changed tactics to gain access into someplace warm. He walked as fast as he could while consistently looking behind him and listening for the sound of any approaching horses.

Before too long, a light in the distance drew his attention to the next homestead but, when he got closer, two large dogs stood in the yard barking and growling at him. The house set back a good forty yards or so off the road but the dogs had come much closer to block the way. The front door of the house opened and a man holding a shotgun stepped onto the porch peering into the darkness while another man held a lantern to cast some light in the direction of the dogs. "Anyone out there?" one of the men hollered. "Duke, Midge. Heel!"

"Who's out there, Pa?"

"I don't know. I don't see anything," the man with the gun answered. He hollered, "You'll be making a mistake if you mess around my property."

Unknown to the homesteaders, Jude had already passed by their house. It was undesirable to be forced to kill two protective dogs while facing another man or two with weapons in their hands. Jude walked for twenty minutes, becoming increasingly aware that time was running out before Matt and his posse came searching for him. There was no option other than to keep moving no matter how cold or weak he was feeling. The road was mud and his boot tracks left a clear trail to follow in the morning's light. He moved over into the grass alongside the road to give him more cover to hide behind and make his trail a little more challenging to follow in the morning. His desperation to get out of the rain would be happily satisfied by a rat-infested chicken coop if he could find one. The rain was heavy and he couldn't get any wetter than if he had jumped into a river.

Out of the darkness, he heard singing. The voices sounded like children and a woman's angelic voice rose above the hooves splattering in the mud and the creaking of a wagon that came into sight. Jude moved further off the road into the tall grass and knelt low to stay out of sight. The wagon was coming from town and pulled by a pair of very large and muscular draft horses. Jude was surprised to see a team of Belgians in this speck of a town. He could see the young family as clear as day as they had two lanterns hung from the undercarriage of the wagon to light the horses and road, and another lantern hung from the frame of the bow of the canvas top. The young woman's angelic voice laughed when the song came to an end. She rode beside her husband on the bench seat in the rain and sat half turned around to sing with their younger girls. The lady was dressed in a long black wool coat and a wide-brimmed canvas hat. She didn't seem fazed by the rain at all. Her husband also wore a long duster and wide-brimmed canvas hat. He smiled contently while holding the reins to his trotting double horse team.

"Okay, I know one. How about this: 'Skip, skip, skip, to my Lou..." The young mother sang and was joined by her daughters and husband. "Skip, skip, skip, to my Lou. Skip, skip, skip to my Lou, my darlin," they sang in unison with a joyful sound on such a miserable night.

Jude watched them pass by and stood. He decided the young family was his best opportunity to get into their home as long they weren't going too far. He didn't want to approach their wagon with the Marshal in the area but, if he could keep up with them, he'd be able to surprise them before they had a chance to get into their house. He assumed they had to live in the area or they would have held up somewhere for the night.

Jude was low on energy and feeling weaker by the minute but he tried not to fall too far behind the wagon. The lanterns glowing in the darkness guaranteed he wouldn't lose them if he kept a steady pace. Ten minutes later, Jude heard horses coming from town at a gallop. Jude was twenty yards or so off the road in a field of what he thought might be winter wheat. He laid down and waited. The galloping horses had stopped the wagon and it became clear in the lantern's light that one of the riders was Matt Bannister and the other was Truet Davis. Appalled, Jude clinched his fingers through the muddy soil with his mouth agape. Matt was riding his buckskin gelding named Rebel . Jude had paid a lot of money for the buckskin, broke and trained Rebel himself. Seeing Matt's saddle on Rebel rivaled a husband seeing another man touch his wife. Jude was tempted to pull his revolver and blow Matt out of the saddle and get his horse back but he forced himself to try to keep a level head. He had to be wiser than a rabid dog nipping at the heels of men with guns. He got to his feet and hunched over, drew closer to hear what was being said.

Jude heard the husband driving the wagon to say, "We haven't seen anyone. We live just up the road."

Matt wore a heavy buffalo skin coat with a hood pulled over his bandaged head. He asked, "Would you mind if we rode along and searched your place before you go in? I want to make sure you and your family are safe."

"Sure, that would be great. What did this man you're looking for do? Are we in danger?"

"Let's get your family home and I'll tell you about it on the way."

Jude stood upright and seethed with anger. He wanted to scream and curse to release his frustration. Not only had Matt stolen his beloved gelding but now Matt was ruining the perfect opportunity to get dry, warm and, more importantly, to eat. The young singing family would never be willing to open the door for him now. He resisted the temptation to level his revolver and shoot Matt. The chances were, he'd miss because he was shivering from being cold. Then he'd have to run back into the woods to escape two mounted, better-armed, warm and better-fed men who were just as deadly as he was. The best he could do was follow and hope an opportunity showed itself after Matt and Truet searched the property and left.

23

Matt and Truet had searched the outside of the house with one of the lanterns taken from the wagon and then searched inside the house before moving to the outhouse, outbuildings and finally the large barn with many stalls containing several draft horses. It was a nice property that would undoubtedly attract someone like Jude Maddox to seek refuge, knowing the owners had a certain amount of wealth. Matt and Truet finished their search while the husband put his team away in the barn for the night. The landowner introduced himself as David and invited them in for a cup of hot apple cider which his wife was making while they searched the barn.

"Thank you, but I think we need to keep looking," Matt said, declining the offer.

David was a medium height young man around thirty with short light brown hair and a square-shaped face. He was a broad-shouldered man with a thick chest and had a friendly smile with a short scruffy beard. "If he was coming this way, you probably scared him off. There's not another farm for another two miles or so. Come on inside for a bit. I've met all the Bannisters except for you. Come on in, Kellie's making some hot apple cider and she made cookies earlier today."

Truet shrugged his shoulders with a sly smile as the rainwater dripped from the brim of his Stetson. "It does sound good to me," he said.

Matt agreed and they went into the two-story home with a large front porch and sat at a lovely oak table with six chairs with leather seats. Kellie had set out a platter of cookies and poured hot steaming apple cider for all of them.

"Thank you, Ma'am," Matt said. "It has been a long time since I've had apple cider."

"Please call me, Kellie. You've met my husband, David Crawford. These beautiful young ladies are Amber; she is eight . Emily is seven and Eva is five years old today. We were just at my in-laws for a big birthday party and that's why we are coming home so late." Kellie Crawford was a small and thin lady in her late twenties with black straight hair pulled up in a quick bun while her bangs fell over her large almond vibrant blue eyes. Her face was triangular and attractive. It was easy to see she was a happily married and gentle-hearted lady.

Matt smiled at the three dark-haired little girls who stood nervously at their mother's hip. "Well, happy birthday, Eva." Matt reached into his pocket and pulled out what coins Tillie had given him.

"I hope you folks don't mind but I can't pass by a beautiful birthday girl and not leave a present. But there are two other beautiful young ladies here whose birthdays I must have missed too. So, how about you two each get forty cents, and the birthday girl gets a whole silver dollar," Matt said. He had to reach into his pocketbook to get a silver dollar for Eva.

"Marshal, that's not necessary," Kellie said uncomfortably. It was a lot of money to give away.

"I hope you'll permit me to give these coins to your girls because it helps me. I don't need change jingling in my pocket while searching for someone. And dividing eighty cents by three would take me too long."

"What do you girls say?" Kellie asked.

"Thank you," they all said over one another while grabbing the coins tightly in their hands.

"You are most welcome," Matt said with a friendly smile. He addressed David, "I take it your part of the Crawford Farm family?"

David Crawford answered, "Yes. As I said, I know your whole family. You are the only one I've not met. Adam and my older brother John are old friends. Adam used to work for my Pa many years ago on the farm for a while."

"I've heard Adam mention him before. How many of you brothers are there?"

"There's five of us. John and Howard are older and Paul and James are younger. I'm the middle one."

Matt explained to Truet, "From what I understand, the Crawford Farms is the biggest wheat grower in the valley and probably the biggest employer in Natoma. I know that much about you, folks."

David nodded. "Yeah, we're one of the biggest landowners and employers around here. Between wheat and potato crops, beans, vegetables and berries, we turn a lot of soil. And a lot of harvesting. This is our place. We grow forty-five acres of hay here and five acres of berries. Kellie and the ladies make various kinds of jam to sell."

"How many acres do you farm altogether?" Matt asked curiously.

David whistled and tilted his head. "A lot."

Truet asked, "Are you folks bothered by the Sperry-Helms Gang?"

David grinned with a touch of humor. "No. We grew up with all of them. They might cause trouble elsewhere but not so much around here. We're on friendly terms because if they did cause us any trouble, there are about thirty men around here that would raise arms against them. We have about thirty full-time employees and we're all kind of family."

When Matt and Truet were leaving, Kellie and David stepped out on the front porch to see them off. Kellie asked Truet, "When I went upstairs to tuck the girls in bed, did I hear Matt say you're courting Annie?"

Truet smiled tiredly as he untethered the reins to his mare. "Yes, I am."

Kellie grinned. "I love her. Are you thinking about asking her to marry you?" she asked with raised eyebrows and biting her bottom lip expectantly.

Truet laughed lightly. "There's nothing like being put on the spot, huh?" he asked Matt. He answered Kellie, "We're taking our time. She wants to get Matt married off before we even talk about it."

Kellie giggled like a little girl. "Then yes, you're talking about it! Awesome. Treat her well because she's an extraordinary woman. Tell her hello for me when you see her."

"I will. Thank you for the cookies and apple cider. Nice meeting you folks," Truet said. He was tired and wanted to go back to the hotel and get some sleep.

As they rode away from the homestead, Truet said, "That's a very pretty lady."

"Yes, she is." Matt agreed. "Very nice family."

Jude waited in the field, watching his horse tethered to a hitching rail in front of the house. It would be easy to step in the saddle and ride away but he could see the curtains to the windows were open and he was sure Matt was keeping his eye on the horses like a baited trap. The fact was Jude was ill-prepared to travel too far at all. The rain had ceased but the temperature was dropping as the clouds opened to reveal the stars above. He was shivering and cared far more about getting out of his wet clothes and getting warm than about riding off on a fast horse. He had watched one of the little girls leave a quilt inside of the wagon and it was the first thing he intended to grab once Matt and Truet left the property. Waiting was hard to do and, if he didn't know better, he would have sworn Matt and Truet were staying longer intentionally so that Jude could die of hypothermia.

He ducked when he saw the two lawmen step outside and get on the horses. They glanced around before leaving and spoke to the young homeowners momentarily. He was getting impatient and the only idle chit-chat of interest was that the young woman was friends with Truet's woman. Jude was too cold to care; he just wanted them to leave so he could grab the quilt out of the wagon. When the two lawmen left, Jude quietly made his way to the wagon and grabbed the heavy quilt left inside. He hurried to the large barn and grabbed a lantern he had watched Henry hang up by the door and turned the oil up just enough to see. The barn was wide and long with multiple stalls with draft horses, quarter horses and three stalls of pigs.

There was a space with farrier tools and a tack room where the harnesses, collars, bridles, blinders and saddles were stored. Jude grabbed an old, weathered saddle blanket off the floor and grabbed another from under a saddle. He followed a staircase to the loft and found what he was looking for - a large mound of hay. Jude grabbed the pitchfork, climbed on top of the hay pile and went to the far end against the wall. He dug a pit in the center of the deep pile long enough for him to lay in. When it was dug, he placed the saddle blankets in the hole, stripped naked and wrapped himself in the quilt before burying his clothes and boots in the hay pile. He laid down in his pit and sat up to pull the loose hay back over him. When he was covered with hay and comfortably wrapped in the quilt, he closed his eyes and tried to relax enough to get some needed rest. The safety, dryness and warmth of the haystack would do nothing for his growling stomach but, for now, he could gradually warm up and sleep. In the morning, he would worry about tomorrow. For now, he needed rest.

24

Jude was rudely awakened by the sound of a pitchfork being driven into the hay mound and someone stepping to either side of the hayloft and dumping the hay into feeding troughs.

"Good morning, Marco," a voice said, coming up the stairs into the hayloft. Jude could hear the boots on the plank boards and the sound of the fork slashing into the hay. It unnerved him, but the person was at the front of the stack and not near where he slept. Jude had his gun belt with him but was hesitant to pop out of the haystack naked. He would wait until it was quiet for a while before he crawled out of the hay to get dressed.

"Good morning, David. I was a little late this morning but I'll be done here in a few minutes and then I'll milk and get the milk to Missus Crawford."

"That's fine. I'm going to my brother Howard's to help him today. When you're finished feeding and milking, Kellie would like you to build her six flower boxes that can be mounted under the lower windows of the house. She drew up her plans and measurements and I put the paper in the tack room. You'll find the lumber and paint in the shed. When you're done, she wants them painted red. You can build and paint those today and mount them on the house tomorrow. When you're finished, keep weeding around the raspberry and huckleberries, okay?" David Crawford asked.

"Sure."

"Good. How are you doing today?" David asked with interest. Marco Hernandez was the oldest of seven children that belonged to Jose and Maria Hernandez. Jose and Maria had worked for the Crawford family for over ten years and become good friends. Marco worked primarily for David and Kellie doing a wide variety of whatever they asked him to do.

"I'm a little tired. We were up late after a deputy from Branson and Jack Sperry came over and told us there was a killer somewhere around and not to answer our door or go outside. That doesn't happen very often. Did they come by here?"

David nodded. "Yeah. Not the deputy but Matt Bannister and one of his deputies. The escaped fugitive knocked on the Johnson's door and they chased him off and then Meryl went and got the Marshal. Mister Williams said they think their dogs scared him off and Matt and Truet think the fugitive came our way. They searched our property and didn't find anything. I think we're okay. But it is a little unnerving, isn't it?"

Marco was surprised. "Matt Bannister was here? Does he look mean?"

David smiled. "Not too mean but I don't think I'd want him after me. Would you?"

"No," Marco chuckled. "I'd like to meet him someday, though. I've heard a lot about him."

"Really? He's downstairs right now searching the barn. Hold on." He walked to the stairs and shouted, "Matt, can you hear me?"

"Yeah," Matt's voice answered. He and Morton Sperry came upstairs. "Did you find something?" Matt's eyes were sharp and focused as he scanned the loft for anything suspicious. They settled on a medium height handsome Mexican teenager with a round hairless face in bib overalls and a flannel shirt with a straw hat. The boy held a pitchfork while standing next to David.

David answered, "No. I wanted to introduce you to our young friend Marco Hernandez. He wanted to meet you."

Matt held out his hand to shake. "Nice to meet you, Marco. I'm Matt."

Marco shook his hand and grimaced slightly from the firm grip of Matt's hand. "Likewise."

"Have you seen anything out of the ordinary today?" Matt asked with all business on his mind. "I'm telling you right now, Jude's trail ends right here. Any horses missing or anything like that?"

"No," David answered. "He must've moved on if he did come here." He put his attention on Morton Sperry. "How are you doing, Morton? I'm sorry to hear about your cousin. How is Henry?" David asked, shaking his hand.

"Thank you," Morton said. "Henry is going to be okay. He's going to have a nice scar, though."

"You got the man that shot him?" David asked.

"One of them. Now we're looking for the rat that killed Bo."

Matt asked Marco, "You haven't seen anything strange or out of place?"

Marco shook his head. "No. Well, the lantern was on the floor this morning, but I may have left it there last night when I finished feeding the animals. I normally hang it back up but may not have."

Matt pointed at the hay pile. "Morton, do you want to take the pitchfork and search the hay mound?"

Morton took the pitchfork from Marco and walked over and began ramming it into the hay mound with all the force he could. Matt had stepped near him and pulled the revolver from his holster in case Jude was hiding in the hay. When Morton had finished going around the large pile of hay, he handed the pitchfork back to Marco. "If he were here, you'd probably know it by now," he said.

Matt agreed. "We have men scouring the area, so don't be surprised if they come by here throughout the day."

David said, "Thank you, I appreciate it. If you need more men, I can round up another ten to fifteen to help, including myself."

Matt waved the idea off. "We have enough men. It's just a matter of time."

Jude had nearly stood up shooting when he heard Matt tell Morton to fork the hay mound. Being stabbed by a pitchfork was by no means worth waiting for. However, he had dug his pit in the center of the large pile and figured a pitchfork to either side of him wouldn't penetrate deep enough to touch him. His only vulnerable spot was from straight above and Morton had not gotten close enough to him to expose his hiding spot. Jude waited until they all left the loft and there was no sound upstairs before he slowly raised his head out of the hay to peek around. He crawled out of the hay wrapped in the quilt and exposed himself to the brisk morning air. He dug his wet clothes out of the hay and took a deep breath before slipping his scratched and cut-up legs into his damp and frigid, ripped long johns. The feel of the wet clothes sent a chill down his spine. He gritted his teeth and pulled the wet long johns over his dry skin quickly to get the worst of it over with. Once in his long johns, it wasn't so bad to slip into his clothes and boots. Once dressed, he was once again cold and miserable. He strapped on his gun belt and slowly proceeded down the stairs holding his Colt .44 in hand. Jude could hear the squirting of a cow's milk hitting the side of the tin bucket as Marco milked the family cow. It was a chore he did every morning and occasionally in the evenings if the Crawfords weren't going to be home.

Jude looked carefully outside of the barn and confident that the other men had left, he approached Marco from behind. He put the revolver to the back of Marco's head and pulled the hammer back. The sound of the hammer's click startled Marco and he jumped up, spilling the nearly full bucket of milk onto the ground. He spun around and stared wide-eyed at the barrel of a gun pointed inches from his head and the cold light blue eyes and snarling lips of Jude aiming it.

"Don't say a word!" Jude snarled. He motioned towards the door of the barn. "You're going to lead me into the house just like any other day when you take the milk in. If you try to run or warn the woman of the house, I'll kill you and everyone in the house too. Do you understand me?" Jude licked his lips, anticipating eating some breakfast and getting into some dry clothes.

Marco swallowed nervously and nodded quickly. He was shocked to be facing the man the Marshal was looking for. The terror showed on his face.

"Then pick up the damn milk bucket and let's go," Jude ordered harshly.

Jude nudged the boy and followed him with the gun pointed inches from Marco's back. His stomach growled loudly while his alert eyes darted back and forth nervously around him, looking for any sign of the posse. "Hurry up!" He jabbed the barrel into Marco's back impatiently.

Marco's heart raced as the blood pulsated through his body in a state of disbelief. Marco loved the Crawford family and was especially fond of Kellie, who always fed him lunch and made him feel at home. He couldn't think clearly with the amount of adrenaline running through his veins, knowing he was one mistake or minute away from being killed. Marco tried to think of a way to stop the fugitive from entering the house and putting Kellie and the three girls in danger. He was afraid to die but he was also fearful of what could happen if the man got inside the house. Kellie and three girls were in no position to fight off a man with a gun. The only man between them and the fugitive was him. It was up to him to try to spare the Crawford girls from the outlaw if he could. Marco held the quarter full milk can and stopped at the backdoor. It was a solid wood door that he had painted red the summer before. Every morning, he would knock on the door and greet the family as he carried the milk in for Kellie.

Marco hesitated to knock, not wanting to expose the family to a threat. He turned his head towards Jude. He could barely speak in fear of being shot, but he spoke, "Sir, I could get you our fastest horse and you can get away. I swear, I won't tell anyone. No one would know until late today when David comes home, if then. You'd have from now until almost dark or a full day or two head start if you left now."

For a moment, Jude considered it but the boy couldn't be trusted and, more important than that, Jude was starving. He needed to eat and he needed to eat as soon as possible. Jude slapped the back of Marco's head with his left hand and pressed the gun's barrel into Marco's back. "Knock on the door!" he hissed, keeping his voice down.

Marco hesitated, not knowing what to do. He

was tempted to yell for Kellie not to open the door and get one of David's guns. He would've liked to have done so, but he was too frightened of sacrificing his own life. "Please don't hurt them," he begged with a quivering lip.

"Knock!" Jude spat out. "I won't tell you again," Jude threatened while looking nervously around him.

Marco had no choice but to hold the milk bucket and knock on the back door. He could hear the three girls running excitedly towards the back door like they always did when he brought the morning milk. He leaned his forehead on the door and closed his eyes with the shame of feeling like he was betraying his friends. He prayed for the Lord to protect the family from the man about to take them hostage. He felt Jude maneuver in expectation of the door opening.

"Wait..." came Kellie's voice over the pitter-patter of her daughters running to open the door. She peeked out the nearest window and saw the silver milk bucket. "It's just Marco." She allowed the girls to open the door and her smile faded when she saw the expression and tears running down Marco's face. "Marco?" she asked with concern.

Jude swung around the side of Marco and pointed the gun at Kellie as he forced Marco into the house and kicked the door shut behind him. Kellie screamed and backed up, startled, as did her girls. The older two, Amber and Emily, clung to their mother's hip while she protectively wrapped her arms around them. Little Eva stood beside the door with a frightened expression on her face.

"Shut up!" Jude shouted. "Who's here? Tell me!" He demanded.

"Just us," Kellie answered, horrified by the sudden home invasion. She waved Eva over to her to hold her close as well. "Eva, come here!"

"You," Jude said to Marco. "Take my knife and go cut the ropes from the clothesline. If you don't hurry and get back here, I'll kill them and then come for you. I'm giving you the count to twenty to get back here with those ropes." He handed him his eight-inch skinning knife. "Go!"

Marco nervously took hold of the knife and stepped outside. Jude glanced out the window and watched Marco run to the clothesline and raise the blade to cut the ropes obediently. He turned back to Kellie. "I'm hungry! Go make me something to eat."

"What?" she asked in a trembling voice. "Please, don't hurt my girls. They're just children."

Jude grabbed her arm in a tight grip. "I have no intention of hurting your children but I will if you don't get in the kitchen and make me something to eat, now!" he shouted. He pushed her arm towards the kitchen.

"Girls, come with me," she said and herded them in front of her towards the kitchen. She told her girls to sit at the table and be quiet. "Play the quiet game. Shhh, for real."

"Mama, I'm scared," seven-year-old Emily said.

"Shhh, quiet game. Jesus will protect us. Pray."

Jude followed her into the kitchen and then walked out of the kitchen to lock the front door and closed the curtain over the window while she settled her children. He returned to the kitchen and found Kellie standing in front of the cookstove staring at it blankly. "Breakfast won't cook itself!" he shouted impatiently. "I'm starving!"

She raised her hands hopelessly. "What do you want?"

"Breakfast! Do you have bacon, eggs, steak, bread, potatoes? For crying out loud, just make something to eat. I'm starving!"

Marco came running back into the house carrying three twenty-foot pieces of the thin rope. "I got it."

Jude pointed his revolver at him. "Lock that back door and then start cutting four-foot pieces off for me. And don't try any funny stuff or you know what will happen!"

"Where?" Marco asked with a perplexed expression.

Jude squinted into a sour grimace. "Right there! Sit down on the floor and start cutting!"

Marco began to lower himself to the floor.

"After you lock the door!" Jude screamed. Jude turned to Kellie. "Do you have to tell him where to piss?" He turned back to Marco. "There are a thousand square miles of woods out there, just find a tree and piss! For crying out loud, do you know which end of a shovel to dig with?"

Marco began to whimper as he returned to the rope after locking the door. He knelt and kept his head down to hide his emotions.

"Please, stop yelling at him," Kellie said, glaring

at Jude. "He's scared. My girls are scared. I'm making you something to eat so, please, stop yelling."

Jude grabbed her by the throat with his left hand and pushed her back against the kitchen cabinets. "Shut your mouth and cook me some food!" His attention went to eight-year-old Amber, who ran over to protect her mother and began hitting his lower back and thighs with open palm slaps. "Let go of my Mama!"

Amber slapped his thigh and hit his open cuts from the fence. The pain induced caused Jude to immediately swing his right hand, which held his revolver, down and hit the side of Amber's head with the back of his hand. The little girl was knocked to the floor abruptly and began wailing while holding her head.

Kellie's hands began swinging to hit, scratch or gouge the face and eyes of Jude. "Don't you touch my daughter!" she screamed and ripped her short fingernails across his cheeks, leaving shallow scratches. He stepped back and turned his hip away from her to holster his revolver while trying to hold her back with his left arm. Quickly, his right-opened palm smacked her hard across the face with a solid blow. Kellie fell to the floor, stunned. She quickly recovered at the sound of her daughter's wails. Kellie crawled to her daughter, pulled Amber into her lap, and frantically searched through Amber's hair for any knots or bleeding.

Marco watched from the family room and got to his feet with a fiery rage warring against the fear within him. He clenched the knife in his right hand

and came forward quickly to stab the man who dared to hit Kellie and Amber.

Kellie's eyes betrayed Marco with a mere glance. Jude drew his revolver and spun around and brought his right hand around and slammed the barrel of the pistol across Marco's head in a display of quickness and hand and eye coordination. Marco dropped to the floor unconscious. Blood spilled onto the floor from a gash on the side of his head. The two young girls at the table both began to scream, horrified by what they witnessed. Kellie tried to crawl on her hands and knees to Marco but Amber held onto her refusing to let go.

Jude grabbed Kellie's hair and pulled up to her feet slowly. "I didn't hit your daughter with my gun. She's fine! He'll be fine too. Just make my breakfast and then you can care for him!" Jude shouted over the chaos of the crying girls. He shoved Kellie towards the stove and grabbed his knife off the floor. Jude grabbed Marco by his ankles and drug him out of the kitchen into the family room and tied Marco's hands behind his back and then tied his ankles as well. He glanced up at Kellie who was holding all three of her girls in a tight bundle, comforting them while they all wept. The girls were scared and Kellie was trying to reassure them that they would be okay. However, she wasn't very confident of that herself.

Jude stood at the entrance of the kitchen. He spoke with an intentional softer tone, "Make me some breakfast and I'll take one of your horses and leave."

Her head raised and she glared at him with her piercing blue eyes. "Promise?"

His lips twitched with animosity. He didn't like the way she was looking at him. "I can't outrun the Marshal and his posse staying here, now can I? I've never heard so much screaming over nothing in my whole life with all these girls around here. Does your husband have any hearing left?" he asked bitterly.

Kellie ignored his words and struggled to break free from her frightened daughters. "Listen, he'll go away once he eats. Let me cook. You girls sit at the table and play the quiet game. The winner gets to choose dessert tonight."

"I don't want dessert, I want you, Mama," five-year-old Eva cried with a troubled expression on her frightened face.

"I know, sweetheart. I'll hold you as soon as I am done here."

Jude watched Kellie put a frying pan on the cookstove and begin to cut pieces off an eight-pound chunk of bacon and put them in the pan. He leaned on the wall between the family room and kitchen to watch her. "Have you ever heard of the Big Z Ranch?" he asked. Jude had overheard her conversation on the porch with Truet the night before regarding Annie.

"Yes."

"Do you know where it is?"

"Yes."

"The Marshal's sister? The one Truet is courting, is she a friend of yours?" he asked.

"Yes." She sounded uninterested in talking to him.

"What's her name again?"

"Annie."

He grinned just enough to show the bottom of his teeth. "And you know how to get there?"

"Yes," Kellie replied without looking back at him. She just wanted to cook breakfast and get him out of her house.

"I'm going to need some of your husband's clothes before I leave," Jude said. "How about when your done cooking, I'll sit with your girls and eat while you go pick me out some of your husband's clothes? I need them all from long johns to boots and a coat. I don't need to tell you what will happen if you come down with a gun instead of clothes, right?"

She turned to glare at him. "Right."

He took a deep breath and exhaled. "You didn't ask why I'm curious about your friend, Annie," he stated with a half-smile.

"It's none of my business."

"It might be if you like your friend. If I heard right last night, it sounds like Truet and her are talking about getting married."

She turned towards him slack-jawed and stunned.

He grinned knowingly. "Yeah, I was listening. I slept in the barn. You'll find your quilt and saddle blankets in the back of the hay mound. My friend Elias and I came here to look for work on the Big Z Ranch until I heard Truet was here. He killed my little brother like a coward." The bacon sizzled with the aroma filling the kitchen, causing Jude's stomach to growl with anticipation. He continued, "My friend Elias is the one that got us in trouble. I didn't hurt anyone; Elias did. I did kill Bo but that was self-defense. The Marshal and the Sperrys are not coming to arrest me. It's doubtful that I'll get out of this valley alive. But I'll be damned if I'm going to let Truet get away with murdering my little brother without losing something too."

"You could turn yourself in. The Marshal won't harm you if you're unarmed," she suggested.

He watched her crack eggs into the pan. "Like my friend, Elias? He tried to surrender. He dropped his gun and had his hands up to surrender and they killed him in cold blood. No, if I'm going to die, I'll go down fighting."

She grabbed a plate out of a cabinet. "Your food's about done. I'll cut you some bread and jam."

Jude sat at the table and ate quickly. The thick pieces of bacon, fried eggs and thick slices of bread with huckleberry jam were delicious. He ate every crumb of it, nearly filling the emptiness of his stomach with a good meal. He cut some more bread and added jam to it and drank a second cup of coffee to satisfy his stomach. True to his word, he sat with the girls and ate while Kellie found him new clothes to wear. Long johns, pants, a flannel shirt, socks and new boots that were just a bit too big, and a straw hat. He had dressed in the family room where he could keep an eye on the family. He raided David's gun collection and took a Remington repeater and ammunition before cutting Marco loose with orders to bring him the fastest horse they owned to the back door.

"How far is it to the Big Z Ranch?" he asked, tying

Marco up again after he returned with an Arabian stallion. It was tall and lean with a snow-white coat and extraordinary blue eyes. The stallion was tied to a small tree by the back door.

"From here about seven or eight miles maybe."

His lips twisted while eyeing Kellie. "Get your coat. You're coming with me."

"What?" she gasped in horror. "No. That's not what you said. You promised you'd leave. I have children. Please just go; we won't say a word."

He pointed his finger at her with a cold glare. "You're coming with me like it or not. I'm not going to become a target without some protection. Those men looking for me won't shoot if you're sharing the saddle with me. You are coming with me. You know where we're going and can show me the way. I promise, I won't hurt you or your kids but, if you refuse, I'll start with the boy and begin shooting right down the line. Get your coat." There was no room to question the sincerity of his threat.

Kellie felt a numb and sickening sensation overwhelm her. To leave her three children, for all she knew may be the last time, left her in a state of panic. Her obedience was the only way to spare their lives. She wept bitterly while she meekly grabbed her coat and put it on. She watched Jude tie all three of the little girl's hands and feet together and left them crying out for their mother on the family room floor. Kellie went to them but Jude pushed her towards the door. Afraid their loud screaming would attract unwanted visitors, Jude tore his wet clothes and made gags to tie around their mouths.

Jude knelt at Marco's head. "When help comes, tell Truet Davis that I am going to wait for him at the Big Z Ranch. Understand?"

Marco nodded.

"Repeat it."

"You're waiting for Truet Davis at the Big Z Ranch."

"Good boy." He cast an annoyed glance at Kellie as she pulled the gag off of four-year-old Eva. Jude grabbed Kellie's hair and yanked her out his way. "Don't touch it again!" he shouted while he forcefully replaced the gag.

"Take the gags off of their mouths, please. They're just babies. Please," she begged through her sobbing.

"No."

"They're just babies!" she yelled with tears streaming down her face. "Eva has an easy gag reflex and she could vomit and drown. Please, I'll do anything, just please remove the gag from her mouth."

Jude grabbed Kellie's arm and shoved her towards the door. "Hope she doesn't puke. Let's move. Don't make me repeat it or I'll end it all right now and take my chances alone." He pulled his revolver and turned back towards the family room.

"No! Please," she grabbed hold of his arm and pulled weakly towards the door. "I'll go. I'll do whatever you want." She was beaten. Her eyes roamed over her girls one last time as they wailed uncomfortably through the ropes and gags. "Lord Jesus, if it's all I ever ask, please watch my over children and keep them safe. Please, Lord." She prayed as Jude closed the door and forced her towards the stallion.

25

Truet Davis and Alan Garrison had spent most of the morning riding along the Modoc River two miles north of Natoma and followed it east for five miles looking for any sign of Jude Maddox. They had not found a single thing except a dead deer that had been shot and injured but never found. They had ridden along the river's bank upstream to the Modoc River bridge where the main road going east and west through the valley crossed over the river. It was about three miles from the Willow Falls junction off the main road. Once at the bridge, they turned back towards Natoma to follow the main road into town. So far it had been an unproductive day.

"I think he's hiding in the woods," Alan stated bluntly. He was looking at the Blue Mountains that towered above them to the south.

"He could be. He might've figured out the valley isn't very welcoming and worked his back up into the woods."

Alan was tired and not used to being on a horse for long. He was saddle sore and grumpy. "If he is, then we're not going to find him in the valley."

Truet yawned and rubbed his eyes with both of his hands. He had not slept well because the hotel bed was too soft and the pillow was too thin. "We'll widen our search area if there's not been any horses reported stolen, no sightings or people missing. We think he's still in the area until we can verify he's not. Matt has made a career for himself by doing this stuff. He knows what he's doing."

"I sure hope so because I want to go home," Alan said, adjusting himself in the saddle. "The good thing about the city sheriff's office is we never have to leave town."

Truet chuckled. "You're spoiled. Heck, we go everywhere. A day in the saddle is no big deal. By the time you get home, you'll be saddle broke and ready to join the marshal's office begging to do more adventures."

Alan scoffed heartedly. "I don't think so, Truet. Matt would not want me as a deputy since I like to be home too much. I have a lady that I'm courting and certainly don't want to get shot now. You fella's do a lot more dangerous work than we do."

"We cover more ground and we don't back down. If Matt caught you backing down from a mere fistfight with Ritchie Thorn, let's say, Matt would give you a choice, turn in your badge or fight. I'd give you the same choice because if you didn't stand your ground, Ritchie would make a habit of trying to humiliate and bully you until it becomes dangerous." Truet paused and then explained, "I learned that the hard way back where I used to live. It's good to be a nice Christian man but there are lines you can't afford to let anyone cross and that's where the niceness must stop. Matt's one of the nicest and biggest-hearted men I've ever known but you don't want to cross a line with him because he'll hurt you. That's why we get into more scruffs than you all do. We cannot be intimidated; Sheriff Wright already is."

Alan was proud of being a Branson deputy and Truet's words offended him but there was a certain truth to it as well. Alan had seen Sheriff Tim Wright sidestep the law and back down to certain people in the community. The sheriff wasn't a man of honor nor did he have Matt's no-nonsense courage and grit to not hide behind his deputies when trouble was at hand. Alan decided to change the subject. He had been working in the jail when Jude threatened Truet the night of the dance. "Why does Jude want to kill you?"

Truet frowned. "I killed his brother and he wants to even the score."

"Is it scary to have someone who wants to kill you running free and we don't know where he is?"

Truet narrowed his brow and compressed his lips in thought. "A bit. Vengeance is a risk you take when you pull a weapon and kill someone. Most of the time, families recognize the error of their loved ones and accept the consequences. But once in a while, they can't let it go and come for your blood.

The Dobson Gang came here clear from Texas to kill Matt's uncle and now they're in the Willow Falls cemetery. That thirst for vengeance for some people has no time limit or distance they won't go to satisfy that quest. So, to answer your question, it's a little unnerving not knowing where Jude is or wondering if he's behind the next bush waiting for me to ride a few feet closer before he pulls the trigger. I look forward to this being over whether Jude goes back to jail or is dead. I tried talking to him but he won't listen. There are times when you can't stop the fight that's coming and there is no option to back down. You have to fight but, unlike a fistfight, this one's to the death. If we run into Jude at this homestead coming up, by chance, one of us will die. He's leaving no other option. And Lord willing, it won't be me because I have a lady I'm courting too," he finished with his handsome smile. "And I like her."

Alan exhaled. "I don't think I ever realized family members can come after you for doing your job."

Truet chuckled. "I guarantee you if we had gotten in a gunfight with the Sperrys and you killed Bo Crowe, you'd be the one Morton and his relatives would be looking for."

"Aren't you afraid one day that the Sperry-Helms Gang and the Crowe Brothers and all their friends will be looking for Matt and you someday? I know Sheriff Wright thinks they'll be the end of Matt sooner or later."

Truet rubbed the whiskers on his chin. "No. I think they know we carry a big stick and aren't afraid to use it. They'd lose a few too and they know it. Hence they haven't done too much robbing since we've been here."

A small home along the road was ahead. It wasn't much more than a shack with a chicken coop and a small barn but Truet and Alan rode to the front door. A mangy-looking dog with gray hair mixing with its aging face barked from a safe distance.

The door opened and a thin, old woman opened the door. "Oh, thank goodness. You are looking for that man that broke out of jail, right?"

"Yes, ma'am. Do you mind if we search your place?" Truet asked.

"No need. He isn't here. However, I did see something. I watched a white Arabian horse run by and it looked to be Kellie on the back. It was her horse; I know that because no one else has a horse like that around here. But it wasn't her husband in front of her. My eyesight isn't too good but she seemed scared to me. I don't have a way to town anymore but you might check her place. It didn't look right and I am concerned. I don't want nothing happening to that family."

"We'll go check right now. Thank you, Ma'am." Truet turned his horse and kicked it into a gallop to hurry towards Crawford's homestead.

Before long, the home of David and Kellie Crawford was in view. They rode up to the house and tethered their horses and could hear one of the little girls screaming. It wasn't a sad cry but a pain-filled and frightened scream. The door was locked and all the curtains were closed. The sound of the little girl's crying haunted Truet. He ran around the house and found the curtains closed. He put his hand on the backdoor knob and turned it. The door opened revealing a teenage boy and the two older girls bound with rope and gags in their mouths, laying on the floor. They were scared and crying but the older girls had gags over their mouths and tied around their heads.

Five-year-old Eva was terrified and screamed. She had tried to break free from the ropes and received rope burns on her wrists. Luckily, the gag had slipped from her mouth, allowing her to vomit on the floor. The vomit was on her face and dress. She had been so distressed it made her physically sick.

Truet immediately went to Eva and cut the binds on her wrists and ankles. He sat and scooped her into his arms to hold her close to his chest, trying to comfort her. His eyes teared, feeling a rage he had not felt in a long time. "Get her some water!" he ordered Marco sharply when he was cut free by Alan. "It's okay, baby, you're going to be okay," he tried to comfort Eva. It was the first time Truet had become emotional on the job and he tried to focus through the moisture that clouded his vision. It enraged him to think someone could tie up a child and leave them lying on the floor. The two older girls huddled together crying as well now that the gags were pulled from their mouths.

Marco came in with a bucket of water and set it on the counter. All three girls were thirsty, but he took a cup of water to Eva while Truet held her.

Truet asked him, "Where's Kellie?"

Marco was upset. "He took her. He said to tell Truman, True…"

"Truet. That's me. What did he say? Where did he go?" Truet's voice was rough and demanding. He remained sitting on the floor, holding Eva. She had urinated herself, but Truet didn't care about that or the vomit. He cared about comforting the child.

"The Big Z Ranch."

Truet handed Eva to Marco. "Take care of her and her sisters. And I mean take care of them!" he emphasized. He jabbed a finger into Alan's chest. "Go find Matt and tell him Jude took Kellie to the Big Z. Tell him I'm going there to kill Jude and I'll meet him there. Go now!"

Truet tried to comfort the three scared girls. "You're safe now. I'm going to get your mama right now."

26

Kellie was repulsed to have her hands around the belly of the man who bound and gagged her daughters. He forced her to hold onto him like she would her husband as they rode away from her terrified children. Kellie would have fought him but the threat of any of her girls being hurt was a price she wasn't willing to pay. She tearfully but willfully allowed him to take her away from her family. Kellie sat behind the cantle on the saddle skirt, forced to lock her hands around his stomach as they galloped towards Willow Falls. They had passed by the widow, Belva Tompkins's, place while the lonesome elderly lady stood outside beating on a rug with her broom. Kellie turned her head in shame before Belva could see her. It was a reactionary movement to hide her face while being carried away by a stranger. Kellie tried to release her hands to avoid touching Jude but he grabbed her hands and forced them back around him. It kept her securely behind him and that's what he wanted, to make sure Truet wouldn't shoot him in the back.

A mile past the Modoc River bridge Kellie got her first glimpse of hope. Coming towards them was a wagon being driven by two Crawford farm employees that she knew. They were returning from Branson with a wagon load of supplies. She knew they would recognize her Arabian and wonder what was going on when they didn't recognize Jude. There was a part of her that prayed Allister Mull, the driver, would ignore them and keep driving and that Norman Westfall wouldn't raise the rifle he carried with him on trips. Neither man carried sidearms but they always had a gun if they ran into trouble or saw a coyote or deer to shoot on the way. She prayed they would pass by with a casual wave for their own safety. But at the same time, she realized they might have been her only chance to escape her captor.

"Who are these men?" Jude asked, having slowed the horse to a casual trot to rest it from the long period of galloping. The two men on the wagon appeared to be quite curious about the strange sight of a stranger riding Kellie's horse and with Kellie straddling the horse like a man while in a long dress. She usually rode a gentler red roan mare with a sidesaddle. The Arabian, named Blue, because of its beautiful blue eyes, was a stunning pure white creature with a long mane and tail. Still, he was a temperamental and fiery stallion that preferred men to women and proved to be more than Kellie could handle as a casual riding horse. The oddity of the sight didn't look right and Allister pulled the reins bringing the team of mules to a stop. Jude had little interest in talking to the men but figured they knew Kellie, which was a threat. He moved his hand slowly towards the butt of his revolver.

"Don't!" she said, suddenly feeling his arm reaching back for his revolver. "They're employees and that's all. I'll tell them you're my brother," Kellie said quickly to ease his hand forward away from his revolver. "Don't hurt them, please."

Allister Mull was a middle-aged red-headed man with a thin build and a kind nature. He moved his head to the right to peek at Kellie behind the stranger. An odd expression was fixed on his face. He could see something wasn't right and also recognized David's coat and hat on the stranger. "Out for a ride today, Miss Kellie?" he asked with a skeptical smile.

"Yes, my brother and I are going for a ride," she said, trying to signal a hint by repeatedly widening her eyes at Norman Westfall, silently beckoning him to grab the rifle beside him. She had grown up in Natoma and the two men knew her only brother as well as they knew her. "You men have a great day," she said as Jude walked the stallion casually by them. She could see Jude's revolver's wooden grip and counted a silent three to collect her courage and then quickly released Jude and grabbed his revolver to pull it out of the holster while she leaped off the back of the horse. It would have been a good plan except for the leather loop around the gun's hammer held it in place. Her body slid off the back of the horse while still holding onto the revolver. She was pulled to the right side of the horse as it lunged forward and kicked, barely missing her. Kellie fell into the mud of the road while the stallion, being startled, began to buck.

Kellie glanced at her two friends and yelled, "Shoot him!"

Jude jerked the left rein back and downward to force the stallion to turn its head back towards his foot to cease the bucking but the horse's mouth widened and stretched for the meat of his calf. Jude jerked the right rein in a quick reaction while at the same time noticing the bigger man on the wagon stand and raise a rifle towards him. The stallion, given some free rein, reared up and then began to buck as a shot was fired at Jude. The bullet whizzed by, frightening the stallion into a crow hop and then it began bucking wildly. Unable to settle the spooked horse and worry about the two men, Jude leaped from the saddle onto the road and allowed the horse to run free.

A bullet hit the mud a mere few inches from him while he scrambled to his feet and ran towards the wagon. The man shooting the rifle was nervous and ejected the cartridge and fired before he could aim, missing Jude by a foot or two. Jude ducked behind the wagon stocked with supplies and pulled his revolver. His heart pounded, knowing if the men were experienced, he would have been hit twice. He didn't need to be told the shooter had never shot at a man before.

Norman Westfall held the rifle against his shoulder, aiming towards the back of the wagon bed. He couldn't see Jude due to a load of hundred-pound bags of grain and other supplies. He was nervous and his hands shook severely. He spoke, "If you start walking away, we'll let you go."

Jude grinned. He could see the men's shadows on the road and knew only one of them had a weapon. The skinny red-headed man had run to help Kellie out of the mud and was holding her protectively by the front wagon wheel. "Really? You will let me go? How can I trust you?" Jude asked with a cold grin.

"If you walk away, you have my word. We don't want trouble, mister. We just want Kellie."

"All right," Jude shouted. "Keep the woman but you'll let me walk away? You won't shoot me, will you?" He could visualize the shooter's face beginning to relax.

"No, sir. Just go away is all I ask."

"Okay," Jude said. Kneeling, he could look under the wagon at the legs of Allister Mull while he waited with Kellie. He aimed at Allister's shin bone just above the boot line and fired. The bullet shattered the bone. Allister collapsed to the muddy road screaming in agony.

"Al!" Norman shouted with concern over the screaming of Kellie.

Jude stood behind the wagon and aimed his revolver at Norman quickly and fired, hitting him just shy of the chest. Jude expected him to fall off the wagon but Norman stood there with a dazed expression and dropped the rifle instead. Jude began fanning the hammer to fire multiple shots quickly. Three of the five bullets had found their mark in Norman's abdomen and chest. Norman Westfall fell out of the wagon into the mud with a heavy thud. Jude quickly emptied the chambers of his revolver and began reloading from his gun belt.

"Run. Run Kellie!" he heard Allister shout.

Jude stepped around the side of the wagon and saw Allister sitting against the wagon wheel. He had no weapon and his left shin was shattered. He was in a lot of pain and it showed on his face.

Allister pleaded with Jude, "Let her go, please."

Kellie was running towards home, about twenty yards away from the wagon. Jude aimed his revolver towards her and pulled the hammer back.

Allister threw a handful of mud at Jude's face which got into the edge of his right eye. "Leave her be!" Allister shouted.

Jude spun his revolver around and pulled the trigger, placing a bullet in Allister's liver. "No," he said as he wiped the mud from his eye.

The sound of the percussion stopped Kellie and she turned around. "Allister? Oh, my Lord, no. Allister!" she wept as she ran back and knelt beside him. Seeing his wound, she cursed at Jude with a parade of tears flowing down her face.

The corners of Allister's lips raised while he watched her. He spoke softly, "I told you to run."

Jude snorted. "That's dumb advice. There's nowhere to run out here."

"You killed them!" Kellie exclaimed while glaring at Jude.

Jude used his revolver to point at her. He shouted

vehemently, "This is your fault! I tried to ride past them; you are the one that caused this! You!"

Allister leaned against the wagon wheel, knowing his time was short. He kept his hand over the blood-soaked wound. "Let her go."

Infuriated, Jude stomped on the top of Allister's hand that covered his liver and pressed downward with all his might. Allister cried out in agony. Jude spoke viciously through gritted teeth, "That's right, scream! Do you want to keep talking? Scream!"

"Leave him alone!" Kellie pushed Jude away from Allister. "What kind of a man are you? How much crueler can you possibly be? Leave him alone! You've already shot him." She peered down at Allister and her face buckled into a display of her sorrow. "I'm so sorry. Allister."

Allister closed his eyes and tried to grin unsuccessfully. "When I told you to run…I meant on the wagon."

Her bottom lip quivered while she knelt to grab his hand. "If it wasn't for me, you wouldn't be hurt. I'm so sorry." She lowered her head shamefully.

Allister reached over and lifted her chin to look into her eyes. He was growing weaker. "I never would have forgiven myself for letting you get by me. At least, now, they know which way you're going. We slowed him down." He winked at her.

Jude kicked Allister's good foot to get his attention. "Are either of these mules saddle broke? It'll be better for her if you answer honestly." His expression revealed nothing except cold brutality.

Allister nodded. "Dolly on the left. Sebastian's

not."

Jude took his knife and cut the leather harnesses before removing the collar of the nearest mule pulling the wagon. He cut the bridle straps to useable size and hopped on. "Let's go." He extended his hand out to Kellie. "Now!" he shouted.

Slowly, she stood from Allister. "I'm sorry, Allister." Her anguish was clear to see in her torn expression.

Allister forced his lips to turn upwards. "It's okay. You're worth dying for, my friend. Never forget that, Kellie."

She buried her face in her hands and broke into uncontrolled sobbing.

Jude rolled his head impatiently. He asked Allister, "Do you want me to put you out of your misery like your friend over there?"

Allister answered, "No, I think I'll just enjoy the sunshine for a little bit longer before I hear the heavenly angels sing. Kellie," he added with a brave smile. "It's okay." He knew he was doomed with a .44 slug traveling through his liver and out his back. It was only a matter of time.

Jude snickered. "Well, I hope you have a while. Tell whoever comes by to send Truet Davis to the Big Z Ranch. That's where I'll be waiting for him with his woman, Annie. Got that?"

Allister peered at Jude with a wry smile and attempted to laugh. "Yeah, I'll tell them where to find your body."

"You first," Jude spat out. He addressed Kellie bitterly with his hand extended out to her. "Get on! Now!"

She was hesitant, not wanting to leave her friend. Allister tossed a handful of mud at her lightly and said, "Go on, my friend. You'll be okay. Go now."

Jude kicked the mule and rode away from the dying man with Kellie sitting on the bareback mule behind him. "What did he mean by that?" Jude asked, directing the mule towards where the Arabian was eating some grass three hundred yards away.

Kellie kept her eyes on Allister for as long as she could. Numb, she answered, "Go back and ask him, I don't know." She refused to tell him about Charlie Ziegler or the other men at the ranch.

He grabbed her hand and squeezed it until she cried out. He warned, "If you try anything like what you did back there again, you'll be the first person I shoot! Those men's deaths are your fault and no one else's." The more guilt he could weigh upon her, the less likely she was to act up again.

She was heavily laden with the deaths of her two friends on her conscience. All she could do was look at the bright blue sky, spotted white cotton clouds and pray for Jesus to forgive her. And ask Jesus to interfere with Jude's plans of hurting Annie.

27

Jude pulled the reins to a stop when the town of Willow Falls came into view. He rubbed the Arabian's neck and spoke softly to it as he carefully maneuvered his right leg over the saddle horn and horse's neck to dismount without startling the skittish horse. He held the reins while speaking to Kellie, "Move up into the saddle, Sweetheart. I want you in front of me."

"Don't call me sweetheart," she said strenuously and moved over the cantle into the saddle. Her dress was caught on the cantle; Jude grabbed the dress material and shoved it down in the saddle seat behind her. She swung her arm around to slap his hand away from her. "Don't touch me!"

"I have more important things on my mind than trying to grab your butt," he answered with a sharp sideways glance. "How far is the ranch?"

They had passed the sheriff, Tom Smith's, house and she hoped to take advantage of being near help.

"The ranch is straight-ahead about two miles on the other side of town. This road ends at their headgate. You can't miss it. You don't need me anymore, so can I please go home to my children?" she pleaded.

He jumped up behind her on the saddle skirt. "Once you get me inside Annie's house and I have control, you will be free to leave. I won't need you anymore." He put his arms around her waist and held the reins to keep control of the spirited stallion. "But until then, keep a smile on your face as we go through town. If you see any more friends, don't be stupid and get them killed like you did your last two. I don't mind killing but I like to have a reason for it other than a woman's stupidity."

"You didn't have to kill them!" she responded bitterly.

"No?" he questioned. "I didn't fire the first shot nor did I plan to until you told them to shoot me. I'd say you had a lot to do with that, sweetheart. Try it again and see what happens." He guided the horse towards town at an easy trot.

"What are you going to do to Annie? Swear to me that you're not going to hurt her or her family."

One side of Jude's lip turned upwards with a wicked hint of a sneer. "How about you do not worry about that. You should keep your mind on getting home to those screaming girls of yours." He took a deep breath and continued in a softer voice, "Truet is the one I want, not your friend, Annie. She is only being used as bait to bring him to his knees. I want to see him beg like a worthless worm before I send him to hell."

Kellie spoke bitterly, "He would've shown up a lot sooner if you didn't tie my girls up. Eva gags easy and if she vomits..." she paused. The chance of Eva vomiting while being gagged terrified her. It was a thought she didn't want to think about. "I told you..." She began to whimper.

"Settle down. I heard you what you said and your daughter's gag is not tied very tight. They all should be able to get loose and untie the boy. If not, they're weak kids and not trying hard enough. But if your girls are weaker than most, then it looks like Annie and I will have plenty of time to get acquainted."

"You could have stayed at our house and sent Marco to get Truet if you wanted him so bad," Kellie said. She wiped her tears from her cheeks.

Jude snickered. "I want to see him beg. Killing you would not hurt him but seeing his woman suffer will drive him to his knees. And that's what I want to do, hurt him where it hurts the most. Like he did to me."

Kellie turned in her seat to look at him. "Annie has never done anything to you. I won't take you there if you're going to hurt her!"

He leaned forward and spoke into her ear, "Sweetheart, you already have." It was followed with a wicked chuckle. "As I said, she is bait."

It repulsed her to feel the warmth of his breath caressing her ear. She took a breath and replied, "You won't get off the ranch alive. That's what Allister was saying to you."

"I don't expect to. Between the marshal, his deputies, and the Sperry brothers, I'm not likely to get too far anyway. Which is fine. I'd rather be dead than lingering in prison forever."

They entered Willow Falls and slowed the horse to a casual walk to not draw any more attention than they already were. He handed her the reins and placed his left hand around her waist onto her belly to keep a hold of her in case she tried something unexpected. They walked past the livery stable on the left and the sheriff's office on the right side of the street. Jude removed the leather thong from the hammer of his revolver just in case he needed it quickly.

Kellie motioned towards a wagon and horse team that was parked in front of the mercantile. "There's Mister and Missus Ziegler right there." An old cowboy with silver hair under his hat was helping his heavy-set wife out of the wagon. The old cowboy had a week's growth of a beard on his tough exterior. His wife appeared to be half Indian with thick black hair that was heavily mixed with gray. She was wrapped in a heavy shawl over her shoulders.

"More friends of yours?" Jude asked, uninterested.

"Mister and Missus Ziegler own the Big Z Ranch."

"I thought Annie did?"

"She's inheriting it. But Charlie and Mary own it."

"Ziegler...Did you say Charlie Ziegler?"

"Yeah."

"Whoa, stop," he said, squeezing his legs together to stop the horse. He gazed at Charlie while he escorted his wife towards the Mercantile. "That's Charlie Ziegler? The old bounty hunter?"

"I believe so. All I know is no one messes with him or his ranch."

"Really?" Jude asked, observing the old man carefully. Charlie turned his head toward Jude with a stern expression that let Jude know he was noticed. Jude gave a friendly nod in return.

Charlie told his bride to wait a minute and stepped towards the road while looking awkwardly at Kellie. Her hair out of place and mud-covered on her face and the front of her dress. Charlie nodded towards the Arabian as he got closer. "Those horses are pretty to look at but a bit ill-tempered for you, isn't it, Kellie?" he asked. "It appears he already threw you off once today. When you're ready to trade it for a gentler one, let me know. I got a few you can choose from."

Kellie attempted a forced smile but failed miserably while feeling Jude's hand squeeze her stomach warningly. "I might," she answered.

Jude spoke, "Kellie tells me your name is Charlie Ziegler. You're not the old bounty hunter by chance?" he asked with interest.

Charlie scanned the stranger up and down with a glance. The question always brought a sense of caution. The man behind Kellie didn't show any sign of hostility but Charlie could see Kellie's reddened eyes and the fear contributing to them. A casual glance revealed the man's hand burrowing into her stomach as a warning and the hammer thong removed from his revolver. By the chaffing of the spur straps on his boots, it was easy to conclude the stranger was a cowboy and by the sweat lathered on the horse, Charlie figured it was the fugitive Matt and Truet were looking for. The new ranch hand, Marvin Aggler, had told him about hooking up with a couple of feisty cowboys that had broken out of jail on Saturday night and killed three men in Branson, including Charlie's friend Gus Fread. Charlie figured the man had no reason to bring Kellie to Willow Falls unless it was to empty David and Kellie's bank account. Charlie nodded in answer, slowly. "I did some bounty hunting long ago."

Jude grinned slightly. "It's an honor to meet you. My brother and I had a book about you that we'd read all the time when we were kids. We used to talk about meeting you someday but I never thought I would." Jude nodded towards Mary. "That must be your beautiful wife over there, huh? Is she why you gave it up?"

Charlie glanced back at Mary and motioned for her to go inside the Mercantile. "Yeah. I gave up those wild times to raise a family. Do you want to hear some stories sometime?" he asked to get the man talking.

Jude's interest peaked. "I really would love to," he answered honestly.

"What's your name?" Charlie asked, stepping closer to shake the man's hand. "Kellie, you better hold on to that saddle horn. Those temperamental breeds spook easily and I don't want to spook it as I shake his hand."

Jude replied, "Um… I'm Henry Jasperson… I just signed on with Kellie's family and she's showing me the town. Well, the next town," he added quickly.

Charlie nodded while keeping his hands down. "Makes sense. We have the only bank in the area. You should start an account to save your money in." He hesitated to shake and kept his hands at his side. "Willow Falls isn't much but we got all we need here. If you don't mind me saying so, you look like more of a cattleman than a sodbuster, in my opinion. I've got a ranch yonder that way a bit but if you're content growing crops then I'm glad to hear it. I'm glad to see Kellie's in good hands." Charlie scanned the street. He was waiting for an older couple to walk across the street.

"Oh yeah? Well, I'll be honest, if I had known you owned a ranch, I'd be begging you for a job. Mister Ziegler, you were a hero to my brother and me growing up. It's an honor to meet you, Sir."

Charlie smiled slightly. "Thank you. I don't get much praise anymore. The folks around here don't even remember that I did that bounty hunting stuff. Nice to meet you, Henry." He raised his hand to shake but kept it low enough for Jude to have to lean down just enough to release his tight grip on Kellie's stomach. Charlie gripped his hand firmly with his right hand and then grabbed Jude's wrist with his left hand and yanked Jude off the back of the horse while kicking the horse in the leg at the same time and yelling, "Yah!" The Arabian lurched forward and crow hopped and bucked, throwing Kellie out of the saddle. She landed on the muddy street while the horse ran off.

Charlie kept a hold of Jude's right hand and planned to force him onto the ground and pull the arm up behind Jude's back to pin him to the ground. Jude quickly rolled through the initial fall and got to his feet. Charlie held Jude's right wrist with a firm grip with his left hand to keep Jude from reaching for his revolver. Charlie reached for his pistol and had removed the thong when Jude crouched low and then exploded forward into Charlie, driving them both to the ground with Jude on top. Charlie was forced to let go of the wrist to protect himself and Jude's left hand was free to block Charlie's efforts to pull his weapon. Jude threw a desperate right fist that connected with Charlie's jaw with a solid blow. The impact dazed the elderly man and Jude pulled Charlie's Schofield out of his holster with his left hand and stood up, aiming it at Charlie, who remained on the ground rubbing his chin and then spat out a mouthful of blood.

"Charlie!" Mary Ziegler screamed and walked briskly out of the Mercantile and onto the street. "Leave my husband alone!" she exclaimed.

"Mary, stand back!" Charlie shouted as he sat on the street and gave a cold gaze at the young man who held Charlie's own Schofield pointed at him. If there was one thing he had drilled into his nephews, it was a real man would never be in a position to be killed by his own gun. He couldn't decide which was more humiliating, having his wife dart out into the street to protect him or losing possession of his revolver.

Jude shook his head with an appreciative grin. "I'm not going to kill you, Mister Ziegler. I have way too much respect for you." Jude noticed the sheriff and deputy both come out of the sheriff's office carrying rifles. Jude raised Charlie's Schofield towards them with his left hand and fired and then drew his Colt .44 with his right hand and fired again. He turned and ran towards Kellie while Mary Ziegler fearlessly stepped onto the street, blocking any shot Tom Smith or Johnny Barso had at Jude.

"Are you okay?" she asked Charlie. She was afraid of losing her husband.

Charlie got back to his feet brushing Mary to the side. His fearless green eyes narrowed as he watched Jude put a gun to Kellie's head, wrap his arm around her waist and rushed her towards the schoolhouse, which was not far from the Mercantile. Everyone on the street could hear the children inside scream as he barged in and slammed the door behind him. Jude began shouting at the children to be quiet.

"Damn it!" Tom Smith yelled, coming to a stop beside Charlie and Mary. "Mary, you got right in my way!"

"Watch your tone, Thomas Smith!" Mary scolded him angrily. "My husband was hurt."

Charlie wiped the blood from his chin. "I'm not hurt!" he corrected sharply. A strange grimace came over his face. Charlie reached into his mouth and pulled out a tooth that had been knocked out and spat out some blood. "He knocked my tooth out."

"Charles Ziegler," Mary scolded, "you're not young anymore! What in the world were you thinking? You could have gotten yourself killed!"

"Yeah, but I didn't," he answered shortly. He was frustrated that he wasn't able to control Jude the way he planned. He turned to Tom, "He took my gun. That has to be the man Matt is after. I say we kill him."

"He was in my sights!" Tom vented with frustration while giving a stern glance at Mary. "Now, he has all the kids as hostages." He handed Charlie his Colt revolver. "Now you're armed. We must get the kids out of there. Any ideas?"

Charlie ran his tongue over the empty spot where his tooth had been. "Yeah. I think I'll kill him for knocking my tooth out."

"I don't want any of those children hurt," Tom said, growing more anxious.

Johnny Barso spoke pointedly, "I'm going in there if one of those children are hurt."

Charlie once again spat out some blood. "You two stay back. I'll talk to him."

"Charlie don't..." Mary pleaded.

He turned his head towards her with a piercing look of danger in his normally gentle green eyes. It was an expression she had not seen on his face in many years and it sent a chill down her spine. He spoke firmly, "I can't stand here and do nothing, Mary. Steven's and Annie's kids are in there too and I'll be damned if I'll wait for any of those children to get hurt. I may not be young, sweetheart, but I'm sure as hell not useless!" He asked Tom, "Is his name Henry?"

"No. His name's Jude Maddox. Farrian Maddox's brother. He apparently wants to kill Truet."

Charlie nodded as the name recognition came to mind. Farrian was one of the men Truet killed in Idaho. He walked to the front of the school-house steps and hollered, "Jude Maddox, can you hear me?"

The door opened a few inches. "I can barely hear you over these whining kids." He turned toward the classroom of kids aged from six to sixteen and shouted at them, "Shut up, before I shut you up!The next brat that cries I'm going to hit you so hard across the head that you'll be out for a week! Shut up, before I shoot you all for the hell of it!"

Charlie listened to Jude yell at those inside the schoolhouse. "Jude!" he demanded loudly.

Jude hollered out of the few inches the door was opened, "I had to shut these kids up. What do you want, Mister Ziegler?"

"I prefer looking at the man I'm talking to. Why don't you open the door so we can talk?"

Jude laughed uneasily. "I'm not going to open the door with a gun in your hand. I think I know better than anyone what you can do with that weapon."

Charlie knew a trapped man under duress could make irrational decisions and a bunch of frightened and crying children was an aggravation that would not help the situation. He had the advantage of being respected and wanted to use that to ease the tension to keep Jude rational. He spoke loudly, "I wouldn't believe everything you read. If things had worked out differently, you could've been working for me and we would've set up some cans to shoot while having a drink or two. We could use a good hand like you. You should have come along with Marvin."

The door opened a bit more. "I wish things had worked out like that because it would have been an honor, Mister Ziegler. It would have been short-lived, though. I would have killed Truet soon enough. Either way, I guess you could say I made my bed in a snake den." He chuckled.

"It sure sounds like it." Charlie agreed. "Listen to me, Jude, I don't know what happened over in Natoma. But you're here now and you have our town's children in there. I need you to send them all out. We don't want no kids getting hurt by you or me or anyone else."

"Hell Charlie, the crybabies make good hostages. No one is going throw dynamite in here with the kids with me."

Charlie spat some blood onto the ground. He could hear the Reverend Abraham Ash and Kellie inside the school, trying to keep the children comforted and calm. "No one's going to throw any dynamite in there anyway. It would cost too much to rebuild the school. Jude, the children, are my concern. Once the children, the reverend and Kellie, are safe, I'll walk away and you can ride out of town free and clear. No one will raise a hand to stop you. I'll even catch that Arabian that Kellie has no business riding for you to take. You have my word on it."

Jude grinned. "I saw a portly sheriff come wobbling out of the sheriff's office. Will he let me go too?"

Charlie looked at Tom with a humored grin. Tom Smith had a sizable belly that was beginning to hang over his pants. He had thinning short brown hair and a well-kept thick brown mustache. Tom's round cheeks were turning red. "Yeah, Tom will do whatever it takes to make sure all those children come out of there unharmed. And you can ride out free and clear with no tricks. Let me get a horse for you."

Jude sighed loudly. "Well, we do have one problem, Mister Ziegler. I have nowhere to run nor a desire to. Kellie wasn't showing me your town. I forced her along to show me where Truet's woman lives. I was going to make sure he knew what it feels like to lose someone he loves."

Any good will for a peaceful ending left Charlie's face. It was now a matter of life and death. "I would have killed you for it. That's my family you're talking about."

Jude chuckled. "Mister Ziegler, I hate to say it but I don't think your warning is as frightening as it was thirty years ago. I could have killed you with your own gun a few minutes ago. You're way past your prime, old man."

Charlie's lips tightened irritably. He had never lost a fight in his life or given up his weapon and it stung his pride for both to happen. "Well, perhaps so, but I'd give it my darndest best try anyway. But that's between you and me. Now, what about those kids?"

Tom Smith stepped to Charlie's side and shouted, "This is Sheriff Tom Smith. If you release all those hostages, we'll lay our arms down and let you ride out of here without so much as a word, just like Charlie said. You have both of our words on that."

There was a pause and then Jude shouted, "I'll make you deal. If you don't kill any of them for crying, screaming and wetting their pants, I'll send these kids out. Because if I don't, I will kill them! I hate kids. Don't shoot and I'm sending the children out." The door opened and he was heard yelling, "Get out of here you, rats! Go have mommy change your diapers you piss ants! Go, get!"

The children of all ages ran out of the schoolhouse knocking over younger students in a panic. Charlie, Tom and Johnny Barso went and helped the smaller children who had fallen down. Some older children ran towards their parents who were beginning to crowd together in front of the Mercantile. Other children who lived out of town ran towards home. Gabriel Smith and Tiffany Foster were the last two students to leave the schoolhouse and both either held hands with or carried the most frightened children.

Jude stood in the doorway and hollered. "Thank you for taking them! Miss Kellie and the good reverend are staying here for a while. I imagine Truet will be here sooner or later. There's no reason to say another word until he is." He closed the door and curtains over the only window to finish any discussions.

Charlie watched the children scamper fearfully towards safety. Annie's two kids attending school, Ira and Catherine, came to Charlie and clung to his hip. Tiffany Foster and Gabriel Smith were urging the younger children with no parents present towards the Mercantile to be safe. They came for

Annie's children and Charlie put his hand on Ira's shoulder. "You're okay." He spoke to Matt's sixteen-year-old son Gabriel. "Take them over to Grandma Mary. Go on," he said softly.

"Now what?" Tom asked Charlie when they stood alone and the children were safe.

Charlie spoke slowly, "Jude just locked himself in the schoolhouse with your father-in-law. How long until you think Jude begs you to go in and arrest him?" he tried to joke. It didn't appear to be very funny by Tom's expression. "I suggest we give the reverend some time to talk to him while waiting for Matt and Truet. Jude's not coming out no matter what until Truet's here to face him. With the door locked and the window blocked, you take a greater chance of dying than killing him if you go bursting in there. But we'll wait here and if we hear Kellie or your father-in-law in trouble, I'll blow that lock off and go in and kill him or die trying."

28

Truet rode over the Modoc River bridge at a consistent gallop pushing his mare far harder than he knew he should. When he was in the Calvary on the Kansas plains, their horses could not compete with the Indians' horses. The calvary horses were smaller, weaker and had not near the speed, agility or, more importantly, the endurance that the Indians' Spanish Mustangs displayed time and time again. It went without saying the Indians were incredible acrobats on a bareback horse. They may have been the enemy, at the time, but the horsemen's skill and the swift animals they rode had greatly impressed Truet. It was a downright criminal to be ordered to kill such magnificent animals but the very horses that the Indians rode seemed to hate the blue coat soldiers as much their owners did. It was said there was no retraining an Indian's horse but Truet always wanted to try. They were beautiful animals and their endurance was top-notch. Truet owned a good horse but she wasn't a Spanish Mustang or another Indian bred breed.

Annie wanted to breed Nez Pierce horses which were similar to the Spanish Mustangs used on the plains. Truet looked forward to having his own Indian bred horse and it would sure help in times like these when he needed to travel a longer distance in a shorter time. His mare was winded but Truet kept her at a gallop. He had no time to lose but he couldn't afford to push too much harder or risk injury if not pushing the mare's heart to the point of giving out.

He could see a wagon stopped on the road with one mule harnessed to the wagon and another meandering away from the wagon. Truet pulled the reins and brought the exhausted girl to a stop. He dismounted to see if the man who was gut shot beside the wagon's wheel was alive and found the man deceased. In the mud, written by a finger, were the words, Big Z Ranch help Kellie.

Truet went to the other man's body and counted the bullet holes. The wagon was full of bags of feed and boxes of different supplies. None of it had been gone through. He caught the loose mule and hopped on it to see if it was saddle broke, which it seemed to be. It had a bridle cut from the wagon's harness. Truet removed his saddle off his exhausted mare and threw it on the wagon to keep it safe while allowing his horse to roam free and find some water. Mules were bred from a male donkey and female horse but their body build was quite different than a horse and his saddle would not fit a mule. Mules could be saddle broke sure enough but needed a saddle designed for a mule. Truet grabbed his rifle out of its scabbard and hopped on the mule's back and gave it a kick. A mule was slower than a horse but, when it came to riding a mule to death, it was nearly impossible to do because a mule would only gallop until it was tired. Unlike a horse that can be run to death, a mule will slow down whether the rider likes it or not. A mule is an intelligent creature with a mind of its own that considers self-preservation before anything else despite what the rider may be trying to do. Truet knew that from his experiences with pack mules in the calvary.

He bent forward and petted the mule's neck. "Sweetheart, my lady is in trouble and I know it's long road but I need your help. We have four or five miles to go and I'm asking you to give me all you have, please." Truet's mind was running faster than he could control and the worst thoughts were coming to mind. Thoughts of what happened to his late wife Jenny Mae filled him with a sickening rage that no man should ever feel. A rage so untamed and savage that he could quickly kill a man with his bare hands given a one-minute time limit and he would if he could get a hold of Jude. One thought brought some hope: Annie was surrounded by men most people wouldn't want to tangle with. Charlie Ziegler, Adam Bannister, Nathan Pierce, Darius Jackson and now the crusty old cowboy that Matt had recommended, Marvin Aggler, all called the Big Z Ranch home. None of them would allow anyone even to raise their voices at Annie, let alone try to harm her, but they could be spread out across the ranch as they often were. Annie was tough for a lady but still weaker than a strong man and, although she might put up a good fight, she probably wouldn't win. She often put on a good show of being more brutal than her brothers but, the fact remained, she wasn't. Truet had been praying for her safety since realizing that Jude was cowardly enough to want to harm him through Annie. If she were hurt or killed, Jude wouldn't live long and Truet hoped he was the first to get a hold of the man.

"Thank you, Jesus!" he prayed as he gave the mule another pat on the neck and a soft kick to let her know he wanted to keep the speed up. His mare could not have run the rest of the way to Willow Falls. In Truet's opinion, it was a miracle to find the saddle broke mule when he did. Mules were often used as draft animals and not for riding. If the mule had not been saddle broke, Truet would have no choice but to push the mare until she dropped. So far along his journey, the mule had not given him any trouble such as slowing down or refusing to gallop.

A mile and a half later, he rounded a bend in the road around a sizeable rolling hill and was stunned to see Matt Bannister and Morton Sperry sitting on their sweat-lathered horses waiting for him. Truet slowed to a stop.

"How did you get ahead of me?" Truet asked, bewildered. He knew Matt and Morton were in Natoma when he sent Alan back to town. Truet thought he was at least three or four miles ahead of Matt.

Matt motioned towards Morton. "He knew a shortcut." Morton had taken the lead and led Matt on an outlaw trail across the Modoc River, through fields, and over a series of wooded hills that cut several miles off the trip. It had been a hard ride over some steep and rough ground but they eventually rode into lower Pearl Creek and followed it to where they were. The outlaw trail had cut off close to six miles of road that went around the hills. Morton had been confident it would put them ahead of Truet and it did. Morton didn't necessarily want to show Matt the trail but he did want to kill Jude more than any of the others and he wasn't about to be left out of his opportunity by needless miles.

"Where's your horse?" Matt asked curiously.

"Wandering around by a wagon, I hope. It looks like two of Crawford's men were killed. Jude took Kellie but he's going after Annie to get me," Truet said pointedly to Matt.

Matt's expression hardened dangerously. There were no words that needed to be said. He turned his horse towards Willow Falls and gave it a hard kick.

29

Jude sat on a child's desk, checking the cylinder of his revolver. It had six bullets and there were four bullets left on his gun belt. Charlie Ziegler's Schofield had five shots which meant Jude had fifteen bullets and then he would be helpless to defend himself against the growing crowd outside of the schoolhouse. He wished he had a chance to grab the rifle he had taken from Kellie's house and tied to the saddle before the horse dashed away. It would have given him more to fight with if it came to a shootout with the town.

Kellie sat at a student's desk staring at the floor quietly while the gray-haired, old reverend sat at the teacher's desk at the front of the room facing the student's desks, flipping through the pages of a book. Now that all the students had left, it was too quiet except for the men of the town surrounding the schoolhouse, armed and ready to gun him down at first sight. Jude's plans had not gone the way he expected and now he would never reach the Big Z Ranch or even get a look at Truet's woman. It figured, though; life always has a way of discouraging his plans. It wasn't his plan to begin with, anyway; it was Bo Crowe's. Having to run for his life, going to the Big Z Ranch became the only option that stood a chance of forcing Truet to his knees and the more he thought about it, the more he had liked the idea.

"Son..." Reverend Abraham Ash said. He was a tall, thin man with a full head of gray hair and long sideburns. Reverend Ash's wrinkled face revealed his sixty-six years of age and was usually in an authoritative scowl. He was dressed in a black suit with a white shirt and black tie. He was filling in for the regular schoolteacher who was sick with the flu.

Jude turned his head towards the old man. "I'm not your son. Don't ever call me that again. Do you understand me, old man?" Jude questioned sharply.

Reverend Ash was unfazed. "Sure. I don't know what kind of trouble you're in but maybe we could talk about it? All these folks around here are God-fearing Christians mostly and not set on shedding blood if it doesn't have to be that way. Of course, you're the one that has to make that decision. You could walk out right now and surrender or ride away as Tom and Charlie said. I know Charlie Ziegler can be a scary man but he's not a bad man. He keeps his word."

Jude chuckled. "Charlie's not a scary man. I took his gun from him, see?" he held up the Scofield. "I'm a scary man. I didn't come here to surrender.

I came here to kill a man and that's what I'm going to do." The truth was he had hoped to tie everyone on the ranch up good and tight and try to disappear. It wasn't a well-thought-out plan, to begin with, and now he didn't have one. He could thank his childhood hero Charlie Ziegler for that. He had not expected Charlie to throw him off the horse. Jude chuckled, thinking about it. If his brother was alive, Jude knew the story would highly entertain Farrian. Charlie, the old coot, was one of Farrian's heroes growing up and it would please him to know Charlie had never lost his fighting spirit.

Reverend Ash continued, "You have not mistreated us in here nor any of the students. You seem like a nice young man who got off to a bad start in life and maybe found yourself in some trouble that might now get out of hand. If you kill a man, and I suppose you mean Truet, you may not have the opportunity to live to be my age. What good would it do you to kill him at the cost of your future? Have you ever heard the Bible verse, 'For what shall it profit a man if he shall gain the whole world, and lose his own soul?'"

Jude stood and walked to the window to glance onto the street. "The only things I own right now are my gun and the clothes on my back, which are her husband's." He pointed towards Kellie. "The marshal seems to have everything else I owned."

"The marshal," Abraham Ash said quietly with a slight proud smile, "wanted to be a minister when he was young. It's funny how the roads in life can lead one to a very different outcome than they hoped in their youth. Have you ever read the Bible?"

Jude snorted and glanced irritably at Reverend Ash. "Parts of it. Do you want to talk about the Bible? Let's talk. I don't think you can believe it. Have you ever read it, Reverend? There's a talking donkey in it! Now, maybe I'm dumb but donkeys don't talk! Horses don't, cows surely don't, and I'll be darned, not even a donkey can talk. Pigs don't fly either," he added sarcastically. "It's ridiculous to believe a fairy tale like that. So no, I don't read it."

Abraham Ash frowned thoughtfully. "The Old Testament does have some things that seem farfetched at times, like the donkey that spoke to Balaam. You see, I do know that story because I do read my Bible. If you think about it, that's not the only time God did amazing and inconceivable things with a voice box. Jesus loosened the tongue of a mute man who had been mute for his whole life. On the day of Pentecost, the disciples spoke languages they did not know through the power of the Holy Spirit. Those foreigners were amazed to hear about Jesus in their own tongue by men that couldn't speak their language. For example, I don't speak French but, if you were from France and Jesus wanted me to tell you the gospel in French, He would make it so I could. It would be through the power of the Holy Spirit and not my knowledge of the language, you understand. What happened to Balaam is more than just a donkey talking to him. Balaam was a sorcerer in modern terms and was summoned by the Hebrews' enemy, the King of Moab, to curse the Israelites. On his way to meet the

King, an angel was blocking the path and Balaam's donkey refused to go near it. Balaam couldn't see the angel and beat the donkey three times before God opened the donkey's mouth and let it speak. That strange thing got Balaam's attention and then God opened Balaam's eyes to see the angel that would have struck him down dead if the donkey had not spared Balaam's life. Instead of cursing Israel, Balaam blessed them to the horror of Malak, the King of Moab. Listen, God is God and no power upon this earth compares to Him. God created this planet and everything on it. Why is it people say 'Faith can move mountains' and believe that but doubt God can make a donkey talk? God can do whatever he chooses to do. If he wanted a pig to fly, it would fly. The laws of nature only apply to God's creation; they do not apply to the creator," he emphasized. "God is not like us. He is God."

"All right, Reverend," Jude said with a smug expression. "Can you explain why the four gospels don't agree with each other? They are all very different even though supposedly they all talk about the same thing. I know the book of John says Jesus had blood and water come out of him on the cross but none of the other books say that. Why? Did no one else know that?"

Reverend Ash stood up and drew a circle on the chalkboard and then four smaller circles on the north, south, east and west sides. In the four smaller circles, he wrote the names Matthew, Mark, Luke and John.

"If we were outside on the street and, let's say,

you, Kellie, Matt and I were on the four corners of town and, suddenly, we all witnessed a dog run under a wagon wheel and die. We all witnessed the same thing but if we were asked what we had seen, we would answer from our viewpoint of what happened. We all saw the same thing but our views were quite different. The four Gospels are very much the same as they are four different books written to four different audiences focusing on four different aspects of Jesus while telling the very same story. Let me explain very quickly that Matthew's Gospel was written for the Jewish people and presents Jesus as the coming promised Savior, the King. The long-awaited Holy Messiah. Therefore, Matthew quotes the Old Testament more than any other Gospel and shows how Jesus fulfilled the prophecies of the coming Promised Savior."

"The Gospel of Mark is the shortest but has more miracles than the three others because it was written for the Romans who preferred action over philosophy. Mark didn't go into Jewish history or customs or prophecy because the Romans didn't care about that. Instead, the Book of Mark focuses on what Jesus did and not so much on what he said. The book of Mark focuses on a Powerful Savior."

"The Gospel of Luke was written to the Greeks who were more intellectual. Luke focuses on the human side of Jesus as being the perfect man. God becoming man and living as one of us. Sharing our heartaches and temptations and his compassion and grace for us. The Gospel of Luke reveals Jesus as fully man and fully God and the Perfect Savior."

"The Gospel of John is different than the others. It was written to all who would believe. The word believe is used ninety-eight times and John's purpose is to show the love and desire of Jesus to be our Savior. Having a relationship with Jesus personally and it couldn't have been written by a better source, John and Jesus were great friends. And yes, John was the only one to witness the blood and water coming from Jesus' side because he was there. The Gospel of John focuses on having a Personal Savior."

The reverend took a deep breath and added, "Promised, Powerful, Perfect and a Personal Savior. Those are the four messages of the Gospels united into one. Of course, they differ according to their audience and their purpose. You see, there is more to the Bible than you know and that means you're missing a lot."

Jude watched Reverend Ash with a half-interested and half-sarcastic smirk on his lips. "Well, thank you for not telling me I'm going to hell."

Reverend Ash raised his slender shoulders in a shrug before he sat behind the desk. "Would it do any good? The truth is, people put up walls of resentment and you cannot break down those walls once they're up. We're just sitting in here and quietly talking. I won't judge you and I hope you won't judge me too hard. I'm just a human being too. I'm not a reverend because I wanted money or power in my community, though I think I have fallen into both of those traps at least once. I came into the ministry because I love the Lord and I wanted to tell others about Jesus and hope they hear me and surrender their lives to him. A life without Jesus is a wasted gift. People my age have been blessed with a long life and people your age neglect to understand how blessed you are and waste it on what? A reputation with a gun? A few dollars that last a short time and a life of crime until those very things you live for come calling and your life is through? Let me assure you, if you were to die today and you stood before the Lord, you won't be so smug. You will be on your knees and you will either feel his great love and be welcomed into heaven to live forever. Or you will be on your knees trembling in fear of his great love that you refused and the terror of facing hell. At that point, I promise you, you will look back on everything that you have lived for and it will mean nothing. Everything that you ever accomplished will be worthless. It's all empty treasures and nothing can change it once your heart stops beating. It's your choice if you go to hell or not. Jesus did all he could do and all you need to do is accept the God-given gift of salvation. It couldn't be any easier. And that's what I invite you to do."

Jude frowned with a touch of sadness in his eyes. "Reverend, I'm..." he paused.

"You're what?"

Jude stood up and turned towards the window when he heard some excitement in front of the school. "I'm afraid you're not going to talk me out of what I have to do." He glared at the reverend. "Truet killed my little brother in cold blood and I aim to correct that sin, to use godly language." He turned back towards the window and saw Matt Bannister, Morton Sperry and Truet Davis talking with Charlie Ziegler.

Reverend Ash said, "I don't know anything about that but I do know the Lord is right here knocking on the door of your soul pleading for you to accept him into your heart."

Jude chuckled. "I'll get the door, Reverend." He stepped towards the door and put his hand on the doorknob and hesitated. He put his ear to the door and then looked at the reverend with a bitter expression. "I don't hear any knocking, Reverend."

"Son, what is your name?" Reverend Ash asked, standing from the desk.

"I'm Jude Maddox. It's time to collect a debt because Truet is here."

Reverend Ash pounded his hand down on the desktop emotionally. "So you can get yourself killed? You know you're not going to walk away with all those men out there, right? Jude, you have other choices. You can ask Jesus to be with you and surrender. You'd serve the penalty for your crimes, whatever they may be, but Jesus will never leave you. He will work on your behalf to change your heart and your life for the better. Any time spent in jail will come to an end and then you still have a future and a chance to live a good life. Jude, please, allow me to walk you outside and hand you over to Matt safely."

Jude's expression hardened to a stone mask that was both cold and deadly. He cared not a cent for anything the reverend was saying. "That's not what I came here for." He demanded Kellie Crawford. "Come here!"

She was startled. "What?" Her breathing became heavy.

"I said come here!" He approached her quickly and yanked her up by the arm. He pulled her in front of him to use as a shield and forced her towards the door. "With all these sorry blood-hungry leaches surrounding me, you're going to be the first to get shot!"

She tried to plant her feet and fight him but he easily forced her towards the door. She cried out, "I have a family! Please, Jude, I have children!"

"Shut up!" Jude shouted, "Your girls will make do without you, just fine."

Reverend Ash stepped sternly in front of the door. "Let her go! This young lady has a family and they do need her. I am the leader of this community and hold far more persuasion over these people than she does. I am also taller and will block more bullets than this little lady. If you're not brave enough to face them alone, please use me to protect you and not an innocent lady. I cannot think of a more cowardly act than that!"

Insulted, Jude pushed Kellie down and grabbed Reverend Ash and turned him towards the door. He snarled, "You want to be brave? Fine!". Jude wrapped his left hand around the reverend's body and pointed his Colt .44 to Reverend Ash's head. "Open the door!"

30

Matt was relieved to hear that Jude had not made it out of Willow Falls and was hiding in the schoolhouse, thanks to Charlie's quick action. Tom Smith had his deputy, Johnny Barso, and Matt's younger brother, Steven, guarding the back door of the schoolhouse that led out to the privy.

Matt took authority over the stand-off and sent all of the bystanders away from the school. He left Johnny and Steven guarding the back door and placed Morton Sperry at the right front corner of the schoolhouse and Truet at the left corner. Both men held rifles and would have side views of the front steps and porch if Jude stepped outside. They were instructed not to shoot unless Matt or Jude fired first. Matt would try to talk to Jude from the bottom of the front steps to convince him to release Kellie Crawford and Reverend Abraham Ash before they were harmed. Charlie and Tom forced the crowd of curious onlookers back from the schoolhouse and kept them there. When the town's people were moved back, Matt chose his Parker double-barreled shotgun as his weapon of choice. He wanted a gun with a broader kill radius if Jude came out shooting or began firing out of the window. He had removed the thong from his side-arm's hammer in case he needed to grab it. Matt approached the four steps to the schoolhouse and pulled both hammers back on the shotgun to shoot both barrels at once. His middle and index finger were on the two triggers.

He was about ready to call to Jude when he heard Kellie begin to plead for her children inside through the closed door. His instinct was to run inside but he hesitated when he overheard the reverend volunteering to take Kellie's place. The door opened and Jude pushed the reverend outside the door, using him as a shield while keeping himself in the doorway. The reverend looked caringly back at Kellie and said, "Get under my desk and stay there."

"Shut up!" Jude hissed in his ear. The barrel of the revolver was pressed firmly against the reverend's head. Jude was alarmed to see Matt ten feet in front of them, aiming the double-barrel Parker at them with both hammers pulled back and his fingers on the triggers. Jude didn't see anyone else except the crowd down the street.

Matt spoke confidently, "Let Reverend Ash go. There's no way out of here, Jude."

"Put your gun down!" Jude yelled. "I'll kill him if you don't."

Reverend Ash spoke loudly, "If I live, the Lord

will be with me but, if I must die, I will be with the Lord. I will not fear either way."

"Shut your mouth!" Jude exclaimed. He found it strange how calm the reverend appeared to be. It was the last thing he had expected. Jude pulled the hammer back on the revolver until it clicked to increase his intensity and kept his finger on the trigger. "I said put your gun down!"

Matt never allowed his focus to leave Jude and Reverend Ash. "Jude, I'm telling you right now, if he falls, you're dead too!" Matt warned with his hardened eyes staring at him behind the barrel of the shotgun. "I don't want to kill you, Jude. Lower that hammer and let the Reverend go. You have no other option."

"Yeah, I do, Marshal. I came here to kill Truet, not harm anyone else. I challenge Truet to a duel. Back-to-back for ten steps, then turn and let the best man win. That's my only offer. If you refuse me my chance at justice, I'll kill the reverend and the woman before you can get me. I promise you that!"

Matt could see Jude's gun hand moving every time Jude spoke and it was making Matt nervous. "Lower that hammer before you do something you'll regret for eternity. If there's anyone here who would want to help you, it's Reverend Ash; so, please, lower the hammer, at least. And then we'll talk."

Jude yelled bitterly, "Don't tell me what to do! I'm in charge here and I said I want a duel with Truet!"

"You expect me to let you have a duel with my deputy for some crazy idea that it is justice? And then what? If you killed my friend, are you going to surrender or am I going to have to kill you anyway?"

Jude chuckled. "I'm not afraid to die, Marshal."

"You ought to be," Reverend Ash said with an uncomfortable grimace. "Please, son, give Jesus a chance to change your life while you can."

"Shut up!" Jude yelled in the reverend's ear. "I don't want to hear it anymore."

Matt shook his head slowly. "I'm not going to let you have a duel. Your brother was never shot in the back. Whoever told you he was is a liar."

The words infuriated Jude. "You heard me! Bring that coward out of his hiding place and let us settle this like men. That's how it's going to be. Your only other choice is burying the Crawford woman and telling her children it's your fault for protecting a coward rather than saving their mother!"

"No. You'd be the spineless coward for having to kill a woman," Matt answered.

Truet had heard enough and stepped out from the corner of the schoolhouse. "I'm fine having a duel, Matt. This piece of crap hogtied and gagged those little girls. I'll gladly put an end to him. Gladly," he emphasized.

Surprised by Truet's voice, Jude turned the reverend's body to face Truet. "I'm not surprised you're hiding behind a corner instead of facing me like a man. It sounds very similar to what you did to my brother."

Truet's voice was harsh, "Think what you will but Farrian's dead and you're about to join him."

Morton Sperry had a perfect shot at the back of Jude's head. Morton could end it right then by squeezing the trigger and placing a bullet in the backside of Jude. But he feared the bullet would pass through Jude and into Reverend Ash.

Jude spoke to Truet, "Ten count step, turn and shoot. Do you agree?"

Truet agreed. "I said I do. Matt, it's your call," Truet put the pressure on Matt to decide.

Matt had no intention of letting his friend take part in a duel to the death with a man that Matt knew nothing about other than his brother was a gunfighter of some reputation for speed and accuracy. Truet had told him in the past that, if Farrian Maddox were sober that day in Gold Hill, Truet would have been killed. If Jude had the same kind of speed and accuracy that Farrian had, then Truet was at the greater risk. It was a risk that Matt did not want to take. A growing crowd was watching and any bad decisions would be on him. He didn't want to risk Truet's life but he also had the more significant responsibility to make sure Reverend Ash and Missus Crawford were unharmed. He had to think quickly and form a plan in his mind.

Matt spoke, "Let Reverend Ash and Missus Crawford go free right now and you can have your duel." He planned on arresting Jude once the two hostages were safe. The duel would never take place.

Morton had Jude's head square in his sights and was waiting to pull the trigger. He wanted to and the temptation was strong despite the risk to the reverend. To hear Matt agree to give Jude a chance at a duel sickened Morton. He wanted to be the one that killed Jude and now his chance was taken away. He lowered his rifle and cursed loudly in frustration.

Startled by Morton's voice so close behind him, Jude panicked and jerked the reverend around to face Morton quickly. He spun around so fast that the momentum carried through in his right arm, and the revolver's barrel hit the reverend's head with the sudden jolt. The unexpected jarring of the barrel transferred to his trigger finger with just enough force to accidentally fire the weapon. The gun's hammer fell, the percussion sounded and a blood-soaked explosion spattered against the schoolhouse wall. Reverend Ash's body collapsed out of Jude's arm to the porch. Stunned by the accidental shooting, Jude turned abruptly towards Matt, intending to tell him it was an accident but he didn't realize until it was too late that he was swinging the barrel of his revolver towards Matt. "I...!"

Matt saw the gun swinging towards him and pulled both triggers of the shotgun at once, filling Jude's chest with two rounds of twelve-gauge pellets that ripped Jude's chest apart and blew him backward through the schoolhouse door. The sound of the percussion echoed and the shocked silence of the crowd was soon interrupted by the screams of the reverend's beloved wife and their daughter. Matt lowered the shotgun and stared with his mouth slack-jawed at the gruesome sight of Reverend Ash lying lifelessly across the small porch and steps while brain matter and blood clung to the white paint of the schoolhouse.

Morton Sperry approached Matt with a bewildered expression. "I wasn't expecting that." He had the reverend's blood spattered across his face.

Matt took a deep breath, trying to focus through the moisture that clouded his eyes. He let the shotgun fall to the ground, stepped away from Morton while running his left hand through his hair, and held his hand on top of his head, shocked by what he had seen. He took a few steps and knelt, fighting with all he had to get control of his emotions. The sound of Elizabeth and Darla Ash's wailing combined with the shock of the others in the community became overwhelming. Matt could hear his son's voice stunned and asking about his grandfather. Matt glanced over and watched Gabriel hugging his mother while both wailed after watching his grandfather being killed. Matt's chest heaved with erratic breaths and growing pressure as the emotions overtook the shock.

"Matt, are you okay?" Truet asked.

Matt stood up. "No, I'm not." He bit his lip, fighting to keep a semblance of control. "Go move his body into the schoolhouse, so they don't have to see it."

"I'll help," said Morton, volunteering to help Truet.

Matt stared at the blood spattered across the white wall and felt a wave of anger overtake him. Matt quickly walked through the curious crowd ignoring anyone who tried to talk to him and shoving others out of his way to reach the mercantile. He heard his Aunt Mary call to him, but he ignored her, grabbed a bucket from inside, filled it with water from a water trough, and carried it back to the schoolhouse. Matt walked up the bloody stairs and threw the water against the wall to wash the grotesque blood and matter off the white paint. He tossed the bucket to his brother Steven who had been covering the back of the schoolhouse with a shotgun. The bucket hit Steven's hip and bounced to the ground. Matt glared at him with eyes thickened with emotion. He ordered harshly, "I need three buckets of water or as many as it takes to get this all washed off the porch and stairs. Now!"

"Sure," Steven said quietly. He spoke to two men close to him, "Robert, Nick, come help me."

Matt stepped into the schoolhouse and slammed the door behind him. He was surprised to see Morton Sperry trying to comfort Kellie Crawford and lead her out of the schoolhouse. Kellie was sobbing uncontrollably into Morton's chest. He questioned Matt, "You don't mind if I take her home, do you?"

"No. You're free to go," Matt replied. He sat on a desktop to look at the reverend's body lying beside Jude's on the floor. Both created a large pool of blood.

Kellie hid her face from the two bodies as Morton guided her out the door. Truet met them on the steps and came inside. "This gentleman down here is making the coffins. He wants to know if we are burying Jude here or are taking him back to Branson?"

Matt shifted his attention to look at Truet irritably. "Branson," he answered in a restrained voice.

Truet knew, immediately, that Matt wanted to be left alone. "I'll close the door and take care of it," Truet said softly.

"Matt..." Carl Snow said, walking up the wet and bloody stairs. "Are you paying..."

Truet put a hand up to stop him. "He doesn't want to talk to anyone right now. Let's go down here and I'll..." Truet said, pushing Carl away from the door.

"Excuse me. I want to talk to Matt!" Carl argued. He pushed Truet's hand away from his chest. "Matt, do you..."

Matt's patience ran out and he shouted, "Go away from me, Carl. Now!"

When the door closed, Matt found it hard to breathe. His chest hurt and tears flooded his vision. Just as shocking as it was to anyone, seeing Reverend Ash killed before his eyes had placed a bullet in Matt's own heart. The elderly man had been not only a lifelong link to his past but also a man that had a more significant impact on Matt's life than he expected.

He wiped his tears and tried to control his breathing as he stared at the old man lying on the floor. Matt covered his mouth with his hand and sniffled. His bottom lip trembled and his vision blurred. His chest heaved while the sobs fought to break free and wail inside him. He could hear Steven and the other men throwing water on the wall, porch steps. He did not want to be bothered and hoped Steven wouldn't come in through the door.

Before too long, there was a soft knock on the

door thenit opened. Mary Ziegler gasped immediately upon entering the schoolhouse after seeing the two bodies' grotesque condition on the floor. She avoided the blood and made her way around a few desks towards Matt and put an arm around his shoulders. His body convulsed with emotion upon her touch. "It wasn't your fault, Matthew," her voice was soft and gentle. She kept her head turned away from the bodies.

Matt sat on a desk top with a tight scowl fixed on his face. He was staring at Reverend Ash. "I couldn't save him. I'm getting so sick of failing!" he exclaimed angrily. "I couldn't save Chusi. I couldn't save Jed. I was there when Christine was shot too, but no, I couldn't stop it! It seems I can't save anyone who means something to me, Aunt Mary. Listen," he paused and raised his hands in defeat. "I can hear Elizabeth out there crying, Missus Ash, Gabriel, all of them, and there was nothing I could do! Reverend Ash..." He exhaled emotionally and sniffled. He raised his hands helplessly and said in a higher-pitched voice filled with emotion, "This one hurts." Tears slipped down his cheek and he squeezed his lips together, struggling not to sob. His breathing was quick and light breaths.

A quiet tear slipped down Mary's cheek. "Reverend Ash was a big part of all of our lives and we're all going to miss him. He was a big part of your life too, Matthew. No one can blame you for what happened; it wasn't your fault."

Matt's mouth opened but he hesitated to speak as another tear rolled down his cheek. "I think of all the things he did and said that hurt me before I left here. I thought I hated him. There were times when I was in Wyoming when I wanted to come back and hurt him for what he did to me. I thought I hated him but I didn't. I loved him and I never told him so." He wiped the tears off his cheek. "I was going to stop by his house and ask him if he would come to Branson to marry Christine and me. We decided to have Reverend Painter marry us but, deep down, I didn't want anyone else to officiate our wedding except for Reverend Ash. He meant that much to me and I didn't even realize it until recently. I never thought he'd die." He took a deep breath and wiped his nose. "And now he's gone. Just like that." Matt rubbed his eyes. "It only seemed right to have him marry us." He exhaled a deep breath slowly. "I can't believe that I'm here looking at him like this. He was such a powerful, influential figure in my life. I think I was blessed to have had Reverend Ash in my life, after all. Despite all the bad stuff and the road I traveled, I think I am."

Mary stood and listened while keeping her arm around his shoulders. "I think so," she agreed. "Reverend Ash lived his whole life wanting to share the Gospel and watching over the hearts and spiritual growth of this community. Something you can think about is that his influence on your life makes you a part of his legacy. There's nothing under heaven that would please him more than knowing his life's work created a lasting garden of fruit and goodness in a wicked world. I think that's a pretty nice legacy to leave, don't you? I know I hope when my time comes that I'm known more for my faith than my cooking," she said, nudging him with her shoulder.

Matt offered a sad smile. He cast the first glance at his aunt since she entered. "You will leave a legacy for having a big heart. And I will leave a legacy of death."

"That is not so," she stated firmly. "Your legacy will be one of justice and doing what's right even when it came to someone's death. You will not be remembered as a killer, not if I have anything to say about it. You'll be remembered as a lawman and a dang fine one. One I am very proud of. Do you hear me?" she asked, giving his shoulders a slight shake.

The corners of his lips rose just a touch. "I do."

Charlie Ziegler quietly opened the door peered inside. "Excuse me. I don't mean to interrupt. I have to grab something." He stepped into the pool of blood and turned Jude's body over just enough to retrieve his Scofield out of the back of Jude's pants. He returned it to his empty holster.

"Ohh, Charlie," Mary said with disgust, turning her body away from him.

Matt raised his eyebrows.

Charlie raised one of his fingers with a roll of his tongue across his missing tooth. "He got lucky," he said as an explanation and walked to the door, leaving bloody boot prints across the wood floor. He closed the door as he went.

Mary asked, "Matt, can we leave here and talk at home? I can't stomach being in here anymore."

Matt took a deep breath and looked at Abraham Ash once more. "I don't want to forget what he looks like, Aunt Mary. But yes, we can go. I better see how Gabriel and the reverend's family are doing. We'll talk more tonight when I come to the ranch." He offered her a sad smile. "Thank you for listening."

She hugged him. "Anytime."

31

Roger King sat on his padded chair, experiencing a depth of loneliness he had never felt before. It was the torment earned after becoming helpless to wipe the tears from Martha's cheek or bring a smile to her somber expression. To ask for forgiveness was one thing but for her to forgive the hurt was another. She stayed upstairs in their bedroom to be away from him and when she did need to walk through the family room, she barely acknowledged him. It hurt Roger more being ignored than it would if she beat his knee with a broom handle. The brace wrapped around his knee to keep his leg straight prohibited his movement. He could walk with crutches but his chair and footstool had become his prison night and day.

"Roger, do you want a piece of the pie that Henry and Sylvia brought over?" Martha asked from the kitchen. The church was having dinner brought over to them every night until they could recover from their injuries. Young Barbara Ballenger came over every day to clean the house and help where she could as well.

"No, thank you. I've had enough."

"Very well," she sounded cold and distant.

A long silence can be a sign of contentment when all is well but it can also be a symptom of a fracture that will only grow and eventually split any marriage in two. Unfortunately for Roger, he alone held the blame for the rock drill and hammer that had fractured the foundation of his home. He had caused the damage but he didn't know how to repair the void separating him and his beloved Martha.

She walked through the family room carrying a saucer with a piece of pie towards the stairs. "Good night." She had not bothered to look at him. He would not see her until the following day and it was still light outside.

"Martha," Roger said, stopping her by the stairs.

She turned back towards him with no emotion on her face except spite. "What?"

"I want you to know that I feel dirty..."

She scowled. "Don't tell me you want a bath," she replied curtly.

"No. It wouldn't do any good anyway. I don't feel dirty because of dust. I feel dirty because of what I did. No matter how much I scrub myself, I still feel dirty. I am more ashamed of myself than you will ever know. I'm not asking you to make me feel better because I deserve whatever happens to me. I just want you to know that I am..." His mouth tightened while tears blurred his vision. "I am terribly sorry. I know I hurt you and I can't forgive myself for that."

Martha hesitated a moment before answering, "I know you're sorry. But it doesn't change what you did. If you expect me to jump on your lap and be grateful that you are not leaving me for some young tramp, guess again. I've been faithful and I've given my life to you for all these years. I've kept my part of the vows and, to my knowledge, you've never been unhappy being married. Or am I wrong? Are you not happy?"

He used a handkerchief to wipe his face dry. "I've always been happily married to you."

"Then why? What did I do or didn't do that led you to her?"

He swallowed hard as his throat tightened. "Nothing. You're perfect just the way you are and I wouldn't want our marriage any other way. I have no excuses, Martha. I just want you to know that I am sorry and I will never be tempted by anyone again. It's not worth the shame and or how it has hurt you. I can see the hurt in your eyes and it's exactly what I never wanted to do. I always wanted to be the best husband to you."

"You were the best husband," she said softly. "I could divorce you tomorrow and no one would blame me."

"I wouldn't blame you either," Roger gasped with a sinking feeling. "But I hope you'll give me a chance to prove myself to you."

There was a knock on the door.

She scoffed with a hint of frustration. She set her pie down on a small corner shelf and left the family room to answer the door. "Lee? Regina?" She questioned upon opening the door. "Do you want to come in?" she asked awkwardly. They were two of the last people she would expect to see at her door.

"Please and thank you," Lee Bannister said as he and his lovely wife stepped inside. "I was wondering if I could speak with you and Roger for a little bit?"

"Sure. Roger is in the family room. Would you like some pie or something to drink?" Martha asked while leading them to the family room.

"No, thank you," Regina answered for them both.

Lee entered the family room carrying a leather case. He frowned when he saw Roger's leg. "How is the leg?" he asked, taking a seat on the davenport closest to Roger.

Roger stared at him with a curious expression. He worried that he might be in legal trouble of some kind. "It's painful to stand on," he answered slowly. "Am I in some kind of trouble or something, Lee?" Roger was curious why Lee and Regina were there.

Lee glanced at Martha and Regina, who both stood awkwardly in the middle of the room. Neither one knew what to say in the awkwardness of the moment. Lee continued, "I'll get right to the point. My childhood reverend over in Willow Falls was murdered earlier today and we are leaving to go to the funeral tomorrow. We're on the way to pick up Matt's fiancé so she can stay the night because we're leaving early."

"Sorry to hear that," Roger stated. He was questioning what they had to do with him.

Lee continued with a smile, "I didn't come here to tell you that." He spoke slowly, "Roger, what you did can't be tolerated and you know that. You helped make the rules. I expected William to do something like that. You'll remember Martha and Regina both were against us hiring William for that very reason."

Roger put up a hand to stop him. "Lee, you don't have to explain. I know what I did and I have no excuses. I'm not angry at you. I'm angry at myself but I deserve what I got." He waved towards Martha. "I hurt Martha and I don't know if I'll ever be able to repair the damage I've done to our relationship. So, honestly, you don't have to explain why I was fired. I already know and you did the right thing. And I'll help William and Pam in any way I can if they need it."

Lee raised his brow and inhaled deeply. "Well, they need it. But I don't want you to help them. I want you to manage the hotel. I came over to offer your job back if you want it?"

"Seriously?" he replied, dumbfounded.

"Are you interested?"

"Of course. Yes. Thank you."

"Good. The only thing is I don't want you going to the hotel until Hiram Stewart is gone. He'll be here for another few weeks but you can work from home. The only people who know I'm giving your job back are William and Pam. For now, I want to keep it that way. Once Hiram leaves, you're back in your office. Pam will be coming over after work every day starting tomorrow and you can work through her over the next few weeks. You're the boss but she'll play the part until your back. You work out what works best for you. I just don't want Hiram finding out and causing trouble. Does that sound fair enough?"

"Yes. Thank you."

Lee stood up. "You know what to do and this case is for you to get started." Lee set the leather case beside Roger's chair. He reached a hand out to shake Roger's. "Everything's the same as it was and you're in control. I'm going to trust you just like I always have."

Roger shook his hand. "Thank you, Lee. I will not let you down ever again."

"I know. I've known you too long not to see that. We have to go."

"I'm sorry to hear about your reverend."

"Me too. Welcome back, Roger. And I hope you two can heal your marriage. You're too well-loved around here not too."

"Wait," Martha said, "Is this a temporary thing until you train Pam or hire someone capable of managing the hotel?"

"No. It's a permanent position. Just like before."

"Why are you doing this?" she asked suspiciously.

Lee answered sincerely, "Because I believe Roger is sincerely sorry and knows what a horrible mistake he made. I also know, as a Christian, there are words we use like grace, forgiveness and mercy. I don't believe he will ever make that mistake again because of his integrity and his love for you. He's a better man than that and he knows it too. The Monarch Hotel is safe in his hands. I'm betting my whole hotel's future on it." He paused and added softly, "You know, Martha, I hope you will too."

When they had left, Martha picked up her saucer of pie and sighed. "Congratulations on getting your job back." She was relieved as well. Having no income had become a frightening position to be in.

He already had the case open and looking through the papers with new vigor on his face. "I'm..." He was speechless. He looked heavenward and raised his hands. "Thank you, Jesus!"

Martha felt the corner of her lips rise just a little. She sat in her chair next to him. "I have been very hurt, Roger. It feels like you took a knife and cut my heart out. I cannot brush that hurt aside or forget about it but I will try to forgive you, day by day, and gradually, I will. We can save our marriage, Roger. Just please, ask yourself then what? if you're ever tempted by anyone again. I promise you, I won't go through it twice. I deserve better."

Roger reached over and took her hand in his. "I don't want anything in this world as much I want to spend my life with you. I don't know how much time we have left in this world but I want to spend the remainder of my life loving you even more than I ever have before. I love you, Martha. And I'm going to tell you that every day for the rest of our lives."

Her embittered lips rose into a recognizable

smile. "I'll hold you to that. I love you too, Roger. I think we're tough enough together to get through this. What about you?"

Her smile was like the warmth of a summer day on his skin. "I've been praying so. I can't get up but do you think I can have a hug?"

She chuckled for the first time. "That would be a nice start."

32

The Willow Falls Christian Church was packed with no more standing room along the walls. The whole town and the surrounding community had gathered to say their final goodbye to Reverend Abraham Ash. His body was in a casket in the Ash family room and would be taken to the cemetery an hour after the church service was over. A large dinner was planned at the church after the interment at the cemetery. Matt sat in a pew next to Christine, holding her hand. He squeezed her hand before standing up to speak in front of the church. Matt was the last speaker and stood behind the lectern that Reverend Ash had placed his Bible and notes every Sunday for the thirty-five years he preached there. Matt let his eyes fall on the first row where Darla Ash and her family sat, wiping their tears. Darla smiled the encouraging smile that she had given him since he was a little boy. It touched him deeply to see the familiar smile and at the same time know Reverend Ash would never stand behind the lectern and see his family again. Matt winked at her in return.

"I'm Matt Bannister," He began. "I can tell you right now, if you knew the story, there is no doubt that it was Reverend Ash who made me what I am today. It is because of him that I am a United States Marshal and a Christian. Someone told you about Jesus and, if you accepted Jesus as your savior, you committed to living your life for the Lord. Most people would say Reverend Ash's legacy is sitting in the front row, his beloved wife of forty-one years, his daughter, son-in-law, and grandchildren. However, for the rest of us, his legacy is what he represented and what he spent his life living. His example of living a holy life is a standard that we should try to copy. Of course, he made mistakes and, if you want to judge him for those, I invite you to take a look in the mirror first. That person staring back at you in the mirror isn't so mistake-free either, right? I honor Reverend Ash today not because I was asked to but because his influence on my life is more valuable than I can explain to you. His legacy in this church shouldn't be the lectern he handcrafted thirty-five years ago or the bell steeple he designed. It should be the lives that he touched and the light that shines within us. The greatest legacy he could leave is the fruit of his labors continuing to grow stronger in the faith and more and more like Jesus, our Lord. I am committed to living my life in such a way that, when I do see Reverend Ash in heaven someday, I can say, 'thank you for your influence in my life because it prepared me to finish the race the Lord set before me.' That is my commitment to Reverend Ash's work on this earth. And for those of us still living, I hope we all want our legacy to have more to do with Jesus and salvation than how many dollars we can earn or the fun times we had or how big and beautiful our homes are. I want to honor Reverend Ash by serving Jesus and reading the Bible for myself like he always reminded me to do. How wonderful it would be if we could all leave a legacy based on our Christian walk. The legacy of a man is not the number behind his riches or debt but the integrity, purpose and honor of the man he was. May we live our lives in that way, in all we do." He put his hand on the lectern and looked towards the ceiling. "Thank you, Jesus, for putting Reverend Ash in my life. He was an influential and big part of who I am today. I never told him so but let him know I love him." Matt let his eyes roam over the people listening to him. "Those of us who knew Reverend Ash, we are his legacy. Let's live a Godly life that honors him."

Darla Ash's graying dark hair was tied in a tight bun as she approached Matt after the service. She dressed in a black dress and wore a black lace veil over her round silver-rimmed spectacles. She hugged him silently and held his attention with her gentle, loving gaze. "Thank you for your words. Abraham was never good about saying how he felt about anyone until he got much older. He loved you, Matthew. He had become quite proud of you.

I want you to know that. You may not remember, or maybe you do, but many years ago, when you were young, you gave Abraham a rock that you painted a white cross on for his birthday. Do you remember that?"

Matt tilted his head, trying to recall a memory he had long since forgotten. "Vaguely."

"A little later, maybe I can have Elizabeth take you over and get it. You might be surprised to see where it has been for all these years. Now," she said with a tap to his chest. "You're Aunt Mary told me you blamed yourself for what happened to Abraham yesterday. Don't do that. I watched the whole thing and there was nothing more you could have done."

Matt's eyes glistened with a touch of moisture. He had no words fitting to say. He wished he had barged into the school and killed Jude instead of trying to talk to him. The memory of the reverend's death repeatedly played in his mind and he regretted not taking another approach. "I just wish it had ended differently."

Darla smiled sadly. "When the Lord calls someone home, he calls them home. We will see him again. Until then, you have a life to live; don't spend any more time blaming yourself. How about we talk about something a little brighter? I came over here to talk to you because I heard a rumor that you're engaged and your fiancé is here. Is this true?" she asked with a knowing smile.

"It is."

"Well, introduce me, Matt." She swatted his shoulder affectionately.

Christine was busy talking to Steven's wife, Nora Bannister, whom Christine had never met. Nora's parents, William and Lucy McDermott, were also engaged in the conversation with them. Matt tapped Christine on the shoulder. She glanced back with a grin. "Yes?" A small floral hat was pinned to her hair that was weaved into a bun. She wore a respectable black dress that was quite plain compared to her usual attire.

"I'd like to introduce you to Reverend Ash's wife, Darla."

"Oh. Yes." She excused herself from Nora and her parents and shook Darla's hand. "I'm so sorry about your husband. Matt has told me so much about him and you. I wish I could have met him. I'm sure Matt told you we wanted him to officiate our wedding."

Darla cast a surprised glance at Matt. "No. He would have loved to have done so. I don't want to be rude but, if it's not too much trouble, I'd love to attend."

Christine's brow furrowed. "Your whole family is already being invited. It would mean a lot to Matt and me if you were there. I haven't met your daughter yet but I love Gabriel."

Darla smiled in response to the wedding invitation. "Elizabeth is here somewhere. There she is. Elizabeth," she called.

Elizabeth Smith came to her mother. She appeared to be physically exhausted and drained emotionally. Her yellow curly hair was held in a ponytail and hung down the back of the black dress. Elizabeth's brown eyes were red from weeping but they widened a touch when she saw Matt. She floated past her mother and hugged Matt tightly. "I'm so glad you're here." She whispered while closing her eyes.

Matt felt a wave of warmth flow through his body, holding her in his arms and a comfortable smile lifting the corners of his lips. He wished he could heal her broken heart. "I wouldn't miss it," he answered.

Darla spoke, "Sweetheart, this is Matt's fiancé, Christine."

Elizabeth ended the hug abruptly and turned towards her with the name recognition. "You're Christine?" Elizabeth's mouth dropped open upon seeing her. "I have been looking forward to meeting you since Gabriel came back from Matt's around Thanksgiving. He and Tiffany have wonderful things to say about you. It's so nice to meet you. As you know, Matt and I are old friends."

"I wish we could have met under happier circumstances. My condolences to you and your family," Christine said sincerely.

"Thank you. It's been quite a shock and very hard," Elizabeth replied with an emotional swallow.

"Of course." Her dark brown eyes looked upon Elizabeth with sincere empathy.

Mary Ziegler hollered across the church, "Christine, can I borrow you for a moment?" She wanted to introduce Christine to some more people.

Christine grabbed Elizabeth's hand in hers. "It was nice to meet you. I hope we can get to know each other later today, maybe?"

"Yes. If you're going to be my Gabriel's stepmother, then yes, we should spend some time getting to know one another."

"Absolutely. We'll talk soon." Christine walked around the front pews towards Mary.

"She's stunning," Elizabeth said to Matt.

"I agree," Matt said with a smile.

Darla touched Elizabeth's hand. "Sweetheart, I am giving the rock Matthew made for your father back to him. Will you take him over to the office and get it for him before I forget?"

Matt followed Elizabeth into the reverend's house. He paused by the casket in the family room. The top was nailed shut but its presence sent a chill down Matt's spine. The burial was in less than an hour at the cemetery.

"Come on, Matt," Elizabeth beckoned him to leave the simple wood casket and enter the reverend's study.

Matt stepped into the reverend's office and felt a wave of nostalgia overwhelm him. He had not been in the room since his youth. It had not changed much at all. The oversized desk, the library of books and the two chairs in front of the desk. A wooden cross on the wall and the framed biblical verses. "It's weird being in here again. I don't even know when the last time was. Yeah, yeah, I do. It's when I came here to confront your father about not allowing you to marry me. I was what, seventeen?"

Elizabeth stood by a bookshelf touching a river rock with a white cross painted on it being used as a bookend. She put her back to the shelf and placed her hands behind her while she gazed at him. "I remember that. I was in my room crying. I could hear every word. I believe that was when my father decided to make me marry Tom." A sad expression had deepened the frown on her face. "I used to come in here after you left and look at this rock you painted as a child. Other than the letters you'd sneak to me before you left, this is all I had to remind me of you. Until Gabriel was born anyway."

Matt picked up the river rock a little larger than his fist. The white lines of the cross were wavy and poorly painted. On the backside were letters painted by a child that spelled out, Happy Birthday, Rev. Ash. Love Matthew Ban. He had run out of space to write any more on the rock. He chuckled.

Elizabeth watched him with a saddened expression. "Tell me about Christine."

Matt shrugged. "She's a dancer at the dance hall. She was married and had a daughter but lost them both on the journey here. That's how she started dancing."

Elizabeth shook her head, annoyed. "No, I mean, how do you know she's good enough to marry you? Matt, you're my..." she paused.

"What?" Matt questioned softly.

Elizabeth took a deep breath and exhaled. "You're my first love and the father of my son. Other than being beautiful, how do you know she's right for you? Convince me."

Matt grinned nervously. "I don't know if I can convince you. But Christine has become my best friend. She's kind, soft-hearted, easy-going and I love her. She always wants the best for me and she loves Gabriel. I guess I don't know what else I can say to convince you."

"You didn't say she was right for you."

"What?" Matt laughed awkwardly. "I just told you she was."

"No. You told me Christine's nice and likes Gabriel," she corrected him pointedly.

"Well, what do you want to know?" he asked uncomfortably.

"Matt, if you marry her, she will become my son's stepmother." She crossed her arms .

"Gabriel's a grown man almost. He's too big to be worried about her being a wicked stepmother. I don't know how to convince you that Christine is right for me. I assume that's for her and me to know and don't need to explain ourselves to anyone else. It just seems like an odd question to me." He was becoming annoyed by the questions and tone of his friend.

Elizabeth rolled her eyes impatiently. "Do you love her?"

"I do."

"More than me?" she asked meekly.

Matt was taken back by the question. He was hesitant to speak.

"Well?" she asked, widening her eyes in expectation of an answer.

He ran his hand through his hair, nervously pulling on the gauze that covered his sutures. "Last year, when I saved you at the cabin, I asked you that question or something similar. You told me you wanted me to move on with my life and find someone to love. And now that I have, you're asking me that?"

"You didn't answer the question, Matt."

He held up his hands. "It's not a comparative question."

Elizabeth frowned and took a deep breath before exhaling. "Let me make this simple for you. Would you leave her for me if I confided in you that Tom and I were divorcing soon?"

"What?" he felt the oxygen leave his lungs.

"You heard me. Would you leave Christine for me if I told you that I'm divorcing Tom?"

Matt was stunned. "No, you're not. Are you?" A knot was growing in his stomach.

"Answer the question. And Matt, answer it honestly." Her brown eyes softly gazed upon him with the same love she had always shown for him.

Matt stared down at the spot on the floor where years before he stood and argued with the reverend for Elizabeth's hand in marriage. He raised his eyes to meet hers and felt a tightening in his chest. He answered softly, "No. I love you, Lizzy, and I always have. I always will love you. But I'm not the same kid I was when I stood here fighting with your father. I'm not the same. Nor are you. I would still marry Christine."

Slowly, a smile came to Elizabeth's lips. "Then she's good enough for you to marry. That's all I wanted to know. I love you, Matthew Bannister, very much. I just want the best for you and I'll give my blessing for you to marry her."

"Are you and Tom...?" he questioned with a creased brow of concern.

She laughed. "Tom and I are fine. We're not getting divorced. I was testing you to see if you were ready and if she was the right one for you."

Matt grimaced. "What if I had said I would drop her like a bedbug for you?" There was no humor in his facial expression.

Her grin fell to a sincere caring gaze. "Then, my friend, I would have told you that you're not ready to get married and she's not the right one for you."

Matt lowered his brow questionably. "How would you know? You haven't spoken to her for more than a minute."

Elizabeth pursed her lips together thoughtfully. "Because, last year, when you saved me up at the cabin, you said you never had another relationship after me because none of the women you met could equal me. It was a nice compliment, Matt, but a sad one too. Now you have found a lady that surpasses me. I wouldn't let you marry her if she didn't."

Matt grinned. "You wouldn't let me?"

Elizabeth took his hand in hers and looked into his eyes with a steady gaze of affection and love. Her eyes watered as she said, "Matt, you have protected me all of my life and saved my life twice. You will always be my hero . Nothing will ever change that. And I know if I needed you for any reason, you'd come running because that's who you are. What I just did to you may have been mean but it is my way of protecting you this time.

I wanted to protect you from making one of the biggest mistakes in your life by marrying the wrong person. I'm just watching out for you like you always do me."

Matt was touched deeply by her words and a faint layer of moisture filled his eyes. He was left speechless with a deep appreciation that humbled him to his core. "Thank you," he said with more appreciation than his tone revealed.

"You're welcome," she said softly. She pointed at the rock in his hand. "Matt, do you really want that rock? Because I'd like to keep it if I could. It reminds me of my father."

"Then you keep it. I wasn't much of an artist, was I?" he asked while looking at the wavy lines of a cross painted on the rock. He held it out for her to take.

"No," she answered quickly. She took hold of the rock and set it back on the bookcase. "But my father loved it. He loved you, Matt. He had high hopes for you when you were young and the Dobson Gang ended much of that. Even though he condemned you for all those years, he never removed this rock from his bookshelf. I think deep down he knew he was wrong because I would see him holding it sometimes. I think he was praying for you like a lost sheep that he drove out from his flock, but still loved. In the last year he became very proud of you and I think that pleased him a lot. The prodigal son had come home." She smiled and wiped her eyes. "It pleases me to have you back too."

They walked to the church where many people were outside socializing while waiting for the procession to the cemetery. Elizabeth gave Matt a quick hug before she went back inside the church. Matt was looking for his fiancé when he was approached by David and Kellie Crawford and their three daughters.

David shook his hand firmly. "Matt, I'm glad we found you. I want to thank you for saving Kellie. You will never know how thankful the girls and I are for you."

Matt's head shook slightly as he answered, "You're welcome, but honestly, it was Reverend Ash that stepped in and saved her."

"That's very true, and he's a hero for that. But Kellie would have been next if you had not killed Jude. So, thank you. We'd be having two funerals today if you had not pulled the trigger."

Matt felt a tug on his suit jacket and looked down. Five-year-old Eva held the silver dollar he had given to her up for him to take.

He could see the red rope burns around her wrists and knelt with a sickened sensation in his stomach. He asked, "How are you today, young lady?"

She held the silver dollar out to him. "This is for you."

"I gave that to you for your birthday. You can keep it," Matt said gently.

Eva's brow rose just a touch while her eyes filled heavily with tears that refused to fall. "No. It's for saving my Mommy."

Matt gasped. He was just a couple of years older than Eva when he lost his mother. Though his Aunt Mary filled in as a loving mother figure, there was always a void that could never be filled within him. He had loved his mother as much as Eva loved her own and if he could have, Matt would have given all he had to save his mother as well. A warm smile slowly spread across his face as he thought of better memories of his mother's smile which was always so warm, inviting and kind. He had a few memories and they were memories that he cherished. He took the coin from Eva's hand and reached for his pocketbook. "How about we make a trade. Happy Birthday, young lady," he said and handed her a one-dollar bill.

Eva took the dollar and then stepped forward quickly and wrapped her arms around his neck to hug him. It surprised Matt and he glanced up at Kellie to see her wiping tears from her eyes. He held the little girl for a moment before she let him go and silently slipped to her mother's side and took her hand.

Once they had parted ways, Matt looked at the silver dollar. It was no different than any other, but it was worth far more than it appeared. It was worth a child's gratitude for protecting what could never be replaced. Her mother.

If you like this, check out

Just John by Reg Quist

About the Author

Ken Pratt and his wife, Cathy, have been married for 22 years and are blessed with five children and six grandchildren. They live on the Oregon Coast where they are raising the youngest of their children. Ken Pratt grew up in the small farming community of Dayton, Oregon.

Ken worked to make a living, but his passion has always been writing. Having a busy family, the only "free" time he had to write was late at night getting no more than five hours of sleep a night. He has penned several novels that are being published along with several children stories as well.

CPSIA information can be obtained
at www.ICGtesting.com
Printed in the USA
LVHW041023150721
692784LV00010B/1097